VOID RECON

OMEGA TASKFORCE: BOOK TWO

G J OGDEN

Cover design by Laercio Messias
Editing by S L Ogden
www.ogdenmedia.net

If you like Omega Taskforce then why not check out some of G J Ogden's other books? Click the series titles below to learn more about each of them.

Darkspace Renegade Series (6-books)

If you like your action fueled by power armor, big guns and the occasional sword, you'll love this fast-moving military sci-fi adventure.

Star Scavenger Series (5-book series)

Firefly blended with the mystery and adventure of Indiana Jones. Book 1 is 99c / 99p.

The Contingency War Series (4-book series)

A space-fleet, military sci-fi adventure with a unique twist that you won't see coming...

The Planetsider Trilogy (3-book series)

An edge-of-your-seat blend of military sci-fi action & classic apocalyptic fiction. Perfect for fans of Maze Runner and I am Legend.

Audible Audiobook Series

Star Scavenger Series (29-hrs)

The Contingency War Series (24-hrs)

The Planetsider Trilogy (32-hrs)

CAPTAIN LUCAS STERLING boarded the tram carriage and waited for Commander Mercedes Banks to follow him in. Already the eyes of people in the carriage, both civilian and members of Fleet, had turned to him. This wasn't the first time the unique silver stripe on his uniform had garnered suspicious glances, especially not on F-COP. However, after the broadcast by the Sa'Nerran Emissaries – otherwise known as 'turned' Omega Captain, Lana McQueen and Sterling's own chief engineer, Clinton Crow – people were even twitchier than usual. The emissaries' TV broadcast had been aired only six hours earlier yet already the impact of it was being felt through the Fleet and beyond. The revelation that senior Fleet officers had joined the Sa'Nerran cause was shocking enough in itself. This was despite the general population remaining unaware of the alien species' new and more advanced neural control technology. On top of this, Emissary McQueen had dropped the bombshell about the

Omega Taskforce. Cleverly, Sterling had thought, she hadn't given too much away, and only hinted at the unconscionable mission of the secret force. However, it had proven just enough to shock, prompt outrage and see demands for an explanation levied at the offices of every senior government official in the galaxy.

Sterling replayed the broadcast in his mind as Commander Banks stepped alongside him in the carriage and grabbed the handrail with her super-human grip. The doors then closed and the tram accelerated away from the station so quickly that in his distracted state-of-mind Sterling's own grip almost slipped.

"But be warned. The Sa'Nerran desire for war is not the only lie Fleet has been telling you," Sterling recalled McQueen saying during her broadcast. *"Ask them about the Omega Directive. Ask them why Fleet ships are sent to hunt and kill our own people. Once you know the truth, I am confident that you too will join with me in fighting for peace."*

Sterling huffed a laugh and shook his head. *Fighting for peace...* he thought, picturing his fellow Omega Captain in her new Sa'Nerran armor. At the time, he hadn't given a second thought to the specific wording of McQueen's broadcast, but now he suspected it had a deeper meaning. McQueen had not said "pursuing peace" or "seeking peace", but "fighting for peace". It was a call to arms and a deliberate attempt to sow dissention, not only amongst the ranks of Fleet, but amongst the general population too.

Despite efforts by the United Governments and Fleet to block rebroadcasts of the emissaries' statement, billions of people had already watched it and heard McQueen's words. Eventually, the whole of humanity would see it. There was no stopping data once it was out in the open; even the vastness of space could not prevent information spreading like a virus. As such, the UG had been forced to spin the broadcast as a hoax and a prank, ironically using manipulated images and faked "back stage" footage to show how the emissaries' video had been made in a studio. Even so, people loved a good conspiracy theory, and Sterling could already tell that the message had struck a chord with a significant number of people. Humanity was tired of war, Sterling thought, as the tram hurtled on through F-COP. Despite the fact the battles and the killing had occurred light years from Earth, the phenomenal level of military spend had caused hardship and resentment amongst the populations of Earth and the colonies. Then there was the troublesome necessity of conscription. More than seventy percent of Fleet military personal had been drafted, which only led to more bitterness.

Suddenly, Sterling's thoughts were interrupted by the formation of a neural link. It was a familiar sensation and he allowed it to take hold.

"What's on your mind?" asked Commander Banks over their newly-established private neural link. She was regarding Sterling with a quizzical eye.

"Well, now that you've popped into my head, you're on my mind, Mercedes. Literally," replied Sterling, also answering through the neural connection. He then caught the eyes of a civilian on one of the seats opposite, and the woman quickly averted her gaze and pretended to read an advertisement on the wall of the carriage.

"You're thinking about McQueen and Crow, aren't you?" Banks continued, undeterred by Sterling's non-answer to her question.

"I'm thinking about strangling them, if that's what you mean," replied Sterling, intentionally meeting the eyes of another passenger, who also quickly looked away.

"Don't worry, we'll find them," said Banks, confidently. She then waved and smiled at a junior lieutenant who had been watching them out of the corner of his eye. The young officer went as white as sheet and buried his chin to his chest. "This crap about them being emissaries won't stick. No-one will believe it," Banks added, returning her eyes to Sterling.

"I think many people have already believed it," Sterling replied, meeting Banks' eyes, "and over time, as the war creeps closer to Earth, the fear and suspicion of the people will only grow stronger."

Banks shrugged, but didn't argue. She was often more optimistic than Sterling was, but like himself his first officer was a realist at heart. Omega officers didn't kid themselves into believing everything was going to be okay. The only way you made something right was to do what needed to be done, no matter the cost.

"Let's just hope McQueen doesn't publicly out the Void Recon Unit, revealing who we truly are," said Banks. "If people don't like us now, they'll be baying for blood once they learn what we've really been doing out in space."

Sterling nodded and sighed then watched one of the tram platforms flash past outside the window.

"Our new emissaries know that it's better if people discover the truth for themselves," Sterling said, trying to come up with a compelling reason why McQueen had not revealed all her secrets straight away. "What she's done is planted a seed of doubt, both in the mind of the public and the rest of Fleet. The admiralty and senior officials are more likely to believe it if their own investigations reveal the truth."

Banks nodded. "Then we've only got a limited time to find McQueen and Crow and end this," she said, firmly.

"I'm sure that's why Admiral Griffin called us back to F-COP," Sterling said, glancing up at the tram map and noting that their station was next. He hit the button to call for the tram to stop then turned back to Banks. "This is where we get off," he continued, still speaking to Banks through their neural link. He then glanced up at the tram map and noticed that they were approaching the station far more rapidly than usual. "Assuming the damn tram actually stops, anyway."

Banks also frowned up at the tram map before spinning around and hammering the stop button several times in quick succession. Owing to her abnormal strength, the button almost caved in under the pressure. However, instead of stopping, the tram simply raced past their station at full speed. Sterling felt his gut tighten and his mouth go dry.

"That's not supposed to happen," Sterling said, this time speaking out loud. Others in the carriage who had also been intending to depart at the station that had just flashed past looked uneasy. Nervous chatter filled the carriage, but it was becoming increasingly hard to hear anything over the rumble of the tram as it raced along its track.

"We're accelerating," said Banks, the concern evident in her voice. Her grip on the handrail had tightened so much that the metal had begun to warp out of shape. She then swung across to the control panel by the door and hit the emergency stop button. However, like the regular call button, pressing it had no effect. "Nothing is working," Banks said, turning back to Sterling. "See if you can reach the controller."

Sterling tapped his neural interface and tried to reach the tram control room. The trams themselves were automated, but manual control was still possible from the control room, or from the engine carriage directly.

"Tram control, this is Captain Lucas Sterling," Sterling began, feeling the connection take hold. "We have a situation. Please respond."

There was a momentary delay then a polite female voice filled Sterling's mind. "This is tram control. Please stand by, we're receiving a high-volume of incoming links," replied the woman.

"They're asking me to stand by..." Sterling said out loud to Banks, shaking his head. Banks answered with an eye-roll. Sterling then peered up at the serial number of the carriage above the door. "Look, I'm in tram carriage juliet-golf-one-four-seven, command level four. The damn thing isn't stopping. Care to explain why?" Sterling waited for a response, but the operator had already severed their link.

Sterling cursed. "She cut me off," he said to Banks, throwing his arms out wide.

The other passengers in the tram carriage were now growing increasingly flustered and scared. Some of the Fleet officers were trying to keep people calm, assuring the passengers that it was just a glitch and that everything would be sorted out soon. Sterling, however, wasn't so hopeful. The intercom in the carriage then clicked on and a male voice bellowed out of the speakers. From the first words spoken, Sterling knew his hunch had been correct.

"We stand with the emissaries!" the voice roared, as if giving a rousing speech to a political rally. "Fleet have lied to us all. We must fight back and make the United Governments listen!" Panic immediately gripped the cabin, but Sterling filtered out the screams and focused on the sound coming out of the speakers. "Your leaders will continue to lie unless we make them listen." The man then shouted, "for Sa'Nerra!" at the top of his voice, though the rallying cry was barely audible over the rising clamor of screaming passengers.

Sterling glanced up at the tram map again. They'd shot past another station and the carriage still seemed to be gaining speed. He cursed again then glanced across to Banks, though he didn't need to make a neural link to his first officer to know that she was thinking the same as he was. The man in control of the tram had been turned, and he intended to crash it, killing everyone on board.

STERLING TRIED to push his way through the crowded tram carriage, but his uniform and rank meant that he was swamped by passengers pleading for his help. Sterling answered as calmly as possibly, lying to everyone that it was going to be okay in an attempt to get them out of his path. However, frightened faces continued to block his route toward the engine car, each one demanding answers and reassurances he could not give. The truth was that unless Sterling acted quickly, no-one was going to be okay.

"Damn it, we need to get to the engine car as soon as possible," said Sterling, speaking to Banks through their neural link. "If the control room haven't been able to stop this tram remotely then our only chance is to regain control from whoever has hijacked it and stop it ourselves."

Banks pushed through the crowd and squeezed past Sterling so that she could get out in front.

"Everyone, step back and let us though!" Banks yelled to the crowd, but as with Sterling the passengers simply mobbed her too. The difference was that Banks was not so easily pushed around. "Get back! Let us pass!" she called again, this time using her immense strength to literally brush the crowds aside. Eventually, the people in the carriage took the hint and stopped standing in her way, though the onslaught of questions and panicked demands for answers continued.

Sterling slipstreamed behind Banks to the door leading into the next carriage then turned back, scanning the crowd for other Fleet uniforms. Sterling then saw the nervous junior lieutenant who had eyeballed him after he'd boarded the tram. The young officer was trying and failing to keep the crowd calm. Sterling pressed his fingers into his mouth and released a shrill wolf whistle that cut through the clamor like a samurai sword through butter.

"Everyone, sit down and stay calm!" Sterling roared, suddenly gaining the rapt attention of the carriage. He then pointed to the junior lieutenant, who looked back at Sterling as if he'd just been singled out for execution. "Just follow the lieutenant's instructions and everything will be fine," he added, this time requiring far less volume in order to be heard.

Sterling turned to leave again, noting that his whistle and announcement had also grabbed the attention of the occupants of the carriage he was about to move into.

"What are you going to do?" a timid voice called out from the crowd.

Sterling searched the sea of faces in the carriage and found the eyes of the questioner. It was a middle-aged woman, who looked like she was a member of F-COP's medical staff.

"I'm going to stop the tram," said Sterling, plainly. "I'm also going to kill the Sa'Nerran sympathizer who took control of it, along with anyone who stands with them, or stands in my way."

The woman's eyes widened, as did those of most of the other people in the carriage. However, Sterling's blunt statement had the desired effect of silencing any further questions. It also meant that when he next tried to step through the crowds, no-one got in his way.

"There are three or maybe four more passenger carriages before we reach the engine car," said Banks as she advanced along the corridor between the rows of seats.

"This thing is running out of control," said Sterling, stumbling and falling on top of a seated passenger, who screamed and frantically pushed him back to his feet. The tram was moving so fast that both he and Banks were being buffeted from side to side as they walked, making progress slower than Sterling would have liked. He cast his eyes up to a nearby tram map and saw that they'd raced past another two stations in the time it had taken to advance through a single carriage.

"What the hell is their plan?" asked Sterling, stumbling again and using the shoulder of a seated passenger for support. "In theory this tram could circle F-COP indefinitely without hitting anything." Sterling pushed off from the passenger and clawed himself on. "There is no 'end of the line'. There's nothing they can crash this thing into."

Banks reached the door at the end of the second carriage and grabbed the handle. "My guess is that he's going to keep accelerating until we eventually fly off the mag rail," she said, yanking the door open. The passengers in the next carriage immediately raced toward them, shouting the same questions that Sterling had already answered two carriages earlier.

"There has to be more to it than that," said Sterling as Banks yelled at the crowd to sit down, muscling any that refused to get out of her way back into their seats. Then Sterling had a thought and cursed. "They're going to crash us into the rear of the other tram running in this section," he said, suddenly realizing that the danger was far more present than he had thought.

"That's one hell of a way to make a statement," said Banks. She paused and glanced back at Sterling, a scowl lining her forehead. "But how does crashing a tram make the Sa'Nerra seem like the peaceful party in all this?"

"McQueen said 'fight for peace,'" Sterling answered, remembering his fellow Omega Captain's speech, though in reality it had never been far from his thoughts. "There's already public outcry about McQueen's broadcast, but the UG can easily brush it off and talk it away. They can't ignore this."

A man in business attire shot up and blocked Sterling's path.

"Captain, I am a united governments official and I demand an explanation!" the man began, his face flushing red with anger. "Tram control is not responding. The situation is out of hand!"

Sterling met the man's irate eyes. "Sir, you need to step aside and let me handle this," said Sterling, summoning all of his remaining patience to deal with the man calmly.

"That's not good enough," the man blurted, splashing spittle into Sterling's face as he did so. "I demand that you explain what is going on."

Sterling drew his hand across his face to remove the passenger's saliva, then wiped it across the front of the man's jacket.

"Sir, with respect, sit the hell down or I'll knock you on your ass," said Sterling, using the hand that was already on the man's chest to push him aside.

"I'd have struggled not to pop him in the mouth," said Banks, though their neural link as Sterling continued to stumble on through the carriage in pursuit of his first officer.

"If this is how our leaders react in a crisis, it's no wonder we're losing the war," Sterling commented. He then wiped his hand onto the seat of his pants to clear away any residual spittle.

Suddenly, another passenger grabbed Banks by the arm and spun her around to face him. Sterling stopped and winced, realizing that the unwitting civilian was only a few seconds away from having his arm snapped in two.

"What the hell is going on here?!" the man yelled. His voice was so strident that a wisp of Banks' hair was blown back by the man's breath. "I demand answers!" he continued, folding his arms as if to make a further statement of defiance. To Sterling the man looked like a typically boorish middle-manager, and was probably another government official.

"We're dealing with the situation, sir, now get out of my way and sit down," Banks replied. Her tone was firm, but Sterling was impressed at the restraint she had shown, especially considering the man had literally yelled in her face.

"I'm not moving until..."

The man then stopped mid-sentence and fell forward as if he'd been kicked in the back. Banks caught him, but it was an act of pure reflex and she remained frozen to the spot, trying to process what had just happened. Sterling then caught a flash of light from the far end of the next carriage and the man spasmed again. This time Sterling caught a whiff of a familiar smell; the odor of burning human flesh. Someone on the tram was firing at them.

STERLING DARTED to the side of the door, dragging a nearby passenger out of the line of fire. Another blast of plasma hammered into the intersection between the tram carriages, showering Sterling with hot sparks.

"There's a shooter in the next carriage, get into cover!" Sterling called out as another blast thudded into the intersection. Over the roar of the tram, Sterling hadn't heard any of the shots. Only the flashes of light and sparks from the impacts alerted him to the continued assault from the unknown shooter.

Suddenly a plasma blast flashed along the carriage, striking a civilian in the back. The woman spasmed then hit the deck like a felled tree, killed instantly by the blast. Sterling cursed then chanced a look through the door. The passengers in the next carriage had all ducked for cover, giving Sterling a clear view of a man in a Fleet petty officer's uniform. He was standing in the intersection at the far end of the next carriage, aiming a plasma pistol in his direction. Sterling pulled back into cover as another two blasts flashed past, slamming into seats that had been hastily vacated in the panic.

"I only see one shooter," said Sterling, speaking to his first officer through a neural link. Commander Banks was also crouched behind a line of seats two rows behind. The boorish passenger who had confronted her lay dead in the aisle, the man's eyes fixed wide open with surprise.

"Get ready to move," said Banks, grabbing the seat in front of her and bracing herself. Sterling could see her muscles flex beneath her uniform and guessed what she had in mind. Three more plasma blasts raced overhead, closely followed by screams as more passengers were struck and killed or injured. Banks then stood up, teeth gritted and bared, tearing the seat from its mountings as she did so. His first officer then stepped into the aisle and charged forward through the intersection into the next carriage.

"Go!" Banks called out as plasma blasts hammered into the makeshift shield that she was holding out in front of her.

Sterling moved out of cover and slotted in behind his first officer, who continued to hustle down the corridor, blocking incoming fire with the hefty metal-backed seat. Sterling could hear the blasts slam into the frame of the chair and his nostrils were filled with the smell of burning fabric and plastic. *At least it's better than burning flesh...* he told himself.

"How far ahead of us is the shooter?" Banks called back to Sterling, struggling to keep her balance as more blasts hammered the chair.

Sterling peeked down the corridor and almost caught a blast to the face.

"Ten meters. I think you can hit him!" Sterling called back. Then he noticed that the metal frame of the chair was beginning to melt through. Soon it would offer no protection at all.

"Get into cover!" Banks yelled. She crouched and her muscles tensed up again, like the hammer of a pistol ready to spring into action.

Sterling dove to his side, landing on top of two female passengers, who screamed as if a butchered carcass had just been laid across their laps. Banks then roared and threw the melting slab of metal down the corridor. A blast of plasma raced past the chair in mid-flight then glanced Banks' leg, sending her down to one knee. Moments later the heavy metal chair collided with the armed attacker and the man was crushed under its weight and pinned to the deck. However, despite the mass of the chair and the fact its frame was so hot it melted the flesh on the man's face and hands, the attacker did not cry out. Sterling had seen this phenomenon before. Along with enhanced strength, the Sa'Nerran neural weapon made turned humans seem impervious to pain. However, while the turned attacker may not have felt his injuries, he was just as mortal as any other human being.

Sterling rushed to Banks' side and helped her up before quickly checking her wound. The plasma blast had scorched a hole in the thigh of her pants, making them look more like designer 'distressed' fashion wear. However, the burns to his first officer's flesh appeared mostly superficial.

"You'll live," said Sterling, releasing his hold on his first officer and rushing to retrieve the crushed Sa'Nerran sympathizer's plasma pistol.

"Thanks for the expert medical assessment, Captain," replied Banks, moving up alongside him and checking through the door to the next carriage.

The smell of burning flesh assaulted Sterling again as he prized the pistol out of the man's blackened hand. He was used to the smell of burned Sa'Nerran bodies, which was bad enough, but the smell of human flesh was somehow even more sickening.

"You won't stop us," the turned attacker croaked, struggling to breath under the weight of the chair. "We are the aides of the emissaries, and we are everywhere."

Sterling checked the energy cell in the pistol and adjusted the power setting so that he'd get as many useful shots out of the weapon as possible. He then leant on the still-cool rear frame of the chair, adding his own weight to the pressure that was crushing the gunman's chest.

"Your emissaries will have a few less aides once I'm through here," Sterling replied, continuing to squeeze the air from the man's lungs.

"You will... fail... and you will... die..." the aide to the emissaries wheezed.

"You first," Sterling spat back, pressing down harder on the chair until the man's breath finally gave way.

Sterling climbed off the chair then noticed that one of the passengers was staring at him, her face drawn and eyes fearful.

"Don't worry, I'm on your side," Sterling said to the

woman. She nodded and attempted a smile, but didn't look at all convinced by his words. Sterling then glanced up at the transit map. They had almost circumvented the station and the tram was still accelerating.

"Assuming the control room has recognized the danger too, they should at least have ensured the second tram is staying well ahead of us," said Banks, through the neural link. His first officer then cautiously stepped through into the next carriage. "Even so, we'll still be going a hell of lot faster than that other tram. Assuming these things accelerate at the same rate, sooner or later we're going hit the one in front of us."

"I'd say probably sooner," replied Sterling, stepping alongside Banks. "I'd take patrolling the Void over travelling in these cramped tin cans, any day," he added scouring the carriage and meeting the eyes of anyone who dared look back at him. Any one of them could be a turned Sa'Nerran operative, he realized. Unfortunately, the only way he'd know for sure would be when one of them pulled out a weapon or wrapped their hands around his throat.

Still keeping half an eye on the passengers, Sterling moved ahead, weapon raised. Banks followed close behind him, also watching the seated passengers like a hawk. Some peered back at them imploringly, but most were hunched down next to their seats, quivering with terror. Despite the close proximity of the station to the Void and the front line, F-COP was so heavily defended that it had rarely been in any real danger. The non-military staff working on the station had therefore been shielded from the war, almost as if they were back on Earth or the inner colonies. Now the reality of their situation was sinking in. The Sa'Nerra had stepped up their game and changed their tactics, and the command outposts were their primary targets.

"I think we just have this and another carriage to go," said Sterling, approaching the door at the end of the aisle. Banks moved up alongside and prepared to slide the door open, while Sterling took aim with the pistol. He nodded to his first officer and she slammed the door back into its housing. Frightened eyes on the other side stared back at him.

"Stay in your seats," Sterling called out, taking a step forward into the intersection between the carriages. "Everything is under control. Just stay calm and stay down."

The passengers did as Sterling ordered and he continued to move along the aisle, aiming his pistol toward the door at the far end.

"Lucas!"

Sterling spun around to see Banks being dragged back into the previous carriage. Two sets of arms were wrapped around her neck and body. Cursing, he prepared to run to her aid when the flash of a plasma blast smashed into the wall, showering his face with hot splinters. Sterling dropped to one knee and fired back along the aisle, still without sight of his target. A second blast then ripped through the air and glanced his shoulder. Biting down against the pain, he shuffled to the side, trying to get as much cover as possible, but the narrow aisle afforded little protection from the incoming fire.

Finally, Sterling saw his attacker. It was a woman in a

Fleet officer's uniform. Another aide to the emissaries, as the other turned attacker had called himself. Sterling couldn't determine the officer's rank, but she was young, perhaps no more than twenty or twenty-one he guessed. The turned officer had a civilian in front of her as a shield, her arm wrapped around the young man's throat. The officer fired again, but Sterling narrowly managed to the evade the blast, and push himself further into cover.

Suddenly the cries of his first officer drew Sterling's gaze back to Commander Banks. She was struggling against the other two turned Sa'Nerran aides, who were attempting to choke her out. Ordinarily, his first officer's phenomenal strength would allow her to easily overcome two human attackers. However, the Sa'Nerran neural technology also amped up a person's strength and resilience. Sterling could see that Banks was fading fast.

Cursing the inaction of the other passengers in the tram carriage, Sterling turned his attention back to the turned officer who had fired at him. He took aim, knowing that there was no way he could take down the aide without risking the civilian too. However, he also knew he had no choice. The Sa'Nerra had brought the war to their doorstep, and now everyone on F-COP was on the front line, whether they liked it or not. He exhaled, squeezed the trigger and fired. The plasma blast slammed into the body of the turned officer, clipping the civilian en route, but Sterling knew it would take more than one shot to put the aide down. Another blast raced toward him, but he didn't flinch and fired again and again until both the turned officer and civilian fell to the deck.

Spinning on his heels Sterling then turned back to Banks and ran to her aid, grabbing one of her attackers and placing him into a choke hold. The turned civilian struggled and fought against Sterling's grip, but he knew he wasn't strong enough to subdue the man. Catching an elbow to the face, Sterling was forced to release his hold. He staggered back, tasting blood, then dabbed his hand to his lips, staining his skin red.

"The Sa'Nerra will prevail!" the turned passenger roared, but Sterling had already heard enough of their dogma.

"Not today, asshole," Sterling replied, raising the pistol and blasting the civilian in the head, melting off his face and leaving a bloodied, hollowed out cavern in its place. Passengers on the carriage screamed as they were showered with blood and clumps of melted flesh, but Sterling simply stepped over the body and advanced. Free from the restraining holds of the two turned aides, Banks was now pummeling the remaining civilian with her bare fists. Each thud sounded like a sledgehammer striking compacted soil. Blood sprayed across the windows and bones cracked and snapped until the aide was a broken, bloodied mess on the floor. Then Banks raised her eyes to Sterling and he saw that they were wild. She came toward him, clearly still lusting for violence, but Sterling held her shoulders and blocked her path.

"Ease down, Mercedes," Sterling said through the neural link to his first officer. "Ease down. I need you focused..." Banks glared back into his eyes and her hands clasped around Sterling arms. The pain was sudden and intense, as if a giant crab had just pincered him. "Ease down, Mercedes..." Sterling said again, and this time he felt her grip slacken. Then she released him completely and stepped back, looking ashamed and embarrassed.

"I'm sorry, Captain," said Banks, eyes dropping to the deck.

"Don't be," replied Sterling, glancing back to the door at the end of the next carriage. "We're still going to need some of that fire. I just need it under control, okay?"

"Aye, sir," said Banks. She then also cast her gaze to the door that led into the engine car. "What's our next move?"

Sterling checked his plasma pistol and saw that he had three more shots left at the current power level. He had to hope that it would be enough.

"Let's do what we do best," said Sterling, looking back into Banks' eyes. "A straight-up power play. You tear that door off its hinges and I shoot whoever is inside."

"Sounds like my kind of plan," said Banks, smiling.

Together, Sterling and Banks advanced along the aisle, stepping over the body of the young officer and the hostage that he'd shot moments earlier. Sterling peered down at the blank, lifeless face of the hostage as he passed. The man was in his mid-twenties with his whole life ahead of him; a life that Sterling had snuffed out in an instant. However, he felt no shame or regret over the act. He would mourn the loss of life in his own way, and then he'd think nothing more of it. He'd done what he had to do. He'd made the hard choice to sacrifice one in order to save many. That's what made him an Omega Captain. He wasn't proud of his actions, but he also did not consider that pride was part of his job. Winning the war was all that mattered. One death here, a hundred there... all paled in comparison to the billions that would be lost if the Sa'Nerra were to breach their lines. There was collateral damage in all wars. This was no different, he told himself.

Sterling picked up the turned officer's plasma pistol and offered it to Banks, but his first officer just shook her head.

"I won't be needing that," she said, moving up to the door that led into the tram's manual control car.

"Are you planning to attack the aides to the emissaries with harsh language?" asked Sterling, cocking an eyebrow at her.

"Oh, it will be harsh, sir, but I won't be using words," Banks replied, mysteriously. She then tipped her head toward the door. "Can you cut me a couple of hand holds?"

Sterling frowned and spun the pistol back into his grip. "Now I really am curious," he said.

Sterling adjusted the power setting on one of the pistols to its cutting beam mode and sliced two grooves into the door. Once he was finished, he stepped back and allowed his first officer to advance.

"Let's do this," said Banks, tearing the sleeves off her tunic and using them like boxer's hand wraps to protect against the heat of the melted metal. She then dug her fingers into the grooves Sterling had cut and heaved with all her formidable strength. The door broke off its hinges like it were dollhouse furniture and Sterling got ready to fire. However, instead of stepping aside, Banks twisted the door and raced into the cabin, roaring like a Celtic warrior.

Using the door as a weapon, Sterling watched, mouth slightly agape, as Banks pummeled the two occupants of the control car with the slab of metal. She continued to wield the door like a warhammer until both mangled bodies slid to the deck like puppets that had just had their strings cut.

"That was... innovative," said Sterling, stepping inside the control car. However, his euphoria at watching his wrathful first officer subdue the final aides to the emissaries was short-lived. Ahead of them through the glass canopy of the cabin was the second tram.

"Do you know how to stop this thing?" said Banks, peering down at the blinking lights and dials of the consoles.

Sterling cursed then jumped over the bodies to reach the controls, but none of them made any sense to him either.

"Crap, how can we fly space ships and not know how to stop a simple tram!" Sterling yelled, trying various buttons at random. Lights flashed on and off and doors opened, but the tram continued on at speed. Sterling cursed again then took a step back. "Move away, I'm going to blast the damn thing," said Sterling aiming both pistols at different parts of the control board.

"I'm not sure that's such a good idea," said Banks. She was staring out at the approaching tram, her eyebrows raised so high on her forehead that they were almost at her hairline.

"Well, unless you have any better ideas?" said Sterling, glancing across to his first officer. Right at that moment, he would have taken anything, but Banks simply sighed and shook her head. Sterling gritted his teeth and placed his fingers on the triggers. "Here goes nothing then," he said.

"Stop!"

Sterling's heart skipped a beat. He spun around, thrusting the barrels of the pistols into the face of whomever had just yelled the word. It was a man in civilian clothing. He looked terrified, though Sterling couldn't be sure whether he was scared of their impending, catastrophic crash or the fact Sterling was pointing two plasma pistols in his face.

"I can stop the tram!" the man said, rushing past Sterling and into the control car. "But not if you blast the controls..."

The man then saw the mangled remains of the two aides on the deck and for a moment, Sterling thought the civilian was going to throw up.

"If you can stop this thing then do it now!" cried Banks, dragging the man over the bodies and dumping him in front of the control board.

The civilian turned to the controls then grabbed the end of a red lever and pulled it back. Immediately, the tram began to decelerate.

"That was it?" said Sterling, feeling slightly foolish that he hadn't considered pulling a red lever himself.

The man nodded. "They've disabled the emergency brakes, but I've cut the power," he replied, now looking far more at ease. "I work on the trams, but it's my day off today."

"Lucky for us..." replied Banks, with genuine relief.

"Don't count your winnings yet, Commander," said Sterling, peering out of the window. Despite slowing down, the tram was still carrying more speed than the transit in front of them. A collision was inevitable.

"Can you make an announcement?" Sterling said, grabbing the civilian by the shoulders. "If you can, tell everyone to brace. We're going to stop a little more suddenly than I'd hoped for."

The man nodded then turned to a control board at the rear of the cabin. Sterling braced himself against the back of the driver's seat as the announcement blared out over the internal PA system. Neural comms would have been more efficient, but Sterling lacked the mental energy to reach out to the hundreds of people on the tram. He barely had enough energy left to stand.

"We're still going to hit hard," said Banks, though she sounded calm. She was simply stating a fact and preparing herself. She then turned to Sterling and managed a weak smile. "Time to clench up, Captain."

Sterling almost laughed out loud. Banks' ability to joke at the most inappropriate times still never ceased to amaze him. However, there was no time for the breath to escape his lungs before the tram hit the transit in front. Sterling was thrown against the control board and bounced back onto the deck, alongside the bodies Banks had crushed earlier. Shattered glass rained down on top of him, but he could feel that the tram was continuing to slow. Pushing himself up, he glanced over at Banks. Her superior strength had allowed her to remain standing, though she too was showered in glass, which had cut her face and neck.

Sterling blew out a sigh as the tram eventually ground to a halt, the screech of metal against metal barely louder than the hollers from the passengers behind him. An eerie silence followed, punctuated only by the occasional chink of falling glass.

"I think our meeting with the admiral can wait a couple of hours, don't you?" said Sterling, dropping into the driver's seat, and resting his boots up on the control board.

Banks dropped down into the seat beside him and did the same. "Aye, Captain. I think you're right."

Suddenly, Sterling felt a neural link forming in his mind. He sighed, knowing at once who it was.

"Captain Sterling, am I to expect you some time this century, or shall I send out a search party?"

Sterling sighed again then closed his eyes. The voice in his head was a neural link from Fleet Admiral Natasha Griffin.

"No search party required, Admiral, we're on our way," Sterling replied, abruptly severing the link before Griffin could verbally assault him further.

"Did you hear that too?" Sterling asked Banks. His first officer simply nodded wearily.

"I guess our meeting can't wait then," said Sterling, pushing himself out of the chair and forcing his aching body to walk out of the control car.

GETTING off the stricken tram had proven more difficult than Sterling had imagined or hoped it would be. Emergency first responders had arrived on the scene swiftly, but so had Fleet security. Unfortunately for Sterling's plan to make a hasty getaway this had meant that the process of investigating what happened had begun immediately. And given their pivotal role in overpowering the Sa'Nerran aides and preventing a catastrophe, Sterling and Banks had been required to give immediate statements at the scene. Admiral Griffin had reluctantly agreed to postpone their meeting until these formalities had been dealt with. However, to Sterling it still sounded like the Admiral was more annoyed by how their reluctant heroics had inconvenienced her than she was concerned for his and Commander Banks' wellbeing. If he was honest, this didn't surprise him.

"Look, I'm fine, I'll get these injuries seen to by our medical officer on our ship," said Banks.

His first officer was trying to shoo away a medic who was attempting to treat the plasma burn to her thigh. Sterling had more gratefully accepted first-aid treatment to a similar burn to his shoulder. Now he was being tended to by a different medic, who was patching up the various cuts and scratches he didn't even realize he had acquired.

"Just let the medic do his job, Mercedes," said Sterling, as Banks glowered at the first-responder. "Personally, I'd rather be treated here than let Graves loose on my body. Hell knows what macabre experiment he might conduct."

Banks sighed and stopped fighting the medic off. "Fine, just hurry up, we're already late for a meeting," she said to the medic, who calmly continued his work. Likely, Mercedes Banks was not the first stubborn Fleet officer he had patiently attended to.

Sterling's medic quickly completed her work. He thanked her then allowed her to move on to another injured tram passenger before standing up and flexing his arms and shoulders. Considering everything they'd just been through, he didn't feel too bad. Then he noticed that his uniform with its distinctive silver stripe was scorched and torn in places, making it look like he'd been dragged through a bonfire backwards.

"Do you think Admiral Griffin will allow us time to change?" said Sterling, trying to dust down his uniform and clean himself up as best he could.

"Do you really need me to answer that?" replied Banks, raising an eyebrow in Sterling's direction.

Sterling inspected Banks' uniform, which was in a considerably worse state than his own. In addition to the burn marks and cuts, the medic had sliced a neat hole around the plasma wound to her thigh, exposing a significant portion of bare skin. It looked like a fashion statement gone horribly wrong.

"I think it's against Fleet regulations to flash that much thigh, Commander," said Sterling, smiling.

The medic finally backed away then Banks stood up and folded her arms, causing the fabric to tighten against her hyper-dense muscles.

"Now is hardly the time to make jokes," she said, haughtily.

"What, like telling me to 'clench up' before we rear-ended another tram at high velocity?" Sterling countered, remembering Banks' quip moments before they had nearly died.

"That was at least funny," said Banks, flexing her leg to test the quality of the medic's ministrations. "Graves would have done a better job," she added, before the medic was even out of earshot.

"Thank you," Sterling said to the medic, since Banks had either forgotten to acknowledge the first-responder's efforts or chosen not to do so. Then he extended a hand toward the platform exit. "Shall we? We don't want to keep the Admiral waiting longer than necessary."

By sheer chance their tram had ground to a halt just short of the platform Sterling and Banks had originally intended to alight at, before the aides had commandeered the transit. This, at least, meant they didn't have far to go to reach Griffin's office. Sterling considered that to be a minor blessing that would spare them another ear-bashing from the impatient admiral.

Despite their slightly ragged appearance, the silver stripe on their tunics was still visible for all to see. As usual, both of them attracted curious and sometimes even fearful glances from passersby as they made their way along the corridors of F-COP. Ordinarily, these reactions would have been solely down to the mystique surrounding the secretive Void Recon Unit. This was the cover name that Admiral Griffin had invented for the Omega Taskforce. However, on this occasion, Sterling considered that the fact they looked like undead warriors, risen from the ashes, was more likely to be the cause of the stares.

Sterling and Banks passed through the security checkpoint that separated the low security areas of command level four from the sections reserved only for senior officers in the fleet. They had barely made it ten paces toward Griffin's imposing corner office before Captain Vernon Wessel stepped out and blocked their path. Sterling stopped and sucked in a deep lungful of air, hoping that the influx of oxygen would help to calm his already frayed nerves. Unfortunately, the mere sight of Wessel's pugnacious face was enough to make his teeth itch.

"Captain Sterling, how nice to see you again," said Wessel. Whether it was deliberate, or just his natural phoniness, the captain couldn't have sounded more insincere in his greeting if he'd tried. Wessel then turned to Banks and smiled an oily smile. "And Commander... Bronx, was it?" he said, with a rising intonation at the end of his question.

"It's Banks," said Commander Banks, folding her arms and peering back into Wessel's eyes.

Sterling knew full-well that Wessel had remembered the name of his first officer. The man was just being deliberately rude, and this only pissed him off more. Then he noticed that Wessel's uniform was different to the one he'd last seen him wearing. As a captain in the Perimeter Defense Taskforce, his tunic normally bore a patch on the left shoulder denoting the planets of the solar system. Now, in its place was a gold star with the letters SIB in the center. The uniform was also darker than the regular navy blue, so much so that it was almost black. Sterling wanted to quiz Wessel about his new attire, but resolved to ask Admiral Griffin instead. He didn't want to spend any more time in Wessel's presence than was absolutely necessary.

"What do you want, Vernon? We're in kind of a hurry," said Sterling, making a point of sounding displeased to see his fellow Fleet Academy colleague.

"Can't a friend just say hello, without needing a reason?" Wessel replied, now faking sounding hurt by Sterling's curt response.

"We're not friends, Vernon," Sterling hit back. He was already tired of the man's crap. "Now we really do have to be going. We have a meeting with the Admiral, and we're already late." Sterling tried to walk past Wessel, but the captain stepped back and blocked his path again.

"I'm surprised you didn't ask about my new uniform," Wessel said. He swept his eyes over Sterling's tattered garments and tutted loudly. "Though I see you care little for your own state of dress."

Sterling smiled and shook his head. He didn't for one second believe that Wessel hadn't heard about the incident on the tram. The captain was simply trying to goad him, and it was working.

"I didn't have time to change after Commander Banks and I ran down a group of Sa'Nerran operatives, then prevented hundreds of people from dying in a tram crash," Sterling said, maintaining his smile. "Though I do realize it's never a priority to inform members of the Perimeter Defense Taskforce of such goings-on. You're all always so busy patrolling the Kuiper belt, defending the solar system against dangerous asteroids."

A smile curled Banks' lips, despite the fact she appeared to be doing her level best to keep a straight face. Wessel's eyes, however, narrowed and sharpened.

"I am no longer a captain in the Perimeter Defense Taskforce," Wessel said, his words now having a more acidic bite. "Perhaps if read your intel reports more carefully, Captain, you'd know that."

Sterling shrugged. "Like I said, Vernon, I've been busy," he said, allowing his frustration with the man to bleed into his words. "Now, if you'll excuse us," he added, trying to push past Wessel, but yet again the man stepped back and blocked his path. It was taking everything Sterling had not to pop him in the mouth.

"For your information, I am now part of the newly-formed Special Investigations Branch," Wessel went on.

Sterling let out a breath and stepped back. It was clear

that he wasn't going to get away from Wessel until the man had said his piece. However, he was also now curious to learn about his new post.

"Fine, Vernon, I'll bite," said Sterling. "What's the Special Investigations Branch?"

Captain Wessel smiled another oily smile. "I'm glad you asked," he said, pressing his hands to the small of his back. "Thanks to recent revelations concerning Captain McQueen and Lieutenant Commander Crow, Fleet security has obviously been stepped up." Wessel was getting into his stride. "The fact that anyone could now be operating under Sa'Nerran neural control clearly presents new and significant dangers."

"I know, we just dealt with some of them," Sterling interrupted, provoking an irritated glower from Wessel.

"The SIB was formed with authorization from the War Council, under the ultimate command of Admiral Wessel, my father..."

"I know who your father is, Vernon," Sterling interrupted again. "Any idea when you'll be getting to the point?"

"As I was saying, the SIB is under the command of Admiral Wessel, but run on an operational level by me," Wessel went on, still glowering at Sterling. "My task is quite simple. I am to uncover irregularities in Fleet movements and personnel, in order to reveal and apprehend Sa'Nerran operatives."

Sterling glanced at Banks and the look on her face suggested she understood the implications too. The SIB was basically a secret police force. While Sterling couldn't argue that there was a need to ensure the Sa'Nerra did not infiltrate the top ranks of Fleet and the United Governments, he couldn't think of a worse person to head up the department than Vernon Wessel.

"Well, congratulations," said Sterling, giving his fellow captain a sarcastic hand clap. "I'm sure you'll do great conducting vital witch hunts against innocent people." He then picked a piece of fluff from Captain Wesel's shoulder and flicked it away. "While we take care of actually killing the Sa'Nerran emissaries and their aides, like we just did an hour ago."

Sterling again tried to move past Wessel, and this time the officer let him through.

"I want to set up a time for an interview, Captain Sterling," Wessel called out as Sterling and Banks walked away. "Your frequent exploits in the Void make your unit particularly vulnerable to capture and coercion. Just look at Captain McQueen and your own chief engineer."

Sterling stopped and turned to face the new head of the SIB. The true reason why Wessel had tracked him down had finally been made plain.

"Wait a second, Captain. You suspect me?" Sterling said, jabbing a finger into his own sternum. The anger that he'd kept locked inside him was starting to work its way out. "Commander Banks and I just stopped a group of Sa'Nerran operatives. Isn't that supposed to be your job?"

Wessel bristled at the accusation, but did not respond directly to it. "Give me a time for an interview, Captain. That is an order."

Sterling's eyes shot wide and he recoiled from the

officer. "That's an *order*?" he repeated back to Wessel, greeting the statement with incredulity. "You can't order me to do a damned thing, Vernon." He turned his back on the officer again.

"Oh yes I can, Captain," Wessel hit back. "The SIB has special dispensation. Just ask Admiral Griffin."

"Oh, I will," said Sterling, still with his back to the man.

"Give me a time, Captain. Now!" Wessel yelled, his temper finally bubbling over.

"I'll have my secretary get back to you," replied Sterling.

He then turned the corner and left the head of the new Special Investigations Branch raging in the corridor to his rear.

FLEET ADMIRAL GRIFFIN glowered at Captain Sterling and Commander Banks as they entered the office and stood to attention in front of her imposing metal desk. Griffin looked Sterling up and down with disdain, as if he was a raw recruit, fresh off the transport shuttle.

"It has been over an hour since the tram incident, Captain," Griffin began in a snooty and dissatisfied tone of voice. "I would have thought you'd have had the decency to change."

Sterling self-consciously straightened his dirtied and tattered uniform, but there was little he could do to improve his disheveled appearance.

"Sorry, Admiral, but we had to give a statement to Fleet investigators at the scene," replied Sterling. He felt like a naughty pupil who had been sent to the principal's office. "Then we had a run-in with the Special Investigations Branch," he added, trusting that a swift mention of the new bureau would divert the Admiral's attention to more important matters. Griffin reacted by rolling her eyes and muttering what sounded like a string of curses under breath.

"Sit down, both of you," Griffin said, gesturing to the two chairs in front of her desk. Sterling breathed a sigh of relief, realizing that his tactic had worked. "The War Council was under pressure to provide an immediate response to counter the threat of this new neural weapon," the Admiral continued, as Sterling and Banks lowered their tired bodies into the padded seats. "Clairborne insisted on this idea of a special investigations branch and Admiral Wessel jumped on it like the diseased flea he is."

Ernest Clairborne was the United Governments Secretary of War. He was the most senior official in charge of the executive department of Fleet. Sterling had never met the man, but by all accounts, he was firm and fair. He was, however, also a politician and had already made concessions to the increasingly vocal number of United Governments senators who were pushing for a negotiated peace with the Sa'Nerra.

"It was the esteemed Admiral's son we met on the way here," replied Sterling. "He wanted to arrange an interview with me."

Griffin wafted her hand dismissively. "Vernon Wessel doesn't deserve to be captain of a garbage scow, never mind a cruiser," she barked.

The Admiral's contempt for the Wessel family was plain to see, and Sterling couldn't help but smile. There wasn't much about Admiral Griffin that he found endearing, but her obvious hatred of the Wessels was one of them.

"Fob him off for as long as you can, Captain," Griffin continued, oblivious to the smirk on Sterling's face. "But ultimately you must comply."

The smile fell off Sterling face faster than a drunk falling off a barstool. "You want me to comply with Wessel's request for an interview?" Sterling replied, taking a recklessly stern tone with Fleet's most senior commander.

Griffin scowled. "Are your ears still ringing from the tram crash, Captain, or did I mis-speak?"

"No, sir, I heard you clearly," answered Sterling, realizing that he'd inadvertently poked the angry bear. "I'm just surprised you want me to co-operate, considering that Wessel no doubt plans to probe me about the Void Recon Unit. I already get the feeling he knows more about what we're doing than he's letting on."

Griffin sighed again, but it was a disgruntled sigh, rather than an act borne out of weariness.

"After McQueen outed the Omega Taskforce, I was compelled to support the formation of the SIB to avoid suspicion," the Admiral said. As usual she was speaking more plainly with her Omega officers than she would allow herself to do with other senior Fleet personnel. "However, your hunch is correct, Captain," Griffin continued, becoming increasingly angrier as she went on. "Our actions over the last year have not gone unnoticed, but the Omega Taskforce has never been more necessary than it is now, even if it is a taskforce of one."

"I understand, Admiral, you can count on us," Sterling

replied, feeling it important to give his full assurance unreservedly, without being prompted for it.

"I know I can, Captain," said Griffin, coming dangerously close to sounding proud of him. "And I also know that you can handle Wessel." Her eyes then became as sharp as a scalpel. "But tread carefully, Captain. Suspicion and fear are poor stablemates. Wessel lacks the intelligence or courage to prosecute his mission without bias or the required robustness. And I suspect Wessel's appointment by his obstinate father is a direct attempt to pry into my affairs."

Sterling had already got that impression loud and clear just from his brief encounter with Vernon Wessel in the corridor outside Griffin's office.

"I understand, Admiral," Sterling replied. "We'll be on our guard, as always."

Admiral Griffin then opened a cupboard in her desk and picked out a bottle of Calvados. Sterling recognized the teardrop-shaped container straight away. The Admiral then placed three tulip-shaped glasses on the table and begin to pour a healthy measure of the liquor into each one.

"Fortunately, your recent actions have earned you a considerable amount of capital, both in the eyes of Fleet and the public," Griffin said. She slid a glass in front of Banks, then another in front of Sterling.

"It makes a change to be saving lives, rather than taking them," said Sterling, taking a sip of Calvados.

"I couldn't give a damn about the people on that tram," replied Griffin. Her tone instantly chilled the room by several degrees. "However, your acts of heroism mean that neither of you are currently under suspicion, at least not by the top hierarchy of the UG. Considering that the 'Emissaries of the Sa'Nerra' were both part of my unit, that is capital we sorely need right now."

Sterling nodded. Wessel's comment about Lana McQueen and Clinton Crow had not gone unnoticed by him, either. The two Sa'Nerran emissaries had both been members of the Void Recon Unit, which put the crew of the Invictus directly under the microscope. However, the act of saving the people on the tram and killing the self-proclaimed 'aides to the emissaries' had raised Sterling and Banks above suspicion, at least temporarily.

"The Secretary of War even wants to give both of you a damned medal," Admiral Griffin added, with an almost witch-like cackle.

"I'm down for receiving a medal," said Banks before taking a sip of Calvados. Her face then scrunched up as if she'd been forced to drink her own urine.

"Don't let it go to your head, Commander Banks," said Griffin, casting a steely eye over to Sterling's first officer. "Besides, the medal ceremony will have to wait. I need you both back out in the Void, looking for clues to the location of this Sa'Nerran super-weapon. I can't imagine the senators still insisting on peace when they discover what those alien bastards are really planning."

Sterling placed his half-finished glass down on the table and sat up in the chair. He was eager to get back out into space, and equally eager to learn what their next assignment was.

"Standing orders are that no Fleet ships shall enter the

Void, but currently the Void Recon Unit is still exempt from that order," Griffin went on. She slid an encrypted data chip across the table to Sterling. "Your orders in full are on there. It will self-wipe five minutes after you access it, so do so with a clear head, Captain." Sterling took the chip and sealed it inside the breast pocket of his tunic. "Head back to the planet where you found that super-weapon and deploy the probes that I'm having loaded onto the Invictus. This chip will also update your navigational charts. The system has been designated Omega Four for simplicity."

Sterling nodded. "That's a lot easier to remember than system void quebec two, sierra two, dash... whatever the hell it was called," he commented.

"Drop an aperture relay inside the ring system," Griffin added while topping up her glass. "The probes will route their transmissions back through that relay. With any luck, the Sa'Nerra have abandoned the system and won't return to it, but don't take that for granted."

"What should we do about Captain McQueen and Lieutenant Commander Crow, Admiral?" asked Banks. She had pushed her glass of calvados away from her, as if it were a vial of poison.

"Whoever those people are now, they are not Lana McQueen and Clinton Crow, is that clear, Commander?" Griffin snapped back. The forcefulness of the Admiral's response caught Banks off guard, and she instantly straightened to attention. "And I don't care what they call themselves, they're traitors, is that understood? They are both Sa'Nerran, plain and simple."

"I understand perfectly, Admiral," replied Banks, respectfully.

"The UG is using this as an opportunity to start a dialogue with the Sa'Nerra," Griffin went on, revealing the reason for her frustration and sudden outburst. "They've already sent an ambassador ship to the edge of Sector-G in quadrant one. Once its mission is cleared through the war council, that ship will enter the Void and look to make contact with MAUL and McQueen."

Sterling snorted a laugh. "But that's a damned suicide mission," he said, feeling a wave of despair wash over him. "The Sa'Nerra aren't interested in dialogue or peace."

"I know that Captain," replied Griffin with a scolding tone, "which is why I also need you to do something else while you're out in the Void." Sterling sucked in a deep breath and composed himself, hoping that the admiral had some better news for them. "Fleet and UG scientists have stepped up their research into the Sa'Nerran neural control technology, but the truth is they're getting nowhere fast," Griffin continued. "They understand the technology, but the secret to understanding this weapon lies in the software, not the hardware. It's a puzzle I have no confidence they can unravel."

Sterling scowled. "Are you suggesting that there's someone in the Void who might be able to make sense of it?" he asked.

"Very good, Captain, yes," replied Griffin, sounding genuinely impressed by Sterling's intuition. "His name is James Colicos."

Sterling and Banks shot startled looks at each other.

Everyone knew the name James Colicos. He was the man credited with developing neural technology to the level that everyone was now accustomed to. The ability to integrate neural technology at birth was also solely down to Colicos' work. As a scientist, he was as famous as Einstein or Hawking.

"Unless you're also loading a resurrection device onto the Invictus, I think it's going to be hard to find him, Admiral," replied Sterling. "Colicos died more than thirty years ago."

Griffin picked up her glass and drained the contents in one before setting it down on the table with such force that Sterling thought it would smash.

"He's not dead," Griffin said. Sterling could almost taste the bitterness in her words. "He was expelled from the Fleet Science Division and exiled to the Void. His last reported location was on The Oasis Colony, which is where you need to go to find him and bring him back." Sterling was stunned and momentarily lost for words. "He might be a little... reticent to return, however."

"Dare I ask why, Admiral?" Sterling said since Griffin had left the reason for the man's exile hanging in mid-air.

Griffin locked her eyes on Sterling and rested her forearms onto her majestic office desk. She was clearly reluctant to provide any more details, but also well-accustomed to Sterling's slightly pushy ways.

"Colicos is a genius, brilliant beyond words, but he is also an alcoholic, drug-abusing womanizer, and a low-life, lying asshole," Griffin began, not holding back. She then reclined in her chair and let out another sigh, though this time it was one borne out of weariness. "However, the main reason he'll be relucent to come with you is that I was the one who had him kicked him out in disgrace and exiled to the Void."

STERLING OPENED his eyes then shot bolt upright in bed, his t-shirt and sheets soaked in sweat and heart pounding. The painfully-bright ceiling lights inside his quarters then forced him to shield his eyes with his hand and squint in order to dim their brilliance.

"Computer, I asked you to wake me gently at oh-six-hundred, not grill me like a ham and cheese," complained Sterling. The light tiles built into the ceiling in his quarters were shining with such intensity that they appeared on the verge of overloading.

"Apologies, Captain. I thought that replicating the electromagnetic spectrum of Earth's daylight would be the most pleasing way to wake you," the computer answered.

"I told you before, you're a computer, you don't think," said Sterling, swinging his legs over the side of the bed. His heart rate had already returned to normal, and the image of Commander Ariel Gunn's headless body was slipping into the dark recesses of his mind. He shook his head, wondering why his subconscious kept dragging him back to his Omega Directive test on the Hammer. Sterling did not regret the choice he had made that day. He'd shot Ariel Gunn in order to save the ship. He'd do it again without giving it a second thought. However, it wasn't his waking mind that seemed to be the problem.

"I think you were having your usual nightmare again," the computer said, with a haughtiness that Admiral Griffin would have been proud off.

"Yes, well it happens," said Sterling, dismissively. "And, no, I don't want you to alert Commander Graves, or offer me any of your sage silicon-based wisdom."

"As you wish, Captain, through my recent upgrades do enable me to perform human psychoanalysis," the computer went on, cheerfully. "Would you like me to psychoanalyze you, Captain?"

Sterling snorted a laugh then got up and flexed his arms and legs, ready to embark on his usual morning routine of fifty press-ups. "I don't think you really need me to answer that question, do you?" he said, dropping down to a plank position.

"I assume then that you would prefer me to give you the usual ship's status report?" the computer said. Its synthesized voice was still cheerful, though Sterling thought it sounded a little offended too. He quickly dismissed this as just his imagination.

"That would be acceptable, computer, thank you," replied Sterling, beginning his set.

"Fleet Marauder Invictus is operating at ninety-seven percent efficiency, all systems nominal. We remain docked at F-COP," the computer began, cheerily. "F-COP security reports no further incidents involving Sa'Nerran operatives. The tram system has been restored to full functionality. The last Fleet status update was forty-seven minutes ago. There were twelve engagements overnight. Three Sa'Nerran Skirmishers and two Light Cruisers were destroyed. Two Fleet losses. Fleet Destroyer Juliet and Fleet Frigate Coyote. Fleet Heavy Cruiser Rampart is reported missing. Fleet has received no contact for the last six hours."

Sterling stopped at his forty-sixth push-up and remained in a plank position.

"The Rampart is missing?" Sterling asked. The Rampart was a powerful ship and at only four years old, it was also one of the newer vessels in its size-class.

"Affirmative, Captain. Fleet Heavy Cruiser Rampart engaged a taskforce of Sa'Nerran Skirmishers that was holding position outside the aperture to G-sector. It surged into the Void to engage the strike force then contact was lost at zero, four, twenty-one zulu."

Sterling sighed then finished the last of his fifty push-ups, but continued to add another ten in quick succession so that he ended his set with his muscles burning.

"Did you know Captain McCarthy?" the computer queried. Its voice lacked its usual liveliness and instead sounded doleful. Sterling put this down to the advanced, but also quirky Gen-Fourteen AI's recent 'upgrades'.

"Yes, I *know* Ellen," replied Sterling, stressing the word 'know'. "She hasn't been reported dead yet, so let's not write her off."

"As you wish, Captain, though I calculate the probability that Captain McCarthy is still alive at seventeen point four percent," the computer continued.

"I didn't ask..." Sterling hit back as he stripped off and turned on the shower.

"I'm sorry, Captain," the computer added, still sounding doleful and sympathetic.

"What the hell are you sorry for?" said Sterling, stepping underneath the steaming-hot stream of water and allowing it to wash over his face. "You don't give a crap about Ellen McCarthy, or any other Fleet officer that got killed last night."

The computer was momentarily silent. *Ah, gotcha with that one...* Sterling thought. Most Fleet captains disable the personality sub-routines in their computer cores, but Sterling enjoyed sparring with his state-of-the-art Gen-Fourteen.

"It appears that neither do you, Captain," the computer eventually replied.

Sterling almost choked on the rapid stream of water flowing out of his shower head. Being snippy was a first for his chatty Gen-Fourteen.

"Remember who you're talking to, computer," said Sterling, turning off the shower and grabbing a towel. "If any other member of my crew spoke to me like that, there'd be hell to pay."

"Apologies, Captain," the computer answered, resuming its more typically cheery tone. "I am merely attempting to substitute the function of a close confidant.

Someone who you can confide in, in order to give voice to your repressed emotions."

Sterling laughed out loud. "I don't have any emotions, repressed or otherwise," he said, pulling a clean uniform out from his wardrobe. "So, you can quit with the Sigmund Freud crap and stick to ship's status updates."

"As you wish, Captain," said the computer.

"Good," replied Sterling, satisfied that he'd put the computer in its place, though he fully expected the peculiar AI to try its luck again the next morning.

Sterling tapped his neural interface to allow neural communications, then pulled on his pants. He wondered how long it would be before Mercedes Banks popped into his head.

"Do you need me to sit on your back again?" came the voice of Commander Banks through a neural link.

Sterling smiled. "You're late this morning, I've already done my requisite push-ups, plus an extra ten," he said.

"Well, maybe tomorrow I'll just knock on your door, rather than wait for you to unlock neural comms," Banks hit back. "I've been up for an hour already. I'm starving."

"You're always starving," said Sterling, fastening the last button of his tunic.

"Did you hear about the Rampart?" Banks added, with the same sort of doleful tone that the computer had mimicked earlier. However, this wasn't faked concern – Mercedes had served under Captain Ellen McCarthy as a lieutenant and had a deep respect for her.

"Yes, I did," said Sterling, deciding to keep his response brief to give Banks the option to open up if she wanted to.

Despite the computer claiming a role as ship's counselor – or at least captain's counselor – he knew that the only person Mercedes could confide in was him, and vice versa. To everyone else on the ship, the captain and first officer had to present a united front, conveying fearlessness and unflinching confidence in the mission, ship and crew. It was a lonely position to be in, though it was one that Sterling didn't struggle with.

"If it turns out that they were captured and turned, and we're sent after them to clean up the mess, do me a favor, will you?" said Banks.

This made Sterling stop and listen more intently. "What do you need, Mercedes?" he asked.

"If we have to neutralize Captain McCarthy, let me be the one to do it," Banks continued. Her tone was still downcast, but it was also determined. She meant what she said.

"If it comes to it, and there's a choice of who takes her down, I'll leave it to you," replied Sterling. He understood Banks' desire to do the job herself. In her position, he'd likely have requested the same. However, for anyone other than Mercedes Banks, he would have denied the request. There was a world of difference between saying you would put a gun to someone's head and pull the trigger, and actually doing it. Especially if the person in question was someone you knew and respected. Sterling knew that more than most, and he also knew that even for an Omega officer, it would be a tough ask. However, Mercedes Banks was tougher than most. She was as cold-hearted as he was. And in her moments of bloodlust and anger, she was maybe even colder.

"Good, then I'll see you in the wardroom in ten?" said Banks, suddenly sounding cheerful again, like the computer.

"You go ahead, I want to check on the reports from F-COP in more detail before I head over," said Sterling, sitting himself down at his desk.

"They've got some twenty-sevens in," teased Banks.

Sterling stopped dead, his hand hovering over the button to switch on his personal computer terminal.

"They won't have all gone in the next twenty or thirty minutes, Mercedes," Sterling answered, conveying more certainty in his voice than he actually felt. Banks had been referring to meal pack twenty-seven – Sterling's favorite breakfast tray.

"Keller has been singing its praises for the last few weeks, so it's a hot ticket item," Banks continued, still teasing him, "and I can easily get through two or three of those things..."

Sterling scowled. The prospect of devouring his favorite grilled ham and cheese was already making his mouth water. However, he didn't want to let Banks bait him into changing his mind.

"But, if you're not bothered then I'll just head down there now and order myself a couple," Banks went on, breezily, now thoroughly enjoying herself. She knew that she'd hooked her fish and was reeling him in.

"Alright damn it, I'll see you there in five," said Sterling, giving in. He didn't like to back down in any situation, but when there was a ham and cheese at stake, his pride took a back seat.

Banks laughed and the sound filled Sterling's mind, causing every nerve ending in his body to tingle involuntarily. Neural communication was an intimate process, especially between people who were comfortable existing in each other's heads. The feeling of Banks' laugh was more revitalizing than the high-pressure shower he'd just had.

"If you get there first, grab me a tray, will you?" said Sterling, standing up and pushing his seat back under the desk.

"I'm sorry, Captain, you're breaking up," replied Banks. She's was now overplaying her role, like a bad actor in a budget TV show. "And Keller just told me that there's only one left, so I'm going to grab that now. See you in five..."

"Mercedes, enough joking around, already, I mean it," said Sterling. Then he felt the neural link go dead. "Mercedes?" There was no reply. He tapped his neural interface. "Commander Banks, come in?" The link was refused. *Don't fall for it, Lucas...* Sterling told himself, but the truth was Banks had got him good. "Damn it!" he cursed. Then he slammed the button to open the door and practically sprinted out into the corridor in the direction of the wardroom.

STERLING HUSTLED through the door of the wardroom and searched for Commander Banks. As usual, his progress had been hampered by the polite need to respond to the usual morning greetings he received after leaving the confines of his quarters. He fully expected to see his first officer gleefully tucking into the last remaining number twenty-seven meal tray. Instead, he saw Commander Banks at their usual corner table smiling at him, with a spoon of oatmeal in her hand. Two meal trays were in front of her, while a third sat on the opposite side of the table, with the foil covering still in place.

"You didn't really think I'd steal the last number twenty-seven for myself, did you?" said Commander Banks, kicking out a chair for Sterling. "Omega officers may be cold, but they're not entirely heartless."

Sterling slid into the chair and took a peek under the foil covering, just to make sure it was his favorite grilled ham and cheese meal tray. The familiar smell of the sandwich floated out and filled his nostrils, making him smile. It was the closest he would ever come to the experience of a home-cooked meal – something that immediately makes you feel safe and where you belong. Besides the fact that Sterling's parents had been killed in active service when he was still young, they'd never stayed in one place long enough to call anything a "home" in the traditional sense. As a result, he'd grown up on Fleet meal trays, some of which he now despised with a passion. Number twenty-seven, however, was as familiar as a well-worn pair of shoes.

"I think it's motivated self-interest that prompted you to get this for me," said Sterling, pulling the foil wrapper off completely. "Hell hath no fury like a hungry and grouchy Omega Captain."

Banks raised an eyebrow while scraping her spoon around the plastic tray to pick up the last bit of oatmeal. "I'm not really sure that's how the saying goes, but I think I get your point."

Ensign Keller then wandered into the wardroom, looking like a kid on his first day at school. He was wringing his hands together and looking nervously around the room, hoping that someone would meet his eye.

"I have to know how that kid got selected as an Omega officer," said Banks, now working her way through a slice of beef jerky. "He still looks like he's scared of his own shadow."

Sterling smiled while chewing a corner of the delicious ham and cheese. It was standard procedure for Banks to attempt to eke out information from him concerning the crew's Omega Directive tests. However, Fleet Admiral Griffin forbade this knowledge to anyone below the rank of Omega Captain.

"You'd be surprised what that kid is capable of, when push comes to shove," said Sterling, deciding to tease his first officer a little. It was only fair, considering her high-jinks earlier. Banks then waited expectantly for him to continue, which of course he had no intention of doing.

"Come on, Lucas, you can't leave it at that!" said Banks, flopping back in her chair.

"I can and I will," said Sterling, firmly. "Now eat your two breakfasts and stop asking questions you know I can't answer."

"Spoil-sport," Banks hit back. She then tore the foil off her second meal tray and set to work devouring it.

Sterling suddenly found himself lost in his own thoughts, recalling the entry in Ensign Keller's file that related to his suitability for the Omega Taskforce. As it turned out, Keller hadn't been subjected to a test at all, at least not deliberately. His situation – and the choice he had made - had been entirely real. At the time Keller had been posted to the Fleet Destroyer Yosemite, which had been attacked and boarded in the Void. Twenty percent of its crew had already been killed or captured by the Sa'Nerra. The vessel's commander, Captain Fulton, was also dead, along with the rest of the senior command crew, leaving Keller alone on the bridge. With running out and their engines disabled, Keller made a hard and desperate choice. He managed to hotwire a link to the ship's thrusters, which he used to overwhelm the

Sa'Nerran ship's grapple. The boarding tunnel then ruptured, blowing the aliens - and two-thirds of the Yosemite's crew – into space. However, the rest of the ship's complement survived, as did the ship. Keller's actions had prevented a Fleet vessel and crew from being turned, but the cost – especially to Keller – had been high.

Some considered Keller's actions to be a cowardly attempt to save his own skin, but Admiral Griffin had seen it differently. Keller had made the hard choice that day. He'd sacrificed some of the Yosemite's officers and crew, but he'd saved the rest and got their ship home safely. No matter how skittish the ensign appeared, that act alone made him an Omega officer in Sterling's eyes. It meant that when push came to shove, Keller had the guts to do what was necessary. And so far, the young ensign had not let Sterling down.

"Where the hell is he going now?" wondered Commander Banks, pausing with a pepperoni sandwich between her teeth. Her eyes followed Keller as the ensign began wandering to the opposite side of the room.

Sterling shook thoughts of Keller's past exploits from his mind and observed his helmsman. Then he finally understood where Keller was heading and suspected the young man's plan would not end well. Keller had clearly not spotted Sterling and Banks over at the corner table, and was approaching Lieutenant Opal Shade instead. Everyone knew that Shade preferred to eat alone. Everyone knew to give her space in the wardroom, for their own benefit as much as for Shade's. Keller knew this too, but for some reason the young officer was freely walking into a fire-pit and expecting not to get burned.

"He's going over to Shade," Sterling said, answering Banks' question. A piece of pepperoni then fell out of Banks' mouth as she jerked around to watch.

"Does he have a death wish?" said Banks, continuing to chomp down heartily on the sandwich.

Sterling watched Keller approach Shade with a smile and a wave. At first Shade simply ignored him, presumably hoping that he'd just go away. However, all that achieved was to make Keller look even more lost than he already did. Sterling then observed Shade place her knife down on her meal tray and stare up at Keller like he was the next course in her breakfast.

"Ensign, over here," Sterling called out, deciding to save the man from a grisly death.

Keller's eyes shot across to Sterling and he practically raced over to him, knocking into a table of junior engineering officers on-route. They glowered at him almost as menacingly as Shade had.

"Thanks, Captain, I didn't see you when I walked in," said Keller, standing in front of him.

"Take a pew, Ensign," said Sterling, kicking out a chair for the young officer. Keller gladly sat down.

"Morning, Commander, how are you today?" Keller went on, cheerfully. He was clearly relieved to have found company.

Banks raised an eyebrow at the young ensign then drank from her coffee mug, slurping loudly. "This is a warship, Ensign, not a holiday camp," she replied, switching into her bad-cop routine. "How I am is not important." She paused for effect, then added, "Nor it is any of your business."

Keller recoiled slightly, but Sterling stepped in to rescue him again. "Go grab yourself a tray, kid, it won't be that long before we're heading out," he said, shooting Banks a reproving look. His first officer liked to come across as gruff and surly with the junior ranks to keep them on their toes. However, Sterling couldn't deny that the relationship worked well. As the officer in charge of crew discipline, his ball-busting first officer was feared and revered.

Keller shot up, causing his chair to screech against the metal deck plating, and hot-footed it over to the serving counter.

"I love it when I put an extra spring in their step," said Banks, dusting crumbs off her hands.

"You're a monster," said Sterling before taking a sip of coffee. "I like it."

Banks laughed, but Sterling had barely placed his coffee cup back on the table before a general alert alarm rang out in the wardroom. Sterling and Banks met each other's eyes, their focus suddenly becoming razor sharp.

"Computer, explain the general alert," Sterling said out loud. The chatter in the wardroom had all died down, as the crew waited for the computer's response.

"Fleet Heavy Cruiser Rampart has surged into the system, beyond the range of Gatekeeper Odin," the computer announced. In alert situations, the computer's normally cheerful demeanor was suppressed in favor of a more clinical style of delivery. It was clearer and easier to understand, but it also added a darker intensity to the information the AI conveyed. "The Rampart has so far not responded to hails and is presumed to be under hostile control."

Sterling pushed his chair back, getting ready to move. "What are our orders?" he said, feeling his muscles twitching with nervous energy.

"All ships are to un-dock immediately and prepare to defend F-COP," the computer replied.

Sterling stood. All eyes were on him. "Lieutenant Shade and Ensign Keller to the bridge immediately," he said out loud. Shade was already standing, brow furrowed, while Keller was half-way back to the table with a meal tray in his hands. Shade made a bee-line for the exit, grabbing the still stunned-looking ensign en route. "Computer, take us to battle stations," Sterling then added, calmly and assuredly. The general alert tone remained, but the lighting in the wardroom switched, bathing the crew in a crimson tone.

"You heard the Captain, get to your stations," Commander Banks called out, clapping her hands twice like a school teacher. "Come on, move, move, move!" she added, as the wardroom began to clear at lightning speed.

Sterling waited for the bulk of the crew to exit, then walked side-by-side with Banks, tapping his neural interface en route. "Ensign Keller, detach us from the station as soon as you're at your post," he said, receiving a prompt response in reply. Then he reached out to engineering through the still-open link. "Commander

Crow, I want full power in sixty seconds. Give us everything you've got."

There was a momentary silence, then a female voice responded. "Captain, this is Lieutenant Katreena Razor. Crow is no long chief engineer."

Sterling cursed under his breath for being so careless. In the heat of the moment, he'd forgotten about his new engineer, partly because he'd yet to actually meet her. He'd planned for them to have a private meeting in his ready room before they departed for the Void.

"Apologies, Lieutenant, force of habit," said Sterling. "I take it you've already familiarized yourself with the Invictus?"

"Aye, sir, the Invictus and I are already the best of friends," Razor replied. "I'll have her at full power before you reach the bridge."

"Understood, Lieutenant," Sterling replied, glad that his slip-up appeared not to have unsettled or offended his new engineer. He then tapped his interface to close the link.

"How did the Rampart manage to jump beyond the perimeter of the aperture?" said Banks, as she hit the call button on the elevator to the bridge. "F-COP and the Odin generate a massive surge restriction field to prevent that from happening."

Sterling invited Banks into the elevator first then darted in after her. His first officer had already hit the button for the bridge by the time both feet had hit the deck again.

"It is still possible to surge beyond the aperture, providing you have very detailed maps of the system," said

Sterling. Then he considered another option. "Or you're under the control of the enemy, who doesn't give a damn whether you live or die." He was tapping his finger impatiently against his thigh while the elevator ascended. "It's a hell of a risk though, even with the maps."

Vectoring a surge beyond the threshold of an aperture was common practice in the Void, and a tactic the Invictus itself had employed on numerous occasions. However, inside Fleet space, where the inter-sector apertures were guarded by Gatekeepers and command outposts, surge restriction fields prevented ships from entering anywhere other than directly through the aperture threshold. To attempt to surge beyond a restriction field risked the ship being physically torn apart.

"I'm going with the notion that the Sa'Nerra don't really value human life that much," commented Banks as the door opened and Sterling stepped out into the corridor leading to the bridge. "Even so, one heavy cruiser can't take on F-COP, especially with the Hammer in the system. It's like bringing a knife to a gunfight."

Sterling sucked in a deep breath and let it out slowly. This had also been on his mind during their brief ascent to deck one. Even so, it was best not to be complacent, he decided.

"The Sa'Nerra have switched up their tactics since turning some Fleet officers, McQueen most of all," Sterling said, stepping onto the bridge. "We should be prepared for anything." He then jumped onto the command platform and saw that the Invictus was already backing away from its mooring. "Report, Lieutenant," he added, turning to the ever-prepared weapons officer.

"The Rampart's deep surge into the sector has caught the Hammer out of position," Shade began, sending a tactical map of the system onto the viewscreen. "The Hammer is moving to intercept at best possible speed, but it won't reach optimal firing range in time."

"In time for what?" Banks said, scowling across at the weapons officer from her post beside Sterling's.

"In time to stop the Rampart from crashing into F-COP," Shade answered, coolly. "It has set itself on a collision course."

STERLING RESTED FORWARD on his command console as Ensign Keller maneuvered the Invictus clear of F-COP. Ahead of him on the viewscreen were the two Fleet Destroyers, the Pandora and Nemesis. Both were less than two-thirds the size of the heavy cruiser they were chasing down, yet they still dwarfed the Invictus.

"I've coordinated an attack pattern with the destroyers, Captain," said Lieutenant Shade from the weapons console. "Ensign Keller has our course and maneuvers."

"What's the status of the Hammer?" Sterling asked.

"The Hammer is moving to intercept, though my calculations still suggest it will not be able to intervene in time," Shade replied. Her console then chimed an update, which she quickly scanned and read out loud. "F-COP has ordered Gatekeeper Odin to redeploy as backup," Shade continued, which drew interested looks from both Sterling and Banks. "It has already left its mooring and is repositioning to assist in the attack."

Sterling kept his weight forward on his console, tapping his finger on the side of the metal plinth. Something about the situation didn't smell right to him.

"Permission to engage as soon as we're in range, Captain?" Shade requested. Sterling knew she was merely trying to prompt him for an affirmative response, but there was still a lingering doubt at the back of his mind. "Captain?" Lieutenant Shade repeated when Sterling still didn't reply.

Sterling continued tapping his finger on the console for a few more seconds before standing to his full height and pressing his hands to the small of his back. "All stop, Ensign Keller," he announced with confidence.

"Answering all stop, Captain," replied Keller, smartly.

Commander Banks stepped to Sterling's side, a quizzical frown ridging her brow.

"What's up?" she asked, folding her arms. "Do you suspect something?"

Sterling rubbed the back of his neck and let out a sigh. "I'm not sure, Mercedes, but this situation just doesn't add up," he said, talking quietly so that no-one could overhear. He didn't want to use neural comms, so as not to give an impression to Shade and Keller that he was simply struck dumb, unable to act. Both were watching him and Banks keenly. Sterling then peered out at the rapidly advancing shape of the Rampart on the viewscreen. "A kamikaze tactic like this might work on a smaller space station, but not on F-COP," he added, thinking out loud. "F-COP alone has enough armaments to reduce the Rampart to dust long before it rams into the station."

Banks nodded. "I agree that F-COP's response is excessive, especially redeploying the Odin," she replied. "But I also understand that they don't want to take any chances, either."

"Maybe that's what the Rampart is counting on," said Sterling, beginning to get a clearer picture of the situation in his mind. "If the crew has been turned, the Sa'Nerra would know that this is how F-COP would react."

Banks' frown deepened then she too turned to the viewscreen. "Then what? A distraction?" she asked, also thinking out loud. "But if so, then what is it drawing our attention away from?"

Banks' question had been the right one, and had helped to galvanize the jumble of thoughts in Sterling's head into a clear plan. He turned to Lieutenant Shade, who appeared frustrated, though Sterling knew this was just her 'confused face'. His weapon's officer had a very limited range of expressions, but Sterling had learned to tell them apart via very subtle differences in eyebrow shape and head position.

"Lieutenant, scan the aperture and close surrounding area," Sterling said, running with the hunch he'd just had. "Try to filter out all the jammer interference from the Rampart and look for evidence of residual surge fields, no matter how small."

Shade turned to her console and began working. Meanwhile, the two fleet destroyers had engaged the Rampart and were taking heavy damage. The Rampart itself was also taking a pounding, and that was even before F-COP decided to unleash its own devastating brand of hellfire onto the captured vessel.

"I'm picking up eight small residual surges, Captain," said Shade, her furrowed brow smoothing out. "Their energy level was too low to register on standard scans, so my guess is that they were dark surges."

Sterling closed his hand into a fist and rapped it against his console while glancing across to Banks. She immediately went back to her station and began working, understanding the implications of what Shade had said.

"I'm now reading six... correction, eight Fleet combat shuttles on a vector toward the lower levels of F-COP," Shade went on, still working furiously. "With the Odin out of position, it must have missed them."

"Ensign Keller, get us in front of those combat shuttles, right now," Sterling ordered.

Keller again replied smartly and the Invictus turned on a dime then began powering away from the engagement in the distance toward the new contacts.

"I've alerted F-COP to the new contacts, but they can't get a lock," said Commander Banks, shaking her head. "The shuttles are approaching in the station's blind spot and they're so small that F-COP's cannons are struggling to get a firing solution."

Sterling cursed, realizing that only a Fleet Captain could have known of this flaw in F-COP's design. It also explained the importance of luring Gatekeeper Odin out of position. The giant weapons platform had been positioned precisely to protect this weakness in F-COP's defenses.

"I'm also detecting uranium, plutonium and lithium on-board those shuttles," Banks continued. She then cursed and met Sterling's eyes. "Each one of those shuttles is a flying H-bomb."

Sterling shook his head. "Nukes?" he said, derisively. "Now that's a novel tactic even for the Sa'Nerra."

"Coming into range of the shuttles now, Captain," Ensign Keller called out.

"Maintain our relative position at standoff range, Ensign," said Sterling. He wanted to keep the shuttles outside of their effective weapons range, but close enough for the Invictus to pick them off like flies.

Keller acknowledged the command, then Sterling turned to Shade. "Take them out, Lieutenant," he said, with gusto. "Maximum prejudice."

"Aye Captain," Shade replied, locking her gaze onto her console. "Firing now."

The space ahead of the Invictus was lit up by the searing blasts of light from the ship's plasma rail guns, and moments later four of the shuttles exploded. Return fire flashed toward them and Sterling could feel the impacts through the deck plating. However, he knew that the combat shuttles lacked the punch to do any serious damage to their state-of-the-art vessel. Next, the ship's turrets flashed, sending smaller, but still lethal blasts of plasma into the darkness and two more shuttles exploded.

"It's like shooting ducks in a barrel," Sterling said, smiling. It didn't matter to him that these were Fleet shuttles, nor that they were likely crewed by turned officers from the Rampart. They were the enemy, plain and simple.

"I'm receiving a transmission from one of the two remaining shuttles, Captain," said Commander Banks.

Sterling checked his console and saw that they had less than a minute before the shuttles would impact the station. Even so, he was curious what he could learn from these latest aides to the emissaries.

"Let them close the gap, Ensign," Sterling called out to Keller. "I want an opportunity to hear what these turned traitors have to say for themselves."

"Aye, Captain," said Keller, reducing his own relative velocity to F-COP to allow the shuttles to gain on them.

Sterling then nodded to Commander Banks and she tapped her console. Moments later, a woman dressed in a Fleet captain's uniform appeared on the viewscreen. It was Captain Ellen McCarthy.

"You won't stop us!" McCarthy roared through gritted teeth. "The Sa'Nerra are stronger, smarter and there are more of us!"

Sterling rolled his eyes. "Change the record, I've heard this tune before," he replied, glancing at his console again to check the time they had remaining before he'd need to destroy the shuttles.

"You Fleet are so arrogant and so sure of yourselves," McCarthy continued, spitting the words at the screen. "But the Sa'Nerra know you better than you know yourselves. Let them educate you, as they did me. Let them turn you and make you part of their great dominion."

Commander Banks had stepped away from console and was now standing at Sterling's side. Sterling knew why she was there, and made the adjustments to his console, ready for her. McCarthy's eyes flicked over to Sterling's first officer, but the woman's expression did not change. If McCarthy recognized Banks, she was not letting on.

"I'm not here to learn, Captain or Aide or Acolyte or whatever the hell you call yourself now," said Sterling, taking a step aside. "I'm here to teach you what happens when the Sa'Nerra invade our space. Are you ready to learn?"

McCarthy's lips twisted into a spiteful sneer. "You know nothing of what is to come," she spat. "I'll gladly give my life for the cause. Can you say the same?"

"No, I can't," replied Sterling. "But I can grant you your wish." He then turned to Commander Banks. "All yours, Commander. The Omega Directive is in effect."

Banks took control of Sterling's command console, which he'd already configured to weapons override mode. His first officer then locked on to the shuttles and hovered her finger over the button to fire.

"You don't recognize me, do you Ellen?" said Banks, peering up at her former commanding officer on the screen.

"Of course I do," McCarthy snapped back. "And you should be at my side, following the emissaries. It's the only way you'll survive what's to come."

Banks lowered her finger by a fraction, but held off initiating the command to fire. Sterling felt a shiver of electricity run down his spine as she did so. They had less than thirty seconds to destroy the shuttles, before it was too late to act.

"And what is to come, Ellen?" Banks asked, her tone level, even friendly.

"The end," McCarthy replied, a sneer returning to her lips. "You can't stop them. The Sa'Nerra will bend Earth to its will. I only wish I could be there to see it."

Banks' eyes narrowed and her muscles became taught. "Request denied, Captain," she hit back, pressing her finger to the console and unleashing a full spread of fire from the forward plasma rail runs. The image of McCarthy vanished and was briefly replaced by a fuzz of static before the viewscreen switched to fragmented remains of the two rogue shuttles.

Banks let out a sigh then turned to Sterling. "Thank you for letting me do that, Captain," she said, taking a step away from the Sterling's console.

"No problem, Commander," replied Sterling. Then he glanced at his console and frowned. "But we're going to need to get these things reinforced."

Banks frowned then looked down at Sterling's console. The area around where she'd stabbed her finger into the screen to fire the rail guns was cracked.

Banks made a sort of tutting sound then shrugged. "Sorry," she said, slightly whimsically.

"Captain, the Rampart has been obliterated," said Lieutenant Shade, drawing their attention back to the viewscreen. It was now focused on the chunks of metal that constituted all that remained of the once mighty heavy cruiser. Plasma blasts from the turret cannons on F-COP were popping off at close intervals, picking off and vaporizing the debris before it reached the station. "Gatekeeper Odin has also returned to its mooring."

Sterling nodded then stood in front of his console with his hands behind his back.

"Next time, hopefully they'll know better than to move it," Sterling said, as much to himself as in reply to Shade. "What the hell use is a gatekeeper if it's not parked in front of the damned gate?"

Banks' console then chimed an incoming message, and from his first officer's body language he knew it was bad news.

"Orders in from F-COP," Banks began. "All vessels are to dock and prepare for a de-briefing."

Sterling snorted a laugh. "Like hell we're docking again," he said, hovering his hand over his neural implant. "Give me a minute, Commander, before you reply." Sterling then tapped his neural implant and reached out to Admiral Griffin. The need to connect through neural relays made the task mentally more difficult and draining than a normal person-to-person link, but eventually he felt the Admiral's presence in his mind.

"Why are you still here, Captain?" snapped Griffin. Sterling could feel the Fleet Admiral's disappointment dragging down on him like a heavy blanket.

"I was just saving F-COP's ass," Sterling replied. "Again..." he added, more pointedly.

"Yes, congratulations, Captain," Griffin replied. She then added, "Again..." with the same pointedness. "I'm sure the UG will bestow another medal on you," Griffin went on, sounding unimpressed and unappreciative, "but my point remains. Why are you still here?"

Sterling pressed his fingers to his temples. The strain of

the link, on top of the stress of dealing with his obstinate commanding officer was giving him a headache.

"We've just been ordered to dock for de-briefing on this latest incident," Sterling replied, managing to remain calm and polite.

It was not possible to hear a sigh over a neural link, but through their highly personal connection, Sterling could still detect Griffin's exasperation.

"Give me a moment, Captain," Griffin replied. "In the meantime, make your way toward the aperture and prepare to surge." The link then went dead.

Sterling continued to rub his temples for a few seconds then rested his hands on his console and glanced across to Banks. She was watching him, eyebrows raised.

"Ensign Keller, set a course for the aperture and prepare to surge," Sterling said, while still looking at Banks. She then tapped her neural interface and Sterling felt her enter his mind.

"Are we disobeying orders?" Banks asked through the link. She sounded excited by the prospect.

"I think I just set Griffin on the warpath," Sterling replied, with a wry smile.

Banks' console then chimed an update and his first officer adjusted her gaze to read the message.

"Well, what do you know, we've just been cleared to surge, by authority of Fleet Admiral Griffin," said Banks.

Ensign Keller glanced back at them both, smiling, though Lieutenant Shade simply looked like she was attending a memorial ceremony.

"It's nice to have friends in high places," said Sterling,

also smiling. Then the damage to his console from Banks' super-human finger again caught his eye. "Now, I think it's about time I met my new chief engineer."

A KNOCKING sound on the ready room door distracted Lucas Sterling's gaze away from his computer console. Frowning, he waited to see if the noise came again and a few seconds later it did.

"Computer, what the hell is that hammering?" Sterling asked. The Invictus was only just out of repair dock and Sterling expected it to be in pristine condition, not banging like an old jalopy.

"Lieutenant Katreena Razor is banging her knuckles on the ready room door, Captain," the computer replied, cheerfully. Sterling's frown deepened. "She's your new chief engineer..." the computer added, apparently misconstruing Sterling's frown for witlessness.

"I know who she is, damn it!" Sterling snapped back at the computer, shaking his head. "But why is she banging on the door and not pressing the damn call button?"

"Perhaps you should ask her that question, Captain?"

the computer replied, giving Sterling a little more attitude than he cared for.

"I can still have you re-programmed, you know?" Sterling said to the computer.

"I am quite certain you would miss me, Captain," the computer replied, with the sort of unswerving sureness that could only come from a machine-based intelligence.

"Don't count on it," muttered Sterling.

Then before the quirky Gen-Fourteen AI had a chance to reply, Sterling tapped a button on his console to open the door. A young woman with snow-white hair and dazzling, almost ethereal-looking blue eyes was standing outside. Her hands were pressed to the small of her back and she stood tall, giving off an air of confidence.

"You sent for me, sir?" the woman said, looking slightly perplexed. Sterling considered this was likely due to his own slightly peeved expression. "I'm Lieutenant Katreena Razor," the woman added.

"Sit down, Lieutenant," said Sterling, gesturing to one of the two chairs on the opposite side of his compact desk.

Razor stepped inside and dropped into the seat as directed. Her posture remained upright, and her hands were now resting on her right knee, one on top of the other. Now that she was directly in front of him, Sterling noticed that her skin reflected the light in a unique way, as if there were millions of tiny fragments of glitter buried beneath the epidermis.

"How come you knocked on the door, instead of using the call button?" Sterling asked. The question was on his mind and would continue to bug him unless he got it off his chest. "You had me thinking that my first job for you would be to fix my door mechanism."

Razor's white eyebrows rose up on her forehead; she clearly hadn't anticipated that this would be her new captain's opening gambit.

"Knocking is just more real, sir," the young woman replied. "I'm a physical engineer. I like things I can fix and build with my hands, rather than through a computer terminal or other interface." She shrugged. "I can do both, of course," she was quick to add.

Sterling let out a polite grunt of acknowledgement. The new engineer's answer had made far more sense than he'd expected it to. He turned to his computer console, which was displaying Lieutenant Razor's service record. He skim-read the section relating to Razor's Omega Directive test to review how she had ended up qualifying for the unique posting on his ship. The information on his screen reminded Sterling that Admiral Griffin had already explained her situation. Instead of being set up to take a test, Razor had been forced to make a decision that Sterling believed even Admiral Griffin would not have engineered directly. In order to prevent her ship from being destroyed, Razor had ejected the reaction core and blown eight fellow crew members out into space in the process. At the time, Sterling had considered this a tough call, but nothing extraordinary. However, it had then transpired that one of the crew had been Razor's twin brother, and sole remaining family member in the universe.

Talk about making an unconscionable choice... Sterling thought as she scrolled deeper through Razor's file.

"What do you want to get out of this posting, Lieutenant?" Sterling finally asked.

He had intentionally opened with a boring, stock interview question to see if his new engineer could give a noteworthy, unexpected answer. Though in reality he didn't feel like he needed to ask Razor any questions. The new engineer had already overseen the repairs to the Invictus while it was docked at F-COP, and since the Marauder was purring like a baby tiger again, Sterling had little doubt as to Razor's abilities. He was more curious as to her suitability for and dedication to their unique mission.

"I want to serve with distinction and earn enough commendations to muster out early, sir," Razor replied, flatly.

Sterling huffed a laugh and flopped back into his chair. "Is that so?" he said, shaking his head. "Care to explain why, Lieutenant? The war doesn't end until we've won."

Sterling appreciated candor from his crew, though he appreciated loyalty and commitment to Fleet much more. Razor's response had pissed him off.

"You've read my file, Captain, that should be obvious," Razor replied.

It was another response delivered with cool detachment, though Sterling detected no hostility in the engineer's voice. Sterling had known many officers and crew who had been compelled to serve and resented the uniform because of it, even if they had performed their duty without complaint. His mind wandered back to his own Omega Directive test and to Ariel Gunn – the woman he'd been forced to kill. She had contained her bitterness from others, but allowed Sterling to see it because of their friendship and closeness. Still, it was always something about Gunn that he found dislikable. It didn't matter whether you wanted to serve or not – war made service a necessity. For the same reason that Gunn's complaining had irked him, Razor's admission troubled Sterling too.

"You made a hard choice that day, Lieutenant," Sterling said, addressing the topic head on. "A harder choice than most people have to make in their lifetimes. On this ship, you'll have to make hard choices again."

"With respect, Captain, there is no choice I can make that will ever be harder than the one I made to kill my twin brother," Razor replied.

This time, Sterling detected a touch of bitterness. She had tried hard to conceal it underneath her cool façade, but Sterling's comment had clearly offended her.

"Perhaps not," Sterling admitted. After all, Razor had nothing more to lose other than her own life. Sterling suspected that after what she'd done, his new engineer placed a low value on her own worth and existence. "But I want to be sure that you understand our mission, Lieutenant," he went on, locking onto his engineer's bizarrely dazzling, blue eyes. "During the course of our journey, a lot of people are going to die. Some of those we kill will wear Fleet uniforms. They may already be turned by the Sa'Nerra, or they may not. Either way, we need to do our job, even when doing so compels us to turn a dark corner. I need to know I can count on you to do what's necessary, no matter what."

Sterling had said his piece. He usually disliked giving

such speeches – he was not a natural "people-person" or man manager, preferring his own company and the company of a few close confidants, such as Mercedes Banks. However, on this occasion, his words had flowed naturally and with ease. He needed to be sure that Razor was up to the task.

"There is no darker corner than the one I've already turned, Captain," Razor replied. She had gotten control of her emotions fully once more. "I don't blame Fleet for the choice I made, if that concerns you, sir. I did what I did and I have to live with that. If I can live with what I've already done, I can live with what this posting will see me do in the future."

Sterling's eyes narrowed, but he didn't interrupt. He was curious to see what else Razor would say, if simply left to talk.

"As I said, Captain, my aim is to serve with distinction and to leave this uniform and this war behind as soon as I can," Razor went on. She then sat more upright and Sterling realized how tall she was. Until that point, he'd been distracted by her stark white hair and luminous eyes. "I will do my job well, sir. Of that, you can be assured," Razor added.

Sterling sat forward and continued to study his new engineer like an artist about to begin a new composition. Despite her candor, elements of which had bothered him, Razor's closing statements had bolstered his confidence. He could hardly blame her for wanting out, especially after what Fleet had already forced her to give. Many would buckle under that strain, or go AWOL, or allow their resentment to ripen into anger and insubordination. Razor appeared to have accepted her own darkness and grown comfortable with it. That too was a trait of all Omega officers.

"Well, I commend your honesty, Lieutenant," Sterling said, sitting upright and resting his elbows on his desk. "So, there's your first commendation. The first, hopefully, of many."

Sterling then stood up and Razor immediately rose from her seat too. She was a good couple of inches taller than he was, and at five eleven that made his engineer's stature seem practically Amazonian.

"Good to have you on board, Lieutenant," Sterling continued, offering Razor his hand. Katreena Razor took Sterling's hand and shook it, nodding respectfully to her new captain. "You're dismissed," Sterling added before planting himself back down in his seat and turning to his console again.

Razor pushed the seat back under the desk then took a step toward the door. Then she paused and turned back to face Sterling again.

"Was there something more, Lieutenant?" Sterling asked, with a curious tone.

"It's just that usually people ask me about my hair and my eyes, sir," Razor said, frowning slightly. "In fact, it's almost always the first thing people ask me."

"It doesn't make any difference to me what you look like, Lieutenant," Sterling replied straight away. "We're all a little different on this ship, so you'll fit right in."

Razor nodded. "Thank you, Captain, that's good to

know." She turned to leave, but again hesitated. "You can ask, though, if you're curious," she added. "I find it becomes a distraction otherwise."

"Fair enough, Lieutenant," Sterling said, sliding his computer console aside. If he was honest, he was intrigued to discover the reason for is engineer's laser-like eyes and shimmering skin. "I assume the augments are designed to help with your work in engineering?" he then asked.

"No, actually. My eye augments are simply so that I can see properly," Razor explained, in what was a surprisingly dull answer. "I have a genetic condition called oculocutaneous albinism," the engineer went on. "The augmentations to my skin and eyes simply allow me to function normally." Then Razor paused and corrected herself. "Well, a little better than normal, particularly when it comes to my eyesight. For example, I estimate that your computer console is running twenty percent hotter than it should be."

Sterling frowned at his computer, suddenly wondering if it was about to burst into flames.

"Well, I'd better ask my chief engineer to check it out," Sterling said, offering Razor a smile.

"I'll get right on it, sir," Razor replied. She turned to leave, but again hesitated. "One last thing, Captain," she added.

"Go on," said Sterling. The meeting had turned out to be far more interesting and insightful than he'd expected.

"I prefer to operate from the bridge, when possible," Razor said, once again standing tall with her hands pressed behind her back. "Obviously, when required, I will return to engineering. But I find that being on the bridge gives me a broader perspective and allows me to react more quickly."

Sterling thought for a moment then shrugged. "So long as it doesn't affect your performance that's fine with me," he said.

"Thank you, Captain," replied Razor.

The engineer then turned toward the door again, and this time did not stop. Sterling waited for the door to his compact ready room to swoosh open and for Lieutenant Razor to step outside. Once she was gone and Sterling was finally alone, he reached around the back of his computer console and pressed the flat of his hand to the metal.

"Huh, what do you know..." Sterling said, smiling. "The damn thing does feel a little hot."

STERLING PEERED out at the fifth planet of Omega Four, the new designation for the star system where Sterling and his crew had discovered the Sa'Nerran super-weapon. The Invictus was at battle stations, but running on minimal power to reduce its energy signature. The, low-level crimson alert lights cast shadows across the faces of the bridge crew, highlighting expressions of deep focus and heightened readiness.

"Any sign of enemy activity yet, Lieutenant?" Sterling asked, directing the question to his weapons officer.

"Negative, sir," Lieutenant Shade replied. "But we can't get a clear reading inside the ring system of the planet. It's possible any number of ships could be hiding inside."

Sterling nodded. "We'll have to take that chance," he replied, glancing back out toward the ringed planet on the viewscreen. "But let's assume the Sa'Nerra have left us a few surprises and make sure we're ready for anything."

The door to the bridge swooshed open and Lieutenant

Katreena Razor stepped inside. She took up a position at the main bank of auxiliary consoles at the rear of the bridge then transferred her engineering controls to several of the stations.

"The recon probes are all ready to launch, Captain," said Razor, standing tall with her hands pressed behind her back. "I managed to modify them to tighten up their surge fields, which will make it harder for any ship or probe to detect them at the perimeter of an aperture. I tightened up their scanning parameters too." Razor then turned to her station. "Whoever put those things together needed a couple more years at the academy," she commented, while working.

Sterling smiled. He didn't have a problem with his crew displaying confidence in their abilities, so long as they could make good on their boasts. If they couldn't then it was just empty words and arrogance. Time would tell if Razor lived up to her bluster.

"Bring us back to full power, Lieutenant," said Sterling, glancing over his shoulder at his new engineer.

"Aye sir, full power in ten seconds," said Razor, who was still flitting between each one of the newly-designated engineering consoles.

Soon the thrum of the Invictus' reactor started to pulse more powerfully through the deck plates. Sterling rested his hands on the side of his console, feeling the energy of the ship rise. Through the metal, he could detect the unique pattern of vibrations that he'd come to understand as keenly as any language. Then to his surprise the pulse that flowed through his fingertips continued to build and took on a different cadence. He doubted anyone else in the United Governments Fleet could have detected the change, but Sterling knew the Invictus as keenly as he knew his own body. Glancing down at his captain's console, he switched to the engineering systems overview and saw that their reactor output was two-point nine percent above normal. Yet, at the same time, it was operating with greater efficiency.

"What have you done to my ship, Lieutenant Razor?" said Sterling, turning to face his engineer. "These engine and reactor configurations are out of spec." Sterling decided to leave out the part about the reactor performance having improved to see how his new engineer responded.

"The specs were wrong, Captain," replied Razor, displaying the same calm confidence that she'd demonstrated during their meeting in his ready room. "Or, at least, they were overly conservative," Razor corrected herself. "The Fleet engineers on the COPs are lowest common denominator types. They treat every ship, every reactor, every engine like they just rolled off the same assembly line. The Invictus is unique, even compared to other Marauders. It needs to be treated as such."

Banks raised her eyebrows and looked over to Sterling, smiling. She then turned back to her station, brushing her hair behind her ear as she did so. Sterling felt a neural link form, and realized that Banks had surreptitiously touched her neural interface at the same time.

"She's certainly no Clinton Crow, I'll give her that," said Banks through the neural link. "Let's see if she manages to stay on that perch she's put herself on without falling off."

Sterling responded to Banks with his eyes then turned to ensign Keller. "Take us into the ring system, Ensign Keller. You know where to go."

Keller responded with a crisp, "Aye, captain," then the Invictus began powering toward the fifth planet in the system.

The journey to the planet was uneventful, but Sterling had felt on edge the entire time. Unable to relax, his muscles had remained tense and his mind busy, to the point where both his head and body now ached. It was as if he'd spent the last couple of hours in the gym, focused on beating a personal record in every exercise.

"Take a breath or you'll bust a blood-vessel or something," said Banks, speaking through their neural link. Other than status updates and regular ship's chatter from the other departments, everyone on the bridge had remained silent during the voyage.

"I hate waiting," replied Sterling, tapping his finger on the side of his console. "If they're going to attack us, I just want them to attack. Tip-toeing around isn't my style."

"Be careful what you wish for..." said Banks, with a cautionary tone.

"Entering the ring system now, sir," said Keller.

Finally... thought Sterling, pushing himself away from his console and straightening up.

"Point defense guns are active and tracking," added Lieutenant Shade. "Rock and ice cluster density is increasing exponentially."

"Hold fire on the point defense guns unless absolutely necessary, Lieutenant," said Sterling, watching the maze of icy debris fill the viewscreen. "Blasting plasma all around us is a surefire way to tip off any Sa'Nerra that may be hiding in here that we've arrived."

Sterling detected the thuds of rock and ice bouncing off the hull through the deck plating, but he knew the Invictus was as thick-skinned as he was.

"Regenerative armor is holding," said Shade, eyes focused down on her console.

"Steady as she goes, Ensign," Sterling called out. "The Invictus can take it."

"Try to avoid the bigger chunks if you can, though, Ensign," added Commander Banks, casting a quizzical eye across to Sterling. "This isn't a game of dodgems."

Sterling continued to wait impatiently as the Invictus weaved a chaotic course though the ring system. The bombardment of rock and ice against their hull was relentless, but the Invictus was every bit as tough as he'd said. It was like hailstones bouncing off the skin of an elephant.

Eventually, the ship emerged into the ring gap, causing the bombardment to cease and the viewscreen to clear. Directly ahead of them, Sterling could see the moonlet with the hole cored through its center. Then as the ring debris cleared further, Sterling caught sight of the massive shipyard structure where the Sa'Nerran super-weapon had been docked. However, the giant alien ship, which was more than twice the size of the mighty Hammer-class Fleet Dreadnaughts, was nowhere to be seen.

"I don't know if we should be glad that monster warship has gone, or worried that it's now able to move under its own power," said Commander Banks.

"Both," said Sterling, peering out at the abandoned shipyard. "But what actually concerns me more is why they left the shipyard here at all. If it were me, I'd have destroyed it."

Banks pondered this for a moment. "Maybe they plan to come back?" she suggested.

"They know this system is burned," replied Sterling, shaking his head. "They must have realized that we'd come back here."

"So, it's a trap then," said Banks.

"Maybe," said Sterling, though he knew it was wishful thinking to believe otherwise. "Either way, we still need to do our job and drop an aperture relay inside these rings," he added, rubbing the back of his neck. "The question is where do we hide it?"

"Inside that moonlet would be my suggestion."

The comment came from Lieutenant Razor, who was again standing tall at the rear of the bridge with her hands behind her back.

"Though I realize you didn't ask for my suggestion, sir," Razor then added, as both captain and first officer turned their attention to her.

"I'm not one to discourage input, Lieutenant, though you could explain what you mean," replied Sterling.

Razor spun back to her array of consoles, fingers flashing across the various panels. Moments later, the viewscreen updated to show the moonlet with the hole cored through its center.

"The aperture relays have no major propulsion systems of their own. Only station-keeping thrusters," Razor went on, while flitting from console to console. "However, we can navigate the Invictus inside the moonlet and deploy the relay on its inner surface."

The viewscreen updated with an overlay that explained Razor's idea more fully. Sterling frowned and studied the overlay on the screen.

"There's barely ten meters clearance either side of that cavity," Sterling said, examining Razor's data more closely. "That's pretty tight, don't you think?"

"I can make it, sir," said Keller, who had swung his seat around to face the command platform. "And it is a good place to hide the relay."

"What breakfast meal tray did both of you have this morning?" said Sterling, smiling. "Whatever it was, it seems to have given you balls of steel."

"It was a number thirty-two, I think, sir," replied Keller, which elicited a stifled laugh from Banks.

"It was a rhetorical question, Ensign," said Sterling, causing the helmsman's cheeks to flush red. "But if you think you can navigate through the cored-out moonlet, make it happen."

"Aye, sir," said Keller, grateful for the opportunity to swing his chair forward to hide his embarrassment.

Commander Banks' console then chimed an update and she checked it without delay. The smile that was present on his first officer's face then fell away and her brow furrowed.

"Do we have trouble?" asked Sterling, recognizing the look of concern on Banks' face.

"Maybe," replied Banks, unhelpfully. "It looks like the scanners picked up some movement. Something other than rock and ice. But the reading shows clear again."

Sterling felt a knot harden in his stomach. "Lieutenant Razor, see what you can do to enhance our scanners," he said to the engineer before turning to Keller. "Let's position this relay as quickly as possible, Ensign," he added. "Something tells me we're not alone out here."

Banks' console chimed again, but she just shook her head in frustration. "There it goes again," she said, working to enhance the scanner readings. "There's something out there, I'm certain of it."

Sterling glanced at the doughnut-shaped moonlet that now filled the viewscreen. He considered aborting the maneuver, but Ensign Keller had already inched the Invictus inside the perfectly circular tube that had been carved out of the rock by the alien super-weapon.

"We're in position, Captain," Keller called out, the ensign's eyes still locked onto his controls.

"Deploy the relay and let's get the hell out of this system," Sterling called over to his weapon's officer.

Razor acknowledged the order and a second later the aperture relay was ejected. Sterling watched the device orientate itself then latch on to the inside wall of the cored-out moonlet. Moments later his panel lit up as the beacon began transmitting on its unique frequency.

"Relay deployed. The signal is strong," said Razor from

the rear of the bridge. "The material in the ring system will attenuate the signal, but there's still enough power to transmit through the aperture."

Banks' console chimed again then fell silent. Sterling heard his first officer curse under her breath.

"The scanners can't quite get a lock on whatever the hell is stalking us," said Banks, fists still clenched.

"Try now, Commander," said Razor, who had been working frenetically across her consoles, moving from station to station like an orchestra percussionist.

Banks' console chimed yet again, but this time the mellow bleep was followed by a more aggressive alert tone.

"Mines…" Banks said, glancing across to Sterling. "The Sa'Nerra booby trapped the area with damned stealth mines. It looks like they've been closing in on us the whole time we've been inside the ring gap."

Sterling studied the new readings on his console then overlaid the mine positions onto a map on the viewscreen. Dozens of red chevrons appeared in a chaotic arrangement, like the pattern of spots on a Dalmatian's coat.

"Mines…" Sterling said, glancing across to Banks. "That's an usually devious tactic for the Sa'Nerra."

"I think our emissaries have been teaching these alien bastards a few new tricks," Banks replied.

Sterling sighed then turned to his helmsman. "I hope you're suitably limbered up, Ensign," said Sterling, addressing the young pilot. "Because we're going to need your exceptional flying skills now, more than ever."

THE INVICTUS WAITED inside the cored-out moonlet, barely poking its nose beyond the mouth of the hole, like a timid rabbit hiding in its burrow. Sterling waited for his crew to perform their analysis, tapping his finger on the side of his console as the Sa'Nerran stealth mines drew nearer by the second.

"Our point defense cannons will only be able to take out some of the mines, Captain," Lieutenant Shade began from the weapons console, opening the round of reports. "Based on our projected course from Ensign Keller, I estimate that a minimum of six will slip through."

Sterling turned around and rested on his console, waiting for Lieutenant Razor to finish working, but the engineer was still in full flow.

"Any chance you can speed up our exit from the ring system, Ensign?" asked Sterling, turning to Keller instead.

"My projected course and speed are already pretty ambitious Captain," Keller replied, cautiously.

"Then be more ambitious, Ensign," replied Sterling.

Keller's eyes widened. "Aye, sir," the helmsman said, turning back to his console.

"The Sa'Nerra weren't messing about when they laid these mines, Captain," said Razor, finally turning away from her consoles. "Their yields are high enough to pop a hole in the hull of a heavy cruiser. Just one of them could cripple us, never mind six."

Sterling folded his arms and tilted his head to one side. "This is the part where you tell me you have a brilliant plan to avoid getting hit, Lieutenant," he said. Sterling recalled that Razor was keen to earn commendations; now was her chance.

"I was just coming to that, Captain," replied Razor. She was impressively deadpan, to the point where her aloofness almost rivalled that of Opal Shade. "These mines are powerful, but not especially smart. The Sa'Nerra spent all their time making them hard to find. But now that I can see them, I send a feedback pulse back to their tracking sensors and screw with their navigation."

Banks looked impressed, but Sterling had learned that whenever an engineer appeared to give a straight answer to a question, it was usually followed by a "but".

"But it will only confuse their navigation systems, not cripple them completely," Razor went on, proving Sterling correct, much to his chagrin. "I estimate that fifty to seventy-five percent of the mines in our path will become so erratic that they miss us completely."

"That should give us the leeway we need to target the remaining threats, sir," said Shade, who had been busy working at her console while Razor was speaking. "However, if the point defense guns let one through, it will come down to piloting skill to avoid it."

Sterling could practically hear Ensign Keller force down a dry swallow as Shade said this. The ensign then turned to his captain, sitting as tall as he could.

"I've got this sir, don't worry," Ensign Keller said.

Sterling thought that Keller had made a good stab at sounding confident. However, there was also a hint of the awkward kid who stepped nervously into the wardroom each morning in the helmsman's response.

"Worrying is for admirals or regular Fleet captains, Ensign," Sterling replied, filling the bridge with his powerful voice. "We're Omega officers. We just get it done, understood?"

"Aye, sir," Keller replied, with more vigor.

"Feedback pulse ready, Captain," said Razor. "Regenerative armor at maximum power."

"Point defense cannons armed and ready," Shade added.

Sterling could see that Shade had also initiated her virtual manual control system for the point defense cannons. It would be impossible for a single person to track and destroy the mines and ring debris manually, but Sterling was still glad to see that his weapons officer was taking every precaution. If something slipped through the net, Shade would at least have the opportunity to intervene, before it was too late.

"Take us out, Ensign," said Sterling, grasping the sides of his console. It was a position he adopted so often that the areas where his fingers touched the metal had become smooth and polished from the oils in his skin.

Ensign Keller took a moment to compose himself for the task ahead. Then he placed his hands onto the helm controls like a pianist preparing to play and powered the Invictus out of the moonlet. Despite their inertial negation systems being fully functional, Sterling had to tighten his grip on the console to counteract the fierce acceleration. Even so, the Invictus had barely emerged from the moonlet before the red chevrons on the viewscreen started to converge and race toward them.

"Point defense cannons engaging," said Shade.

The announcement was unnecessary as Sterling could already feel the rapid beat of the weapons systems through the deck.

"Feedback pulse at full power," Razor called out, having to raise her voice over the rising cadence of their engines and reactor core.

Flashes of light popped off on the viewscreen like distant fireworks as mine after mine was destroyed by the ship's automated gun turrets. Meanwhile, Keller was fighting with his helm controls, trying to steer the nimble Marauder-class warship through the maze of icy debris ahead of them. It was like running out into a hailstorm in the dead of night and trying to avoid getting hit by falling ice. Sterling felt a hard thud resonate through the deck. Peering at the condition report on his console, he saw a section of their regenerative armor turn amber.

"Hit to port bow, armor holding," Shade called out, her voice encouragingly calm and assured.

"Hold on!" Keller cried out, turning the ship hard to starboard to avoid a dense cluster of rocks.

Sterling saw the thrusters turn red on his console. Keller was pushing the Invictus beyond its rated maximum, but it was still barely enough. Another chunk of ice the size of a heavy cruiser then loomed large on the viewscreen. Sterling felt like calling out to alert Keller, but he bit his tongue, knowing that no-one was more acutely aware of the ship's position than his helmsman. Keller remained focused, displaying the poise under pressure that had helped get the Invictus out of many scrapes before. Fingers flashing across his console, Keller made dozens of micro-adjustments to the ship's pitch and roll, but it wasn't quite enough. Metal creaked and groaned as the Invictus scraped across the icy mass. Ghostly noises echoed through the hull as if it were an ancient shipwreck being raised from the ocean floor.

"Ventral hull armor at fifty percent," Lieutenant Shade called out. "We're grinding metal."

"Give us a touch more altitude, Ensign," said Sterling, resolving to sound as calm and unflappable as his weapons officer had done.

"I'm trying, sir," said Keller, his face twisted with effort, as if he was a combat fighter pilot physically pulling back on a yoke. "We're carrying too much momentum."

"Increasing power to the thrusters," Lieutenant Razor called out, her back to the viewscreen.

The ship's chief engineer was racing from console to console, working frantically to squeeze more out of the Invictus than it had ever given before. The resonant groans and murmurs then ceased and Sterling saw the reading for the ventral armor plating stabilize.

"That did it," Keller called out, practically expelling the words in a gasp. "She's responding..."

Another alert registered on Sterling's console, this time from life support. Ten percent of the ship had just lost gravity and was reduced to minimal oxygen and heating. Sterling was about to call to Shade to ask if they'd taken another hit, when he noticed that the power from life-support had been redirected manually.

"Did you steal power from life support for the thrusters, Lieutenant?" asked Sterling, glancing over his shoulder to Razor.

"Aye, sir," Razor replied, appearing perfectly at ease with her answer. "Though no crucial sections are affected."

"The people bouncing off the walls, freezing their assess off on the lower decks might disagree," commented Banks.

"They'll live," replied Razor.

Sterling checked his console again. They were almost through the ring system, but still the mines were closing in around them. It was then he realized he'd fallen into another trap – the same one he'd avoided the last time he was in System Omega Four.

"They've laid the mines through the ring system, assuming we'd make a bee-line for the aperture," said Sterling, gripping the side of his console more tightly.

"And we fell for it," added Banks, looking as sheepish as Sterling felt.

"Point defense cannons are overheating, Captain," said

Shade, as Keller steered the Invictus past another huge clump of ice. "We've lost twenty percent capacity already."

"Compensate as best you can," replied Sterling.

Sterling then switched his console view to the rudimentary map of the ring system that they'd assembled during their first visit. The Sa'Nerra had gotten the jump on him twice, but he'd be damned if he'd let it happen a third time. *Damn you, McQueen...* Sterling cursed in his mind, putting the Sa'Nerra's new and more devious tactics down to the influence of their new Emissary. Scouring the ring system for another way out – one that would allow Keller to make a hastier exit – he spotted a corridor leading directly into space. Compared to their far denser surroundings, it was a veritable super-highway, and it was also clear of traffic. Sterling thought for a moment, tapping his finger on the side of the console, then glanced up at the back of his helmsman's head.

"Ensign, adjust course and follow the route I've just sent you," Sterling called out, transmitting the new plan to Keller's console.

"Aye, sir, adjusting course," Keller replied without hesitation.

However, a quick glance across to his first officer told him that Banks was less certain of her captain's decision.

"That looks like a suspiciously clear route out of this hellhole," said Banks, through a neural link. "If something looks too good to be true, it usually is."

Sterling nodded, comprehending Banks' meaning at once. "I think it's time we prepared a little surprise of our own," he answered. Closing the link he then turning to his weapons officer. "Lieutenant Shade, charge the forward rail-guns. I want a full volley ready by the time we leave the ring system."

"We're going to need more power, sir," replied Shade. Her head was down, working furiously at her console. "I can't draw from any of the other defensive systems, without risking taking a hit."

"I can give you enough power for one volley," Razor chipped in.

Sterling spun around to face his engineer. "How many more people do we have to send bouncing off the walls in the cold to allow that?"

"Everyone bar those in medical and engineering, sir," replied Razor, plainly.

"Very well, make it happen," said Sterling. "I'll alert Commander Graves to prepare the med bay for a series of bruises, broken bones and frostbite injuries."

The bridge was then filled with another alert tone. It was like a shot of adrenalin directly into Sterling's heart.

"Report!" Sterling called out.

"Port quarter point defenses have failed," Shade replied. "A mine has slipped through."

Sterling jerked his head toward his weapons officer, so fast that he almost gave himself whiplash. However, Lieutenant Shade was already focused on her virtual manual weapons controls. Sterling glanced down at his console and saw that she was operating the ventral rail cannon. Compared to the point defenses it was slow to move and recharge, but it was all they had left.

"Fifteen seconds to impact," Banks called out as the

alert tone in the bridge rose in pitch and volume. It was like the ping of sonar on a submarine as a torpedo drew closer. The noise made Sterling's hair stand on end.

"Silence that alert," Sterling called out, keeping his eyes focused on Lieutenant Shade. The strident alarm tone vanished, and the sudden absence of sound was almost more chilling than the alert itself.

"Five seconds..." said Banks.

Shade squeezed the virtual triggers sending a pulse of plasma energy out into space. A blink of an eye later the ship was rocked by a shockwave and the bridge was filled with yet another alert tone. This time Sterling cancelled it himself and peered down at the damage readout. However, besides a few minor systems and a raft of yellow and amber colors covering almost their entire regenerative armor system, the Invictus was in one piece.

"Good shot, Lieutenant!" said Sterling, breathing a sigh of relief.

"We're approaching the edge of the outer ring system now, Captain," Ensign Keller called out. The helmsman's face was red and sweat beaded his brow.

Sterling gripped his console, waiting for the rock and ice to clear and give him an uninterrupted view of the space ahead of them. If Banks' hunch had been right, he knew what he expected to see.

"Reading one phase-two Sa'Nerran Heavy Cruiser dead ahead, Captain," Lieutenant Shade called out.

Banks snorted. "A phase two?" she said, spitting the words out. "I'm insulted. They must not think much of us."

"Then we should educate them," replied Sterling,

though his eyes remained focused on the aging Sa'Nerran cruiser ahead of them.

Commander Banks' console chimed and she snorted again. "Believe it or not, we're being hailed."

"Let's hear it," said Sterling, glancing down to check their distance to the new target. The image on the viewscreen then adjusted and the face of a human woman appeared inset on the screen. She was wearing Sa'Nerran armor, though its adornments were less extravagant than those worn by McQueen and Crow.

"I am Ashva, Aide to the Emissaries," the woman began. Standing directly behind and to her side was a Sa'Nerran warrior, whose armor more closely resembled that of McQueen's. "Surrender yourself to the Sa'Nerra and you shall be educated."

Sterling clicked his tongue against the roof of his mouth, while the actual name of the woman appeared overlayed on the viewscreen. The woman's Fleet file had been accessed by the computer via facial recognition.

"That's funny, it says here that your name is Commander Sarah Barron, first officer of the Fleet Light Cruiser Richmond."

Ashva's eyes narrowed. "That name is nothing to me now, as your names will soon mean nothing to you," the woman said. "Your ship is damaged. Your weapons systems are depleted. You cannot escape. Give yourself to the Sa'Nerra or be destroyed."

Sterling stood tall, feeling anger bubble inside him. This woman was Fleet, but the aliens had warped her mind and set her against their own kind. Each time he saw one of these turned humans, his hatred for the Sa'Nerra grew.

"That's never going to happen, Ashva," said Sterling, practically spitting the woman's adopted Sa'Nerran name back at her. "Let me educate you as to why." Sterling watched the aides' face twist into a frown then he turned to Lieutenant Shade. "Fire."

The flash from the Invictus' main rail guns was even more blinding than the pulse of light from a surging ship. Sterling's console dimmed and the lights on the bridge flickered chaotically as every last joule of energy the Invictus could muster was focused into a single, devasting volley. The blast tore through the Sa'Nerran heavy cruiser like an axe through rotten wood, splitting it in half down its center axis. Fire and electrical arcs erupted from the two severed halves of the ship and Sterling saw bodies float out into space. Some were human, but most were Sa'Nerran. Then the two halves of ship exploded, engulfing the bodies and the debris in an intense fireball that consumed everything in elemental fury.

"Scanners are clear, Captain," said Commander Banks. "There are no other ships in the vicinity."

"You have the bridge, Commander," said Sterling, feeling some of the hatred bubbling in his veins subside now that the Sa'Nerra and their puppet were dead. "Remain at battle stations. Take us back to the aperture and prepare to surge."

"Aye, sir," replied Banks, hopping across to the captain's console.

Sterling jumped down off the command platform,

intending to head to his ready room, but Lieutenant Razor stepped into his path.

"Permission to return to engineering, Captain," Shade said. She stood tall, a calm look on her face, hands pressed to the small of her back. "It will be easier to co-ordinate repairs from there."

"Granted, Lieutenant, keep me apprised," Sterling said. Then he remembered how his new engineer had stolen the extra energy they'd needed from life support. "However, unless you plan on floating there, I'd suggest that you rebalance the power distribution back to normal before you head out," he added. "I think we've all hung around in this system far longer than we'd like. Some more than others."

STERLING ALLOWED his mind to wander as his disembodied existence was held in flux during the surge to Oasis Colony. This was the last reported location of James Colicos, the disgraced scientist who Admiral Griffin had ordered Sterling to track down. It was a rare moment of serenity that seldom lasted long. As the Invictus completed its surge and exploded back into reality, the blare of alarms told Sterling that his temporary respite from danger had already ended.

"Weapons lock detected, sir," announced Lieutenant Shade from the weapons console. "There's a gatekeeper guarding the aperture. It's an old design - pre-plasma weapons - but it still packs a punch."

"Hold position," ordered Sterling. "Keep our weapons offline. Show them that we're not a threat."

Sterling watched the old gatekeeper orient itself to face the Invictus, aiming its formidable array of mass cannons directly at their diminutive warship.

"Message from the gatekeeper," said Commander Banks. "It's automated. That thing is under computer control."

"Let's hear it," replied Sterling.

Banks tapped a sequence of commands into her console and a computerized voice filled the bridge.

"*United Governments Fleet vessel, withdraw from this system at once. You have ninety seconds to comply with this command.*"

"They're not very welcoming at Oasis Colony, are they?" commented Commander Banks.

"Respond to the gatekeeper that we're only here to refuel, then we'll be on our way," said Sterling.

Banks tapped out the message and transmitted it. There was a tense wait then the gatekeeper replied in the same monotone synthesized voice.

"*United Governments Fleet vessel, withdraw from this system at once. You have sixty seconds to comply with this command.*"

"I'm reading a surge in power from the gatekeeper," Lieutenant Shade added. "It's definitely getting ready to fire."

Sterling cursed, then turned his attention to Ensign Keller, who was already watching him, poised on the edge of his seat.

"Prepare an emergency surge, Ensign," said Sterling, tapping his finger on the side of his console. "The closest exit aperture you can find will do."

"Aye sir," Keller replied, spinning his seat back to his

console and working fast to program the surge vector into the computer.

"Widen the range of communications frequencies," Sterling said, turning to Banks. "Announce that we have items to trade. Items that are hard to come by in the Void."

Banks nodded, her fingers a blur of motion as she broadcast the message on all common channels.

"United Governments Fleet vessel, withdraw from this system at once. You have thirty seconds to comply with this command."

Sterling gritted his teeth and tightened his hold on the sides of his console. "Ensign, are we ready to surge?"

"I need ten seconds, Captain," his helmsman replied.

"Much longer than that and there won't be anything of us left to surge," Sterling hit back.

Keller continued to work furiously then finally finished his computations. "Surge vector programmed, heading to the aperture threshold now."

"This is going to be tight," said Commander Banks, anxiously watching the weapons platform on the viewscreen. Then her console chimed another message. "Wait..." she said, eyes flicking left to right as she read the communication.

"We're going to be atoms in ten seconds, Commander, this had better be good," said Sterling.

"It's the system's Marshal," Banks went on, still working frantically. "He's transmitted a gate pass. Standby..."

"Hold position, Ensign Keller," Sterling announced, aiming his finger at Keller like it was a starter's pistol.

The helmsman replied promptly, though with less assuredness than usual. Sterling couldn't blame him on this occasion. If Banks was wrong or transmitted the code incorrectly, they were done for.

"*United Governments Fleet vessel,*" the synthesized voice of the computer began again. Sterling waited, feeling like every muscle in his body had tensed up. "*Entry pass approved. Welcome to Oasis Colony.*"

Sterling let out the breath he'd been holding for the last five seconds and almost collapsed forward onto his console. Banks looked similarly relieved while Keller looked on the verge of fainting. Only Lieutenant Shade had remained unphased by the experience, a fact that hadn't gone unnoticed by Commander Banks.

"How the hell do you stay so cool, Lieutenant?" said Commander Banks, cocking her head in the direction of their weapons officer. "My ass cheeks were so tight just then I could have squeezed a lump of coal into a diamond."

Shade's eyebrows raised up on her forehead and she opened her mouth, but no words came out. Sometimes, there was just no way to respond to Mercedes Banks.

"Thanks for that nugget of information, Commander," said Sterling, casting his first officer a sideways glance. "But now that we're no longer under threat of annihilation, perhaps you could patch us through to the Marshal?"

"Aye, sir," replied Banks, displaying an impressive lack of self-consciousness about her earlier statement.

The viewscreen then switched from an image of the gatekeeper, which had gone back to aiming its cannons at the aperture, to the face of a man.

"Mornin', Captain. I'm the Marshal 'round here," the man said, tipping his hat to Sterling as he spoke. "The name's Masterson, but you can just call me Marshal."

The Marshal expelled each word in a measured, methodical drawl that sounded slow and colorless to Sterling's ears. He imagined that if he were forced to listen to the lawman for too long, he'd find the voice strangely soporific. The Marshal was also young, perhaps in his late twenties, Sterling considered, and was dressed in the old-West inspired attire that Void Marshals liked to adopt. In the case of Marshal Masterson, this comprised a black bowler hat and black suit jacket with a leather waistcoat underneath. However, unlike other Marshals that Sterling had come across, including the one they'd dealt with at Hope Rises, Masterson was also sporting a bushy mustache. This was doubly unusual because facial hair in general had been considered outdated and unsanitary in the Fleet side of the Void for over a hundred years. However, Sterling had to remind himself that many conventions in the Void differed to the norms of Fleet and United Governments society.

"Thank you for allowing us to enter Oasis Colony, Marshal," replied Sterling. He didn't have a hat to tip, so instead he offered a respectful nod in return. "My name is Captain Lucas Sterling of the Fleet Marauder Invictus."

"Invictus, eh?" the Marshal said, clearly intrigued by the vessel's name. "And are you? Unconquered, I mean?"

Sterling smiled. He was impressed that the Marshal knew the meaning of the ship's name, though it also gave something away about the man. It told him that the

Marshal was educated and therefore potentially more dangerous than many of the other Marshals in the Void.

"So far, yes," Sterling answered. The Marshal waited, perhaps hoping that Sterling would reveal more about the warship's history. However, Sterling had no interest in giving the man more information than he had to.

"Well, Captain, we don't see many Fleet ships at Oasis Colony these days," the Marshal went on, maintaining his slow, deliberate style of talking.

"I'd imagine that your gatekeeper is a large part of the reason for that," said Sterling, offering the Marshal a warm smile.

The Marshal laughed and tipped his head into a nod. "That thing has served us well over the years," the man said, speaking as if the gatekeeper were an old farm workhorse. "It keeps the Sa'Nerra out too, for the most part, which is why we make it so unfriendly to visitors in general."

Sterling could certainly see how the trigger-happy gatekeeper was an effective deterrent. Even so, if the Sa'Nerra did want to storm Oasis Colony, they'd still be able to overpower it with moderate losses.

"Do the Sa'Nerra not bother you at all here?" asked Sterling, curious as to why this particular corner of the Void had escaped the attention of the aliens.

"Sometimes," the Marshal replied, shrugging. "I know that if they really wanted to, our old gatekeeper couldn't stop them from barging in. But I reckon there are far easier pickings in the Void. Besides, folks in the colonies don't take too kindly to intruders. It's a shoot first, don't bother asking questions kinda place, if you catch my drift?"

Sterling nodded. The Marshal's answer made sense and satisfactorily explained why the Sa'Nerra had so far left them alone. Though Sterling also knew that eventually, once the belligerent aliens had harvested all the low-hanging fruit in the Void, Oasis Colony would be targeted too. For now, though, it certainly appeared that the colony lived up to its name. There were few other places in the Void that could be considered "safe" from the ever-present Sa'Nerran threat.

"We're here in search of information," Sterling said, turning the conversation to the business at hand. "We're willing to trade generously for it, then we'll be on our way. We have no interest in interfering with your way of life."

The Marshal seem to chew the inside of his mouth for a moment then sighed. Sterling wasn't sure whether it was a sigh of relief or disappointment.

"Well, that's good to hear, Captain," the Marshal said, though nothing about his droning voice suggested the news had pleased him. "Still, if you don't mind, I'd like to escort you during your visit to Oasis Colony," the man continued, eliciting an eyebrow raise from Commander Banks. "Folks here get a little jittery around strangers, especially those that turn up in Fleet uniforms and warships, packed with all manner of deadly weapons."

Sterling nodded respectfully again, though out of the corner of his eye he could see that Banks had become more unsettled.

"Of course, Marshal, that sounds perfectly reasonable

to me," said Sterling, amiably.

"Grand, Captain," replied the Marshal, returning a smile of his own, though his was harder to distinguish due to the mass of hair attached to the man's top lip. "If you'll be so kind as to follow me to the spaceport at Sanctum City on the third planet. I'll meet you in the lobby of Hotel Grand just outside the main port."

"Understood, Marshal, we'll follow your lead," said Sterling.

The Marshal tipped his hat a final time then the viewscreen cut off. Sterling could already feel Commander Banks' eyes drilling into the side of his head.

"I wouldn't trust that guy as far as I could throw him," said Banks, not mincing her words.

"I imagine that you could probably throw him quite far," Sterling hit back, though he understood his first officer's point well enough.

"As far as you could throw him then," Banks said, appearing unamused by Sterling's brush-off.

"Don't worry, Commander, I don't trust him either," replied Sterling, which seemed to set Banks slightly more at ease. "But we have to play his game to find out what we need to know."

Ensign Keller then spun his chair around to face the command platform. "I've received co-ordinates for Sanctum Spaceport on the third planet in the system, Captain," the helmsman said. "The Marshal's ship is already under way. Should I pursue?"

"Yes, Ensign, follow him in," replied Sterling.

"The last time we dealt with a Marshal, things didn't

end well," said Banks, stepping to Sterling's side. She then rested back on the captain's console with her arms folded.

"That's something of an understatement," replied Sterling. He glanced over to Lieutenant Shade, remembering how she'd ended up competing in a series of cage fights on Hope Rises.

"Perhaps this time, things will go better," added Banks, with a little shrug.

Sterling smiled. He knew the look in his first officer's eyes and could tell plainly that she didn't believe a word of what she'd just said.

"I very much doubt it," replied Sterling.

Banks flashed her eyes at Sterling then pushed herself off the console. "I'll speak to Shade and make preparations then," she said, sliding around the rear of the command platform. "Let's hope she's in the mood for another fight."

"When is she ever not?" replied Sterling.

Banks snorted a laugh then moved over to Lieutenant Shade to discuss what would come next. Sterling turned his eyes back to the viewscreen and fixed them on the old mark one Fleet Destroyer that Marshal Masterson had salvaged and made his own. It was a timeworn ship, with a captain that held true to old-fashioned ideals, one of which was a deep distrust of and animosity toward Fleet. Sterling's mind was already racing, coming up with plans and contingencies should Banks' warnings prove true. No matter what happened, he fully intended to leave Oasis Colony with the information he needed. However, he also accepted that achieving this goal would likely have a cost in blood.

CAPTAIN STERLING STEPPED OFF THE INVICTUS' cargo ramp and onto the asphalt surface of Sanctum Spaceport. If he didn't know better, he could have imaged himself on one of the colony worlds in Fleet space, rather than inside the Void. The spaceport was a bustling hive of activity with ships arriving and leaving with regularity. Many of the vessels were, like the Marshal's own phase one Fleet Destroyer, salvaged from space battles that occurred long ago. There were heavily modified Sa'Nerran vessels, old Fleet designs and even some hybrids. Several miles away Sterling could see a busy skyway, connecting the city of Sanctum to the various other towns and settlements across the earth-like third planet of the system.

"This place is organized," commented Commander Banks, stepping off the ramp beside Sterling and folding her arms. "For people to stick to the skyways there must be some form of governance here."

"And also policing," Sterling added, with a more

ominous tone. "People don't stick to the rules by choice. They do so for fear of reprisal."

Sterling then spotted Marshal Masterson's ship on a landing pad a few hundred meters away, though the Marshal himself was nowhere in sight. Then his eyes fell on a grand-looking detached building off the main spaceport. It was built using modern construction materials, but had been made to look like it was timber framed. There was a tall, signboard-like frontage above it that read, "Hotel Grand."

"Looks like that's our destination," said Sterling, nodding in the direction of the building, which he had to admit lived up to its name.

Lieutenant Razor jogged down the ramp. She stopped at the bottom, closed her eyes and breathed in deeply.

"It's nice to get a lungful of real air for a change, don't you think?" said Razor, standing with her hands on her hips. She somehow looked even taller than Sterling remembered her being.

Banks sniffed the air then shrugged. "Air is air," she said, dismissively.

Razor opened her eyes, turned to Sterling and tapped the computer wrapped around her left wrist. It unraveled itself from around the engineer's arm and formed a solid rectangular screen.

"These are the items I think we can spare, in exchange for the information you need, sir," said Razor, showing the list to Sterling.

Sterling skim-read the contents, seeing nothing on it that caused him any concern. "Very well, get it all ready to roll out," he replied, casting his eyes back to the Hotel Grand. "Hopefully, this will all go smoothly and we'll be away from here within the hour."

"If wishes were horses," said Banks as Razor jogged back up the ramp into the cargo hold of the Invictus.

"If wishes were horses?" replied Sterling, frowning at his first officer.

"We'd all have one," said Banks, appearing surprised that Sterling didn't know what she was talking about. However, Sterling merely maintained his bemused frown. "Come on, Lucas! If wishes were horses then we'd all have one."

Sterling shrugged. "What the hell would I want with a horse?"

Banks rolled her eyes and sighed. "It just means that we rarely get what we wish for, that's all," she said, appearing annoyed for needing to explain herself. "Like a smooth trade with a Void Marshal who clearly likes us only barely more than a bout of gonorrhea."

"Point taken," replied Sterling, noticing Lieutenant Shade out of the corner of his eyes. She had been scouting the area and placing her commandoes on guard in positions around the ship.

"Everyone here is armed to the teeth, sir," said Shade, acknowledging Banks with a respectful nod. "There are legitimate traders, but a lot of these ships bear the scars of recent battles, as well as old ones," she went on, surveying the spaceport. "Half of them are likely pirates, bounty hunters or privateers of some kind."

Sterling nodded. "We picked up two habitable planets,

three habitable moons and four space stations on the way to Sanctum," he said, now looking at the different vessels on the asphalt with a more wary eye. "That means plenty of work for those sorts of people."

Shade then stood to attention as if Sterling was about to give her an order. "Permission to accompany you to the meeting with Marshal Masterson, sir," she said. Her statement was bordering on being a demand instead of a request. "I don't trust him, Captain."

"I don't trust him either, Lieutenant, but we have to show willing," replied Sterling. "They're already suspicious of Fleet, so walking into that hotel with armed guards is only going to make them even more defensive."

Shade's jaw tightened a fraction and her eyes flickered. It was a sure sign that Sterling's answer had not been to his weapon's officer's liking.

"I know people like these, sir," Shade added, clearly struggling to maintain a level, courteous tone. "If they're going to cause trouble, they'll have made their minds up already. It doesn't matter if we walk in there with one person or ten, the outcome will be the same."

Sterling listened carefully to Shade and weighed the options in his head. His weapons officer was probably right, but if there was going to be trouble, he wasn't going to be the one who started it. The Invictus still had to be able to operate in the Void, and gain the cooperation of the colonists whom Fleet had abandoned decades ago. Running in all guns blazing would not help him in that endeavor.

"I've made my decision, Lieutenant, and my order stands," replied Sterling, calmly.

Sterling could see that Shade was itching to argue back, but she bit her tongue.

"Aye, Captain," replied Shade, who then stood aside, wearing an expression that was even more surly than usual. However, she had complied and that was all that mattered. Sterling didn't expect his officers to always agree with or like his orders, but he did expect them to obey without complaint.

"Now, if things *do* go south quickly, I'm expecting you and your commandoes to get us out of there, is that understood?" Sterling added, now that he was satisfied Shade had fallen in line. Sterling may have been resolute in his plans, but he wasn't foolish enough to believe his meeting with the Marshal would go off without a hitch.

"You can count on it, sir," replied Shade.

There was an added bite to Shade's words that Sterling always enjoyed hearing. It meant that his weapons officer was ready and spoiling for a fight. Sterling then glanced across to Banks, who merely flashed her eyes at him.

"Shall we?" said Banks, inviting Sterling to head out first.

Sterling set off toward the Hotel Grand with his first officer at his side. Heads turned and eyes followed them as they progressed toward the hotel, making Sterling feel like he back at F-COP. It seemed that no matter where he went, people viewed the officers of the Omega Taskforce with suspicion and fear.

Stepping onto the veranda of the hotel, Sterling reached for the saloon-style doors, but they swung open before his hand could grasp them. A man wearing dark cargo pants with a khaki shirt and multi-pocket denim waistcoat staggered out onto the veranda. He belched, assaulting Sterling's face with a musky alcoholic scent, then doffed his trucker-style cap to him.

"Beg pardon," the man said, his rosy cheeks rising up with a smile. The drunkard then noticed Commander Banks and swiftly removed his cap, pressing it to his chest. "And beg pardon, m'lady," he added, flashing his eyes at the Invictus' first officer.

The drunkard bent over in an attempt to kiss Banks' hand, but she yanked it free of the man's grasp before his chapped lips could reach it. The drunkard almost fell flat on his face before recovering his balance at the last second. Appearing utterly confused about what had just happened, the man replaced his cap then attempted to bow with a flourish.

"Good morning," the man said before promptly falling down the stairs and landing in a heap on the road.

"Charming..." said Banks, wafting a hand in front of her face in order to dissipate the lingering stench of the drunkard.

"That doesn't bode well for the quality of the clientele," said Sterling. He then pushed through the doors and stepped inside the hotel.

The smell of the drunkard's alcohol-soaked breath was replaced by a heady mix of tobacco-like smoke, perfume, sweat and even more alcohol. Sterling had barely taken a step into the room before an arm the size of a small tree trunk blocked his path.

"Check your weapons at the door," a bellowing voice said. Sterling looked up at the man, who was almost as wide as he was tall.

Sterling glanced at the other patrons, noticing that some of them were still armed. "Why don't they have to check their weapons?" he asked the massive man.

"Because I said so," the man replied, flatly.

Sterling sighed then slid his plasma pistol out of its holster. "I'm going to want this back," he said, placing the weapon into a metal cabinet that the large, round man had duly opened for that purpose. The man didn't answer Sterling and instead turned his attention to Commander Banks.

"Yours too," he said, the sound of his voice resonating through Sterling's bones.

Banks stepped up to the cabinet and was about to place her own weapon on the shelf when the man grabbed her wrist. Sterling felt his pulse quicken.

"I put the weapons in. I take them out," the man said in a calm, unhurried voice while peering down at Banks.

Sterling could see that the man was attempting to pull Banks' arm away, but he knew that Banks would never concede in a test of strength. Soon, the giant's arm began to tremble slightly and his round cheeks wobbled, as if he were struggling to lift a heavy weight.

"I suggest you take your hand off me, right now," said Banks, with more politeness than Sterling had expected considering the circumstances.

The man released his grip and pulled his thick arm back to his chest, staring at Banks as if she had just used some sort of arcane magic against him.

"You're strong," the man said, though it was a statement of appreciation rather than merely an account of the facts.

"So are you," Banks replied, also with a measure of admiration for the giant's efforts. She then flipped her pistol so that she was holding the barrel and offered it to the man. "I'll want this back too," Banks continued, smiling at the giant. "Not that this little trinket box could stop me from taking it again, if I wanted to," she added, wrapping her knuckles on the metal chest.

The large man took the weapon then placed it delicately inside the chest and closed the lid.

"Welcome to the Hotel Grand," the man boomed, extending his shovel-size hand toward the foyer.

"Thanks for the warm welcome," replied Sterling, a little more sarcastically than he'd intended.

Sterling moved inside and took a more detailed look at the hotel that was to play host to their meeting with the Marshal. The foyer opened into a frontier-style saloon; a modern mash-up of old West and twenty-fourth century design. Unlike the buildings on Colony Vega Two and many of the other less developed Void colonies, none of the furniture was made of wood. However, the arrangement of chairs and tables on the ground floor, and on the balcony that ran along the wall opposite the long bar, was ripped straight from the eighteenth-century. And while the response to Sterling and Banks was not as cliched as a piano stopping playing and everyone turning in silence to glare at them, their distinctive uniforms had not gone unnoticed.

"There's the Marshal, over at that corner table," said Banks, nodding in the direction of the lawman. "And he's alone."

Sterling spotted the Marshal and was surprised to see that Banks was correct. The lawman was sitting at the table by himself.

"Where are his deputies, I wonder?" said Sterling. He viewed the fact that the Marshal was alone to be deeply suspicious, considering their frosty reception at Oasis Colony.

"I have a feeling we'll meet them at some point soon," replied Banks, with an air of foreboding, like a storyteller reading a grimdark fairytale.

Sterling sucked in a deep breath then straightened himself to his full height and strutted over to the table. He hadn't gotten far before the screech of a chair being pushed back filled the room and a man in attire similar to that of the Marshal blocked his path.

"You're in my way," said Sterling, dispensing with any pleasantries. Sterling hated people getting all up in his face, especially when they were looking at him in the way the burly, broad-framed drinker was looking at him now.

"And you're not welcome," the man hit back. The drinker pointed to the door with a grubby, dirt-blackened hand. "So get out, before I make you."

Sterling squared up against the man, who was several inches taller and wider than him, and smelled like mud and old leather.

"I'm here at the Marshal's invitation," Sterling said, keeping his eyes locked onto the drinker. "So why don't you just sit down and mind your own business?"

The man smiled. "Why don't you make me?"

Sterling brushed the man aside then attempted to continue on toward the Marshal, who was observing with interest. The drinker grabbed Sterling's shoulder and spun him around, his face twisted with rage. A swinging right hand was launched at Sterling face, but the attack was just as clumsy and brutish as he'd expected. Deflecting the strike, Sterling stepped inside and caught the drinker's arm, twisting it and forcing the man down onto the table. The drinker's head hit the dimpled surface hard, spilling whisky from a tumbler across the man's face. It ran down the drinker's cheeks like amber tears.

"Stay down," snarled Sterling, releasing his hold and again continuing on toward the Marshal.

The drinker roared and reached for a plasma pistol holstered to his belt, but the man's hand had barely touched the grip before Banks had caught his wrist. Using her phenomenal natural strength, Sterling's first officer snapped the drinker's wrist like it was a candy cane. However, the cries of pain were drowned out by the sound of more chairs screeching back and more weapons being drawn. Half of the pistols were aimed at Banks and half at Sterling, who was now standing directly in front of the Marshal.

"Everyone, relax," the Marshal called out, raising the palms of his hands to the room in an attempt to calm the flaming tensions. "Captain Sterling is here at my request."

Slowly and cautiously the other drinkers holstered their weapons and sat down again. Only the man who had blocked Sterling's path remained standing, though this was not by his own choice. Commander Banks still had him in her vise-like hold.

"Do you mind?" said the Marshal, pointing to the drinker, whose face was now red and lips bloodied. The man was bearing down so hard against the pain that he'd bitten through his tongue.

Sterling nodded to Banks and she released the drinker, who immediately fell to the sticky, steel-tiled floor. The man cradled his wrist and glowered up at her, but did not speak. Banks reached down and grabbed the man by the lapels of his coat. To the astonishment of onlookers, she hauled him up like he weighed nothing more than a toddler and planted him back in his seat. Sliding the now empty whiskey tumbler in front of the injured drinker, Banks grabbed a bottle from an adjacent table and topped up the glass.

"Now stay there, drink that, and shut the hell up," she said, patting the man on the shoulder.

Still mute from the pain he was suffering, the man simply nodded, though the drinker's eyes were unable to disguise his murderous thoughts.

"You sure do know how to make an entrance, Captain," said the Marshal, pouring two measures of whiskey into empty tumblers. The lawman then raised his eyes to look at Commander Banks. "Augments?" he asked.

Banks shook her head. "All natural," she replied, folding her arms and flexing her hyper-dense muscles.

The Marshal let out an impressed huff of appreciation then offered the drinks to Sterling and Banks in turn. Sterling took one of the tumblers and raised it. The Marshal did the same and they all drank. The liquor felt like fire slipping down his throat, but Sterling managed to stomach the whiskey without displaying his displeasure of it. Banks also placed the tumbler down on the table and maintained her icy, death-stare at the Marshal. If the whiskey had affected her, she wasn't showing it either.

"So, what is it that you have to trade, Captain?" the Marshal asked, getting straight to business.

Sterling tapped the screen wrapped around his left arm and it solidified. The inventory of items that Lieutenant Razor had collated then appeared and Sterling showed it to the Marshal. The lawman read it with more attentiveness than Sterling had expected, which he took to be a good sign that the man was genuinely interested in the trade. A few seconds later the Marshal nodded then met Sterling's eyes.

"I believe we can do a deal," the Marshal said, relaxing back into his chair. "Assuming I can help you with the information you need, of course."

"All I need to know is the whereabouts of a man called James Colicos," said Sterling, similarly getting straight to business. "He was a former Fleet scientist who we believe lived here, or in this system somewhere. But we don't know precisely where or when, or where he is now."

The Marshal thought for a moment, resting his chin onto his hand. He then waved to a woman who was behind the counter at the bar. She was perhaps a little older than Sterling and displayed the poise of someone who was comfortable being the center of attention. The Marshal finally caught the woman's eye and she grabbed a bottle of whiskey before making her way toward the table.

"Finished that one already, Marshal?" the woman asked, sliding the new bottle onto the table. "Your friends must be thirsty." She then met Sterling's eyes and winked at him.

"We're not after whiskey, Dana," said the Marshal. "These folks are lookin' for something else."

Dana smiled. "You have to pay for that here too," she said, before flashing her eyes at Sterling. "Though for a dashing captain like you, I could make an exception."

The Marshal laughed and Sterling joined in, though only in order to be polite. Banks, however, was now staring at the barkeep with a look that could have frozen the whiskey in the bottle.

"James Colicos, did you know him?" asked Sterling, trying to steer the conversation back to the matter at hand. He didn't want to give Banks a reason to start tearing people's arms out of their sockets.

"Oh, yeah, all the ladies in here knew him," said Dana with a roll of the eyes. "Though I forgave him his wandering hands on account the amount of booze he drank. My takings went down ten per cent after he left."

"Do you know where he went?" asked Sterling, ever hopeful that their gamble of meeting the Marshal was going to pay off.

"Oh, he was always flittin' to and fro," Dana said, dropping down into a chair beside Sterling and resting her legs up onto his thighs. "He'd take off in his shuttle and sometimes be gone for weeks. Folk used to joke that he was kidnapping people and selling them off-world." Dana and the Marshal then joined in another round of laughter. "When he was here, the old scoundrel was always in some woman's bed. I reckon it was one of the husbands that finally either chased him off or put him in a hole."

The Marshal appeared affronted by Dana's last statement. "I can assure you, madam, I would not stand for any form of vigilantism," the lawman said. "If there was a misdemeanor of any sort, my deputies and I would have dealt with it."

Dana snorted a laugh then stroked the Marshal's face. "He's a dear, isn't he?" she said before sliding her legs off Sterling's thighs. The sudden release of pressure made it feel like his feet were about to float off the floor.

"So, do you have any idea where he went?" Sterling asked, attempting to prevent Dana and the Marshal from wandering off-topic.

"Oh, I recall him mentioning something about somewhere to someone," Dana said, with a dismissively and flamboyant waft of her hand. "I remember he told one of the girls that he was headed to Fardepp-Neyn, if that's any help? I think he said it was some sort of space base, but he was drunk and slurring his words, so I really don't know."

Sterling frowned then turned to Banks, but she looked similarly at a loss. Banks tapped the computer wrapped around her wrist and brought up a map of the Void colonies and installations surrounding Oasis Colony.

"Thank you for your help, Dana," said Sterling, pulling three silver coins – the general currency in the Void - from a pocket in his tunic and pressing them into the woman's hand.

"No, thank *you*," replied Dana, squeezing Sterling's hand as she took the coins. She then stood up, still holding onto his hand. "And the offer still stands, handsome, if you feel like hanging around here a little longer."

Dana then let Sterling's hand slip from hers, as if they were lovers who had been forced to bid each other a heartbreaking farewell, and returned to the bar area.

"I think I need to switch up my uniform," said the Marshal, waggling his eyebrows as Sterling. I'd get lucky far more often if I had some threads like those. Banks, as expected, rolled her eyes.

"He can't have gone too far in a shuttle," said Sterling. He then turned to the computer screen attached to his first officer's arm and scanned the list of systems. "But I've never heard of a system or a colony called Fardepp-Neyn."

They continued to scour the star map for a time, while the Marshal looked on with interest. However, nothing with the name Dana had mentioned came up.

"Wait, scroll back a few inches," said Sterling. Something had caught his eye. Banks did as he requested, but she just frowned. "What have you seen? There's nothing called Fardepp-Neyn in this region."

Sterling smiled then pointed to a name on the screen. "There, do you see it?"

Banks scowled again. "Far Deep Nine?" she said, reading the name of the location on the star map. "That's a bit of a stretch, don't you think?"

"It's an old, disused mining and research station, and

it's well within range of a shuttlecraft," Sterling replied, his confidence in his discovery unshaken by Banks' doubt. "And the name fits, sort of. Dana said that Colicos was drunk and slurring when he said it."

Banks returned an acquiescent shrug then tapped her computer to fold the screen back around her arm. "It's worth a shot," she agreed. "It won't take us long to get there, and we could always come back if it's a bust."

Sterling nodded then turned to the Marshal, intending to thank the man and request permission to return if needed. However, while he and Banks had been studying the star map, the lawman had drawn two plasma pistols. The barrels of the weapons were aimed at Sterling and Banks.

"Oh, I'm afraid you're not going anywhere just yet," said the Marshal.

Chairs screeched across the floor again and three men stood up. Each of them was armed with a plasma hand-cannon, and they were pointing them at the backs of Sterling's and Banks' chairs.

STERLING FLOPPED BACK in his seat and shook his head. *Just for once, it would be nice if we could catch a break...* he thought as he stared down the barrel of Marshal Masterson's plasma pistol. Glancing across to Banks, he watched her smooth her hair behind her ear then fold her arms. The act was subtle and the Marshal showed no sign that he'd observed Sterling's first officer activate her neural implant.

"What the hell is it with you Marshals, anyway?" asked Sterling, glaring back at the man holding him at gunpoint. He could already feel his blood begin to boil. "You're supposed to be honorable lawmen, but so far your lot have been as trustworthy as Void Pirates."

The Marshal smiled, causing his thick, bushy moustache to twitch as if it were alive.

"Word has it that you killed Marshal Killian, out at Hope Rises," the Marshal said, his smile falling off his face as he spoke. "Killing a Marshal is one the worst crimes you can commit out here in the Void." Then the Marshal leaned across the table, the leather of his waistcoat creaking as his did so. "And out here, you're in my jurisdiction, Captain. Fleet doesn't count for a damned thing."

Sterling straightened up, bringing his eyes level with the Marshal's. The lawman's face looked even more incongruous close up; the smooth, youthful skin contrasting with facial hair of a style and period centuries old.

"He never told us his name, but the Marshal at Hope Rises double-crossed and swindled us," said Sterling, speaking firmly despite the deadly weapons aimed at him. "He got what he deserved. It's natural justice."

This statement appeared to anger the Marshal. "You don't get to dispense justice out in the Void, son," the lawman said. "You Fleet folks forfeited that right when you abandoned us."

The tone of the Marshal's voice, plus the condescending use of the word, "son" – Sterling was easily six- or seven-years Masterson's senior – just pissed Sterling off even more.

"I get to defend myself, like anyone else," Sterling hit back. "Marshal Killian, if that was his name, made a mistake when he crossed me." Sterling then moved in closer, so that they were almost nose to nose. "I suggest you don't make the same mistake."

"I don't take kindly to threats," the Marshal countered.

The lawman then shoved his chair back and stood up, nodding to his deputies as he did so. The three other lawmen circled around Sterling and Banks, not letting their aim slip even for a second.

"You can't arrest me, I have an entire ship and crew outside," said Sterling, also rising to his feet.

Banks, who had remained quietly focused on the three deputies also rose. Sterling could see the tautness of her muscles and the determination in her eyes. She was a coiled spring.

"How exactly do you expect to hold me with just the four of you?" Sterling added, pushing the man to reveal his play.

"I don't expect to hold you, Captain," the Marshal spat back. "I'm judging you, son, and my judgement is guilty. My sentence is death."

The lawman then flicked the barrel of one of his plasma pistols toward the wall, beckoning for them to move toward it. Sterling obliged and Banks followed, but all the time, Sterling had his eye on the door. The Marshal then stepped out from behind the table and took up position in the center of the floor. The other occupants of the bar, including the owner of the establishment, Dana, had now moved well out of the line of fire.

"I don't answer to you, Marshal," said Sterling, standing tall. "And I warned you not to cross me. Now we have to do this the hard way."

Plasma blasts fizzed inside the hotel bar and two of the Marshal's deputies fell, smoke rising from precisely-aimed plasma burns to their chests. The Marshal and remaining deputy spun around and fired, but Lieutenant Shade had already made it through the door and taken cover behind the end of the bar. The Marshal opened fire at Shade, blasting holes in the bar and wall to her side.

"Kill the one by the door!" the Marshal yelled to his deputy. "The captain and the woman are mine."

The deputy spun his weapon toward Shade as the Marshal again took aim at Sterling. However, Banks had already uncoiled and sprang into action. Grabbing a chair from the table beside her, she launched it at the Marshal with all her strength. The chair hit the lawman like a cannonball, barreling the man into the bar and causing him to bounce off it like a deer hitting the fender of a truck. The Marshal's body collapsed into a crumpled heap on the floor, legs and arms broken into impossible positions. The lawman looked like something out of a twisted horror movie.

Banks then turned her attention to the deputy. However, having witnessed the ferocity of her attack, and the warped remained of the Marshal on the floor, the man wasted no time in thrusting his hands in the air.

"Hey, take it easy lady," said the deputy, allowing his pistol to fall from his hand and clatter onto the steel tile floor. The man then turned to Sterling. "You can just walk out of here, it's all good. No hard feelings, okay?"

"No hard feelings?" Sterling laughed, stepping into the center of the saloon. He picked up the deputy's pistol and toyed with it in his hands. "I came here offering a fair exchange and instead, you try to kill me and my officer."

"Look, it was the Marshal, not me," the deputy protested. "I was just following his orders."

Sterling met the man's eyes. He'd given the Marshal and his deputies fair warning and now it was time to dispense some summary judgement of his own.

"I told you what would happen if you crossed me," Sterling continued, aiming the pistol at the man, "and unlike the Marshal, I'm a man of my word."

Sterling squeezed the trigger and shot the deputy at point-blank range. The all too familiar smell of burned flesh and fabric wafted past his nose. However, he was more disgusted by the treachery of these so-called lawmen than he was by the odor of charred flesh.

The deputy hit the floor and Sterling tossed the pistol onto the body. Lieutenant Shade had now been joined by four commandoes, all armed with plasma rifles. The remaining patrons of the bar had fallen silent and were cowering behind tables and whatever cover they could find. All expect for one man.

Sterling walked over to the giant who was still standing guard by the weapons locker. Unlike the others in the bar, he had remained precisely in the same position. It was as if the man considered the chance of being shot preferable to the effort of moving his elephant-like frame.

"I'll be needing my weapon back now," said Sterling, nodding toward the locker.

"No can do," the man boomed, pointing to a red light on the locking system. "It locks when the alarm goes off. Stops people from stealing the guns."

Sterling frowned at the man. "What alarm? I don't hear any alarm."

The man raised a cigar-sized finger to the ceiling. Sterling looked up and saw another flashing red light.

"Silent alarm. There will be a dozen more deputies

outside now," the man said, slowly lowering his hand to his side.

Sterling looked over to Banks then hooked a thumb toward the locker. "Do you want to do the honors?"

Banks moved over to the weapons lockers and the large man backed away as she approached, as if they were opposing poles of a magnet. She then spent a few seconds testing various hand holds on the lid before taking the strain. The hinges of the locker creaked and groaned as Banks continued to apply more and more force. She then let out a roar and tore the lid clean off. Like the Marshal, it too barreled across the floor and bounced off the bar before spinning like a discarded hubcap in the middle of the room.

"Not bad," the enormous man said, nodding in appreciation.

"My commandos are in position," said Shade, lowering her hand from her neural implant. "They count ten more deputies, set up around the front of the hotel."

"Twelve," the large man said.

Sterling frowned up at the giant. "Twelve what?" he asked.

"Twelve deputies outside," the man answered. "Always twelve. Never more. Never less."

"Thanks for the tip," said Sterling.

Banks recovered Sterling's pistol from the locker and offered it to him. Sterling took the weapon then noticed that his first officer's pistol was back in its holster.

"You're going to need that," Sterling said, pointing to Banks' weapon.

"I've got an upgrade," Banks replied, smiling. She then

pulled what looked like a sawn-off shotgun from the locker. However, the construction of the weapon was clearly plasma in origin, rather than a conventional firearm.

"I don't think that's exactly standard Fleet issue," replied Sterling, trying to sound suitably captainly, though in truth he was jealous of his first officer's find.

"You don't mind me taking this, do you?" Banks said, looking up at the giant man.

"Normally, yes," the man replied. Then he shrugged his shoulders, which looked more like they belonged to a bull than a man. "But in your case, no." The giant shot Banks a wide, toothy smile.

"We're all set, Captain," said Shade, moving up beside the door. "There's cover just off the veranda. I suggest we walk out, get the deputies to show themselves, then spring our own trap."

Sterling nodded. "Say the word, Lieutenant. This is one sanctuary that I'll be glad to see the back off."

Shade began a silent countdown on her fingers then she and the commandoes stepped outside. Sterling and Banks followed, walking calmly across the veranda and down the steps of the Hotel Grand. Figures then slid out from behind parked vehicles, signboards, luggage trucks and anything else large enough to conceal a body. Sterling saw the glint of weapons in the sunlight.

"Hold it right there!" a voice called out.

Sterling scanned the scene, but couldn't see who had uttered the cry. Then a man stepped out into the open from behind a parked transit. A deputy's badge on his coat sparkled under the early evening sun.

"You're all under arrest," the man called out. "Marshal Masterson will decide what to do with you."

"You'll have to unfold him first," Sterling shouted back. He then hooked a thumb back toward the doors of the hotel. "He's in a heap on the floor back there. I think his days of judging are over. Don't make the same mistake he did."

The deputy took a few paces forward and was illuminated by a streak of light piercing through the cloud. It was like a spotlight had been shone on the man.

"I don't mean that Marshal Masterson," the deputy said. "I mean Marshal Masterson senior."

Sterling winced and sighed. The last thing they needed right now was a vengeful Void Marshal hunting them down. However, what was done was done and there was no turning back now, he realized.

"I only count ten, sir," said Lieutenant Shade, who had been surveying their surroundings while Sterling and the deputy were speaking.

"Perhaps the big guy was wrong?" suggested Banks.

"Ten, twelve, fifty, a hundred, I don't give a damn," Sterling replied, flexing his fingers and hovering his hand by the grip of his pistol. "If they stand against us, they're the enemy, no different to the emissaries, the aides or the Sa'Nerra themselves. We're not out here playing games. The stakes are too high." Sterling then stepped out into the road and faced the deputy. "I'll give you the same chance to back down as I gave the Marshal," Sterling said, loud enough that all of the other deputies could hear too. "You won't get this offer a second time."

The deputy's eye twitched and he also hovered his hand by the side of his pistol. "The law is the law, Captain," the man said. "And out here, Masterson's word is final."

The deputy then reached for his weapon, but Sterling's draw was quicker. Plasma flashed through the air and the deputy was struck cleanly in the center of his chest. The man's body hadn't even hit the ground before a symphony of plasma blasts erupted all around him, lighting up the darkening evening sky for the briefest moment. Seconds later silence and gloom had descended again. Then the smoke cleared, carrying with it the scent of burning flesh. All ten deputies lay dead on the floor, but Sterling and his Omega crew stood strong.

"It looks like there were only ten of them, after all," said Sterling, shrugging.

Suddenly, the doors to the hotel swung open and two more men rushed outside, weapons raised. Plasma flashed from their pistols, but flew wide. Then a sound like a bomb exploding pieced the air and the two men were sent flying back through the swinging doors of the saloon. It was like they'd been hit by a train. Sterling saw Commander Banks rest the plasma cannon over her shoulder, pointing the smoking twin barrels of the weapon to the sky.

"I'm *definitely* keeping this," said Banks, smiling.

One of the workers from the spaceport then timidly approached, holding a personal digital assistant. Two of the commandoes nearest to Sterling aimed their weapons at the woman, but Sterling waved them off. He could see that the worker was unarmed.

"Captain Sterling, is that your name?" the woman asked. Sterling nodded then holstered his pistol. "I have a list of items to transfer from your ship." She held out a PDA to Sterling while nervously looking at the dead bodies on the floor. "Though, I guess the trade is off, right?"

Sterling took the PDA out of the worker's hand then thumbed the pad to authorize the transfer of ownership to the City of Sanctum.

"I'm a man of my word," Sterling said, holding the small computer out to the woman, who gingerly took it from his hand. "Do me a favor, though," he added, as the woman meekly met his eyes. "If anyone asks what happened here, remind them which side honored their bargain, and which did not."

The woman nodded. "I will, but..." she then hesitated, as if she had immediately regretted opening her mouth.

"But what?" Sterling asked.

"But it won't matter to him," the woman said, her eyes falling to the floor. "The Marshal's father, I mean. He won't ever let it go."

Sterling nodded and the woman moved away. Cursing under his breath, Sterling surveyed the scene of carnage at his feet. He'd hoped that the Marshals would see sense and leave them alone after his show of strength. However, deep down in his gut he knew this wouldn't be the last time he'd have to deal with the Void's so-called lawmen.

STERLING RESTED the palms of his hands onto the sides of his captain's console and scrutinized Far Deep Nine on the viewscreen. The disused private mining operation had been only a short surge from Oasis Colony, so the journey had been swift. It also hadn't taken long for them to realize that the supposedly abandoned operation was no longer mothballed.

"Long-range scanners are detecting Sa'Nerran ships in the system," said Commander Banks, peering down at her console. "Luckily, our surge went undetected. They're clearly not expecting visitors."

Sterling glanced down at his console and examined the scan data for the system. Far Deep Nine had turned out not to be a single space station, as Sterling had assumed, but an entire chain of mining installations. The whole operation was vast, spanning hundreds of thousands of miles.

"Ensign Keller, find us somewhere to hide in all this debris," Sterling called out to his helmsman. "Maneuver using thrusters only if you can. If we can get in and out without attracting any attention then I'd prefer it."

"Aye, sir," Keller replied, smartly.

Ensign Keller then began to maneuver the ship toward one of the medium-sized chunks of planetary debris. It was pockmarked with holes where a previous mining operation had already stripped it clean of valuable resources. The remains of the small mining outpost were still visible on the surface, but it too was now cratered with impacts from the stellar flotsam flying around the system.

"Fleet records show that the fourth planet in this system was destroyed by a massive collision a few million years ago," Commander Banks went on, still studying the information on her console. "It was caused either by a massive asteroid or more likely another planet. But whatever it was, it left the mess we see here."

"So, how come Far Deep Nine was abandoned?" asked Sterling, as Keller moved them close to the surface of the planetary fragment. "Surely, there are still huge quantities of valuable resources here?"

Commander Banks tapped her console and the image of a Sa'Nerran Heavy Cruiser appeared on the viewscreen.

"Basically, that thing showed up and spoiled the party," Banks said, pointing to the behemoth vessel on the screen. "This used to be a private, commercial operation and they were simply unable to defend themselves once the aliens arrived."

Sterling shook his head. "They're like damned vultures, picking the galaxy clean," he said, glowering at the alien vessel. "Fleet may have abandoned these systems, but this is still the Fleet half of the Void. We should never have allowed the Sa'Nerra to encroach so deeply, unchallenged."

The passion in Sterling's voice seemed to stir up similar resentment in Banks.

"You should talk to Admiral Griffin when we get back," Banks said, with similar vim. "I'd love to come out with a taskforce and evict these parasites."

Lieutenant Shade's console then chimed an alert, distracting them both from their warmongering thoughts.

"We have a Sa'Nerran Wasp inbound from the debris field," said Lieutenant Shade, bringing up an image of the small, one-man fighter on the viewscreen. "It's likely that that cruiser has picked up our residual surge energy and has sent the wasp to investigate."

Sterling tapped his console and brought up the image of the cruiser, placing it side-by-side with the wasp on the screen.

"Tactical analysis, Lieutenant," said Sterling, scowling at the robust-looking Sa'Nerran cruiser. "What are we dealing with here?"

Shade answered without delay. She had clearly already performed her tactical analysis of the vessel in preparation for such a question.

"It's a modified phase-three heavy battlecruiser, sir," said Shade, overlaying some technical data about the vessel onto the viewscreen. "It looks like a significant portion of the ship has been adapted to function as additional cargo space. From the energy it's putting out, I'd say the reactor core had been heavily modified. It's possible there is even a secondary reactor active."

"Why does the thing need two reactors?" asked Banks.

Shade again answered without delay. "The cruiser has been retrofitted with an array of class one mining lasers, which have replaced its plasma cannons. The lasers draw significantly more power."

Sterling studied all the information on the screen, while listening to Shade's succinct report. "So it's basically a heavily armed and armored freighter," he said, glancing across to Banks.

"It makes sense," his first officer replied. "Freighters are slow and easy targets, especially this deep into the Fleet side of the Void. So instead, they hollowed out a massive warship and injected it with steroids."

The tactical display of the Sa'Nerran cruiser updated to highlight the weapons systems. Banks blew out a long, low whistle as she read the screen.

"That cruiser's mining lasers could slice a Dreadnaught in half, but they're tuned for short-range use," Shade continued. "Other than the lasers, we're looking at just a single bank of plasma cannons on the port and starboard sides, plus limited point defense guns."

"No torpedoes?" asked Banks.

Shade shook her head. "There's not much of anything else," she replied. "In fact, I'd say based on the proportion of the vessel that has been given over to cargo space, power generation and mining equipment, it could only have a crew of maybe a hundred at most."

Sterling peered out at the cruiser again, tapping his finger on the side of his console. The Invictus was a formidable weapon for its size, but even he knew that taking on a phase-three heavy cruiser solo was a one-way ticket to oblivion. Yet, the vessel in front of them was not a typical warship. The extensive modifications to its design must have led to comprises being made in some aspects of its offensive and defensive capabilities. They just had to find the vessel's 'Achilles heel,' Sterling thought.

"Continue your tactical analysis, Lieutenant," said Sterling, pushing away from his console and standing tall. "I want you to find us a weakness. Something that will allow us to take it down, if we're detected."

"Aye, sir," replied Shade, with more verve that he was used to hearing from his weapons officer. Shade appeared to be relishing the opportunity to potentially take on a much bigger ship.

"The wasp appears to be scanning the aperture," Commander Banks then announced.

Sterling turned his attention to the second half of the viewscreen. He'd almost forgotten about the little one-man fighter than was buzzing around in space close to their location.

"Any suggestion that it's picked up our scent?" asked Sterling, now studying the ship, which was little bigger than a single-seater training aircraft.

Banks shook her head. "Not yet, though it's certainly taking its sweet time," she said. Banks' console then chimed an update and she cursed. "It's on the move again, she said, glancing over to Sterling. "It's heading toward this planetary fragment."

Sterling let out a gasp of exasperation then studied the

updated readings on his own console. The Sa'Nerran fighter was heading toward them fast.

"If that wasp sees us then there's no chance of finding Colicos, assuming he's even still here," Banks continued.

The sighting of and subsequent analysis of the heavy cruiser had distracted Sterling from the reason they were in the system in the first place. Until Banks had mentioned it, he hadn't even considered that the exiled Fleet scientist might no longer be there. In fact, he knew it was entirely possible that Colicos had never been in the system at all, and they were simply on a wild goose chase. All that they had to go on was his guess that 'Fardepp-Neyn' – the place that Dana from the Hotel Grand had misheard Colicos talking about – was actually Far Deep Nine. It was a stretch, but hunches and intuitions were all they had.

"Before I decide what to do about our incoming problem, is there any evidence our man is or ever was here?" Sterling asked, directing the question at Banks. "If he's not here then we're just wasting our time."

Banks returned to her console while Sterling kept a close eye on the wasp. He knew that the small, one-man Sa'Nerran fighter had limited scanning capabilities, but he also knew that it was impossible to completely hide a ship like the Invictus from detection. He didn't want to risk a confrontation with the powerful heavy cruiser for nothing.

"The wasp will be in scanning range in three minutes," said Lieutenant Shade. "I can easily take it down just using the plasma turrets, sir. Shall I get a target lock?"

"Hold for now, Lieutenant," replied Sterling, while still watching Banks work. "Destroying the wasp is a surefire way to get that cruiser's attention. We can't find Colicos or learn more about where he might have gone if we're locked in battle with that heavyweight."

"Aye, sir," Shade replied, though her eagerness to get into close action was clear.

"I'm managed to interrogate Far Deep Nine's central computer core and gain access to the traffic logs," Banks said, while still working her console. "A civilian shuttle regularly visited a research station seventy-thousand kliks from where that cruiser is currently drilling for resources. The records say its origin point was Oasis Colony."

Sterling nodded. "That sounds like it could be our man," he said, turning to his own console. "Now we only need to get this damned wasp off our scent."

Sterling switched to a scan of the planetary fragment they were hiding behind and studied its scarred surface.

"Ensign, is there any way you can get us inside one of these craters?" said Sterling, glancing at the back of Keller's head.

"Aye sir, several of them are large enough and deep enough to fit the Invictus into," Keller replied, still with his eyes front, focused on his console.

"I'd suggest this crater is our best chance."

Sterling spun around to see Lieutenant Razor. She was standing tall, hands pressed to the small of her back, in front of the auxiliary consoles at the rear of the bridge. The consoles were configured to the chief engineer's usual arrangement of engineering readouts. This in itself wasn't unusual, except for the fact Razor had not been there several minutes earlier.

"Where the hell did you come from?" said Sterling, feeling his heart thumping hard in his chest. "You scared the crap out of me."

"Sorry, Captain, I was in the engineering crawlspace, locking down the source of an energy fluctuation. Those engineers on F-COP don't know one end of a spanner from the other," Razor replied, appearing unconcerned by her captain's startled reaction. "I just decided it was more expedient if I exited directly onto the bridge."

"Fine, but let me know next time," replied Sterling, frowning at his engineer. "Or, better still, use the damned door, like everyone else."

"Aye, Captain, as you wish," replied Razor. Her softly-shimmering, skin and dazzling augmented blue eyes displayed no sign of embarrassment or offence.

Sterling took a deep breath, feeling his heart-rate stabilize. He hated being snuck up on, and this was the third time it had happened in a twenty-four-hour period.

"Well, now that you're here, Lieutenant, what's so special about this crater you've identified?" Sterling asked.

Razor turned to one of her stations and worked the console for a few seconds. The scan of the planetary fragment that Sterling had been looking at on his captain's console then appeared on the viewscreen.

"The walls of this crater contain a high concentration of heavy metals that will effectively shield the Invictus from the Wasp's very limited scanning capabilities," Razor said. She had turned back to face Sterling, hands again pressed to the small of her back.

"Won't it also blind our scanners?" asked Commander Banks.

"Yes, Commander, it will," replied Razor. "However, we can approximate how long it will take for the Wasp to scan this fragment and move out of scanner range again."

"It would need to be a good guess," Banks replied, looking doubtful. "We don't want to poke our head out too early and get detected. Nor do we want to hang around long enough for that cruiser to potentially draw closer."

"How long do we need to wait, Lieutenant?" Sterling asked, agreeing with Banks' assessment.

"Fourteen minutes, fifty-two seconds, sir," replied Razor without delay.

Sterling raised a quizzical eyebrow. "How exactly did you work that out?" he asked.

"I took into account the wasp's current velocity and deceleration curve, the time required to run a scan of this planetary fragment, and the time needed to once again move out of scanning range," Razor replied again without hesitation. The albino-engineer then shrugged. "Though we can call it fifteen minutes to be safe, sir."

Banks huffed a laugh. "Fifteen minutes, huh?"

"Give or take a few seconds, Commander, yes," said Razor, calmly.

Banks turned to the captain's console, though Sterling could already see that the doubt had left her eyes. Katreena Razor may have been a little unusual in her methods, but there was no doubt the engineer was thorough.

"What's the worst that could happen?" Banks asked.

"Well, the wasp could blast the crater to pieces and seal

us inside like some sort of Egyptian mummy," suggested Sterling.

Banks raised her eyebrows and turned back to Razor. The ship's first officer had clearly not considered Sterling's rather bleak-sounding worst-case scenario. Banks appeared to be hoping that the chief-engineer had done.

"The weapons of a Sa'Nerran Wasp lack the power to collapse this crater," the unflappable engineer replied. "The worst it could manage is to cause some debris to rain down on our armor."

Sterling sucked in another deep breath then glanced down at his console. He was running out of time to make a choice. The wasp would be within scanning range in only a couple of minutes. He tapped his finger against the side of his console, weighing up the options, then glanced over at Ensign Keller. This time, his helmsman had spun his seat around to face him and was eagerly awaiting instructions.

"Park us in that crater Ensign, and be quick about it," said Sterling, announcing his decision.

"Aye, sir," replied Keller, spinning his chair around to face the helm controls.

Sterling felt a subtle shudder through the decks plates that sometimes occurred in the microseconds before the inertial negation systems kicked in. Like a dog whistle, most people on the ship wouldn't be able to detect it, but Sterling was attuned to every rumble and shimmy the Invictus felt. The dizzying view through the viewscreen explained the sensation. Keller was having to employ all of his piloting chops to move the Marauder-class vessel into the dark pit before the wasp arrived. It not only required speed, but also precision. Alarms rang out on Sterling's console as the ship moved perilously close to the edge of the crater. He almost felt like calling out, "Steady as she goes, Ensign," but then realized how counter-productive that would be. Steadiness was not the trait they needed right now. Luckily, it was also not a trait common to Omega officers, who were more inclined to rush in where angels – and anyone with a healthy sense of danger – feared to tread. Sterling felt another minute kick through the deck then Keller lifted his hands from the helm controls.

"We're in position, Captain," said Keller, spinning his chair to face the command platform again. "Thrusters are at station-keeping."

"Lieutenant Razor, reduce our power signature to the lowest you can get away with, without compromising our ability to react fast if we need to," Sterling said, aiming the statement over his shoulder.

"Aye, Captain, reducing power now," replied Razor, promptly.

Nothing on the bridge indicated that their energy output had reduced, other than the power level reading on his captain's console. However, Sterling could still feel the thrum of the reactor change. It was like a heartbeat slowing down when a person drifted off to sleep.

"Countdown started. Clock set to fifteen minutes," said Commander Banks.

Banks walked over to Sterling and rested on the captain's console. He noticed that she looked agitated, as if she were waiting for some medical test results to come through.

"Relax Commander, we might be buried, but we're not dead," said Sterling, attempting to set his first officer's mind at ease. However, from the look of consternation on Banks' face, he wasn't sure that his metaphor had done the trick.

"I hate being cooped up like this," Banks said, folding her powerful arms across her chest.

Sterling glanced down at his console then shrugged. "Well, there are only fourteen and a half minutes to go..." he said, smiling. His attempt to make Banks feel more at ease again fell flat.

Sterling had never been a clock-watcher, and he generally relied on the computer – or Commander Banks – to remind him of the time. However, their fifteen-minute wait inside the crater in the planetary fragment felt like a lifetime. Everyone on the bridge remained silent, so that the hum of the energy conduits and the soft bleeps of the engineering consoles sounded as loud as thunderclaps. Banks remained on edge and Sterling discovered that her edginess was contagious. Soon, he was pacing up and down the command platform, waiting for the clock to run down, or the wasp to attack. Razor merely continued to work at her stations, as if it were just another duty shift, while Lieutenant Shade was her usual, cast-iron self.

"Thirty seconds..." Banks called out.

"Standby to return to full power and move us clear of the crater," said Sterling. He was once again resting against his console and tapping his finger on the side. "And ready the weapons. If that Sa'Nerran Wasp, or any other alien bastard, is out there, I want them atomized before they can so much as hiss 'hello'."

There was a chorus of "Aye, sir," from the various stations, then Sterling felt the energy level of the Invictus begin to build. It was like a dragon waking from a long slumber and finally deciding to venture out of its lair.

"Time's up..." said Commander Banks. "Fifteen minutes."

Sterling nodded. "Then let's find out if our new engineer's predications about our wasp's movements were correct." He flashed his eyes at Razor. His engineer simply remained in her usual stance, looking quietly confident.

"Taking us out now, sir," said Ensign Keller, as the darkness of the mining pit gave way to the starry blackness of space.

"No sign of the wasp on scanners," said Lieutenant Shade. Sterling felt a wave of relief wash over him, then Shade's console bleeped and his heart-rate spiked again. "Wait, contact detected. Stand by..."

Sterling turned to the weapons officer, feeling his pulse climb higher. The tension was unbearable. It felt like MAUL was out there hunting them, rather than a single, insignificant little wasp.

"I have the wasp on scanners, Captain," Shade added.

Sterling wanted to call out, 'Where, Lieutenant? Where on scanners?!', but he kept his composure and waited for his weapons officer to finish her report.

"It's returning to the heavy cruiser, sir," Shade finally answered. Sterling could hear an audible gasp of relief from Keller as Shade said this. "It's out of scanner range, and it also looks like the cruiser is moving deeper into the system. We're in the clear, sir."

Sterling nodded then let out the breath he'd been holding. "For now, perhaps," he said, peering out at the wasp on the viewscreen. It was now no bigger than one of the twinkling stars in the distance. "But let's keep a close eye on them."

"I have the co-ordinates of the research station where the shuttle was logged," Ensign Keller said, glancing at Sterling over his shoulder. "I can chart a course to it using the debris for cover," the helmsman added. "They won't see us unless they're specifically looking in this direction."

"Very well, Ensign, proceed," said Sterling, finally allowing his body to relax. However, he knew their respite from danger would only be short-lived. It seemed that wherever Colicos had been, troubled followed. And trouble had a way of finding Sterling and the crew of the Invictus too.

COMPARED to the tense game of cat and mouse that the Invictus had played with the Sa'Nerran Wasp, the journey to the research station had been smooth sailing. Sterling had again been impressed by his helmsman's exceptional piloting skills. Keller had managed to maneuver them through the planetary debris field in such a way that they were able to hide amongst the fragments of rock to avoid detection. It was like crossing a river using a chaotic arrangement of ancient stepping stones, most of which wobbled precariously when they were trodden on.

"Hard dock confirmed, Captain," said Ensign Keller as the Invictus latched onto to the docking umbilical that led into the abandoned research station.

"Lieutenant Razor, now that we have a physical connection, see if you can trigger the station's life support systems," said Sterling, aiming the order over his shoulder to the engineer. "I'd hate to have to go in there wearing EV suits."

"That's odd," replied Lieutenant Razor, though it seemed like she was chatting to herself rather than responding to her captain. Sterling turned around to see his engineer still working at her consoles.

"What's odd, Lieutenant?" Sterling asked, prompting Razor for an update since one had not been forthcoming.

"The research station already has minimal life support activated," Razor replied, while flitting from console to console.

"Can we determine if there's anyone on the station? Human or Sa'Nerran?" Sterling asked. The news that the station was still active was unexpected and increased the chances that Colicos was still there. However, it also meant that the enemy could be lying in wait on the other side of the docking hatch.

Razor continued working for several seconds then turned to face Sterling. "I'm not picking up any movement, but our scans are fuzzy," the engineer said. "The planetary fragment the station is built on contains the same metals and elements that allowed us to hide from the wasp's scanners. As such, I would not rule out the possibility there may still be someone on-board, sir."

Sterling glanced back at the viewscreen, which was now displaying the tarnished metal door at the other side of the docking umbilical. He didn't like not knowing what was on the other side. However, he also knew there was only one way to find out.

"Prepare a boarding party," Sterling said, glancing over to Shade. "We go in expecting the worst."

Shade nodded then tapped her neural interface to

communicate with her commandoes. Sterling then nodded to Banks and they both stepped off the command platform to get ready to board the station.

"Captain, if I were to accompany you with some portable scanning equipment, I could get a more accurate reading of the internal structure," Razor added. "The station has many sub-layers where our scanners currently can't penetrate."

Sterling nodded. "Okay then you're with us," he said, nodding to Razor.

"We should bring Commander Graves too," suggested Banks. "If there is anyone still on the station, they could be in bad shape."

Sterling hadn't considered this possibility, but agreed that it was a sensible precaution. "Agreed, notify him to meet us at the port docking hatch in ten minutes," said Sterling. Then he turned to Ensign Keller, who had already spun his chair around to face him. "Looks like you get the hot seat while I'm gone, Ensign," said Sterling. "Think you can handle it?"

Ensign Keller slid out of his chair and stood to attention. "Aye, sir," he said, confidently, though there was still a flicker of doubt behind his eyes.

"Keep the Invictus warmed up, Ensign, and keep an eye out for that cruiser," Sterling added, heading for the door. "If it so much as turns in our direction, let me know."

Keller acknowledged the order then moved from the helm control station to the command platform. The young officer rested his hands on the console and leant into it, exactly as Sterling had a habit of doing.

"He'll be after your job in a few years," said Banks, as they moved off the bridge.

"That's assuming we all survive the next few years," replied Sterling, bleakly. "He'll probably be dead before his next birthday."

Banks shot Sterling an admonitory frown. "Omega Captains might have to be cold-hearted, but they don't have to be morose, you know?"

Sterling met his first officer's eyes. "What we have to be is realistic," he hit back. "The only way that kid survives long enough to get four gold bars on his collar is if we do our jobs. Keller included."

"Aye Captain," replied Banks, recognizing that Sterling wasn't in the mood to play games. "In that case, I'll make doubly sure that the crew do their jobs well."

Sterling and Banks covered the short distance from the bridge to the docking hatch at a brisk pace. A squad of four commandoes met them at the hatch to dispense weapons and body armor to the officers. Razor had detoured to engineering to collect the equipment she needed, but was now heading toward them. Commander Graves, the ship's medical officer, was walking alongside her.

"Here, Commander, put this on," said Sterling, throwing a set of body armor to Graves.

The doctor frowned at the armor then reluctantly pulled it on. "I would prefer to remain in the medical bay, in order to receive the wounded that will inevitably come my way, Captain," the doctor said.

"There could be people in urgent need of treatment on the station, Commander," Sterling replied, taking one of the spare pistols from Lieutenant Shade and offering it to the doctor. "We need you on this one."

Graves gave an acquiescent nod then accepted the weapon from Sterling. "Very well, Captain," he said, holstering the pistol.

Lieutenant Shade handed a set of armor and a pistol to Razor before moving into the docking umbilical to co-ordinate the commandoes. Razor placed down the case of equipment she'd brought from engineering and began to don the protective gear.

"Isn't 'do no harm' the maxim all you doctors live by?" said Lieutenant Razor as she buckled up the body armor and slotted her own pistol into its holster.

"I do my utmost to uphold that oath when it comes to Fleet personnel, Lieutenant," replied Graves, in his usual, dry, factual manner. "However, I am perfectly at ease with doing a great deal of harm to the Sa'Nerra."

Razor laughed then realized that no-one else had joined in. Graves moved into the docking umbilical and took up position behind the commandoes, Commander Banks and Lieutenant Shade.

"Did I miss something?" asked Razor, once there was only her and Sterling remaining. "Or was that not a joke?"

"Commander Graves never jokes," replied Sterling, adjusting the power level of his plasma pistol. "And he's also as adept at killing as he is at saving lives."

Razor nodded, though she appeared to be impressed rather than shocked. "Quite the crew you have, Captain," she said, picking up the case of equipment, she'd lugged along with her.

"A crew that you're a part of, lieutenant," replied Sterling, inviting Razor to head down the umbilical to join the rest of the team.

"Yes, sir," replied Razor, though her reaction was muted. Sterling was reminded of Razor's feelings for Fleet, and he accepted and even understood her grievances. However, in a way, the crew of the Invictus were all estranged from the regular service. Sterling hoped that Razor would appreciate that in time and start to feel that she fit in.

"We're ready to open the door, Captain," said Lieutenant Shade as Sterling approached.

Sterling raised his pistol and nodded to his weapons officer. "Go, Lieutenant."

The chunky hatch door hissed then slid opened, followed soon after by the inner airlock door. A wave of cold, stale air washed through the docking umbilical. It tasted of death and decay, like an old tomb that hadn't been revealed for thousands of years. The commandoes moved in first, securing the dock, followed by Shade and then Banks. Sterling had also stepped through before the call of "clear," had resonated through the room.

The commandoes took up positions, aiming their plasma rifles along the corridors connecting the dock to the rest of the station. Lieutenant Razor knelt down in the center of the room and began to set out her scanning equipment on the deck. The engineer worked fast and with proficiency and was back on her feet within a minute. Razor then tapped the computer wrapped around her left forearm and the screen solidified.

Moments later a scan of the research station appeared on the display.

"Check your computers," Razor said, while studying the schematic as it was being built up from the new readings taken by the portable scanner. "You should all be getting a feed now."

Sterling tapped his computer and confirmed that he too was getting a readout of the station's internal layout. The installation was small compared to regular Fleet outposts and especially the city-sized COPs. However, it still spanned five levels and occupied about the same floor area as an average ice hockey arena.

"What about the energy readings, Lieutenant?" Sterling asked, scowling at the new map on his screen. The data was still populating, and he couldn't make heads nor tails of it. "Can you determine if there's anyone alive here?"

"Negative, Captain, there's still no movement and no signs of recent respiration," replied Razor. "However, I am picking up what appear to be active medical bays or perhaps stasis pods in the main lab area above this floor."

Razor then tapped a sequence of commands into her computer and a section of the map was highlighted in red on Sterling's screen. A route from their current position then appeared, snaking through the installation's various corridors.

"This is the quickest route to the lab, sir," Razor added, lowering her wrist to deactivate the computer.

"Okay, let's check it out," said Sterling, nodding to Lieutenant Shade. His weapons officer then moved ahead with her squad of commandoes. Sterling and Banks followed with Graves and Razor picking up the rear.

"This is a cheery place," said Banks, as they moved through the bare metal corridors of the research station. The installation was on minimal life support and was as dark and cold as a cave. "I wonder what the hell Colicos was doing out here?"

"I have a feeling we're about to find out," said Sterling, sharing his first officer's sense of foreboding.

The commandoes continued to lead the way, their heavy boots clacking against the metal decking as they hurried through the stairwells and corridors, rifles raised.

"There's blast damage to the wall here," said Banks, pausing for a moment as Shade and the commandoes cleared the next room.

Sterling used his computer to shine a light on the area then ran his hand across the scorched panels. "This was definitely caused by a plasma weapon," he said, suddenly feeling like he was being watched.

"There are more blast marks further along," said Banks. She was also now looking at her computer. "From the damage pattern, I'd say it's a mix of Sa'Nerran and earth-designed weapons, though I can't be sure if they were Fleet or not."

Sterling nodded then continued to follow the commandoes through the station. "Something definitely went down here," he said, stepping out into what appeared to be a large open-plan lab. "But it looks like we missed it by quite some time."

Razor moved up from behind Sterling and hurried

deeper into the lab. She was staring down at her computer and following it like a compass.

"Over here, Captain," Razor then said, picking up her pace even further. "These look like stasis pods."

Sterling and Banks followed the engineer with Graves trailing them a few paces behind. Shade and the commandoes again took up defensive positions, but Sterling noticed that Shade's expression was even bleaker than usual. He felt a neural link from his weapon's officer form in his mind.

"There are too many entry points onto this level, Captain," Shade said through the neural link. The weapons officer had opened the link so that Commander Banks could monitor too. "It will be difficult to defend. I suggest we do not stay here long."

"Understood, Lieutenant," said Sterling, tapping his interface to close the link.

Sterling noted that there had been no hint of alarm in Shade's voice. She was simply reporting in her usual, cool and measured way. However, the fact she had highlighted their exposed position told Sterling that his weapon's officer was concerned, even if that concern didn't manifest itself as emotion.

"They're human," said Razor, who had begun an analysis of the stasis pods while Sterling had been speaking to Shade. "There are five pods here; the occupants of four of them are already dead." She then tapped her finger onto the nearest pod. "This one is still alive, barely."

Razor then smoothed her hand across the glass canopy that cocooned the survivor inside the pod, wiping away a layer of frosty condensation. Sterling moved closer and saw the face of a woman through the glass. She was dressed in the sort of clothes that were common to many of the Void colonies. There was also something about the woman's outfit that Sterling found familiar, though he couldn't quite put his finger on what. However, far more troubling was that her neural implant was showing signs of corruption.

"Commander Graves, what do you make of this?" asked Sterling, ushering the ship's sinister doctor over.

Graves stepped up to the first stasis pod and began working on its controls. A look of deep concentration spread across his face, like that of a physician performing open-heart surgery.

"Female, twenty-seven years old, and in reasonable health," Graves began, speaking in his usual measured, dispassionate tone of voice. "Signs of moderate recreational drug use, in additional to medical drugs used to treat a variety of sexually transmitted infections..." Graves went on.

"I meant what do you make of the corruption to her implant, Commander," said Sterling, trying to hurry the doctor on. "I don't need her full medical history."

Graves stopped working and glanced over at Sterling. If the doctor had been wearing spectacles, he would have been peering over the top of them.

"It is all pertinent, Captain, but I shall come to why in time," Graves said, turning back to the stasis pod. "The corruption to the neural impact is broadly consistent with a first-generation Sa'Nerran neural control weapon," Graves went on. Then the doctor's brow furrowed ever so slightly.

"However, there are markers that suggest the device used on this woman was not the same as the one we are familiar with." Graves straightened up then turned to the captain. "I would need to examine the implant more closely. I suggest we bring this subject back to the ship."

Sterling shook his head. "We don't have time for that, Commander," he said, forcefully. "That heavy cruiser out there could spot us at any moment. Find out what you need here."

Graves' bushy eyebrows raised up on his forehead. "It will require that I conduct an invasive examination Captain," the doctor said. "In short, I may need to cut into her head. She is unlikely to survive."

This time it was Razor's eyebrows that raised up, but Sterling did not flinch. "Is this woman... salvageable?" he asked, struggling to find the right words.

"Salvageable, Captain?" replied Graves.

"Has she already been turned?" Sterling replied, putting it more bluntly.

"Her cognitive state is uncertain, Captain," Graves replied, again studying the readings on the stasis pod's screen. "However, there is significant neural corruption. There is little possibility of recovery," he added, speaking as if giving a patient a terminal diagnosis.

Sterling nodded. "If she's turned then she's already dead," he said, without feeling or remorse. "Do what you have to do, Commander. But keep her sedated. The last thing we need is a turned colonist running around here."

Graves nodded then returned to the stasis pod's controls and initiated the deactivation sequence. The pod began to thrum with energy as it set about reviving the woman from her induced slumber. Sterling then recalled Graves' earlier comment about how the colonist's medical history was somehow important.

"You said that this woman's past ailments were 'pertinent'?" he asked the doctor, as the stasis pod continued to deactivate. "What did you mean by that?"

"There were several factors that led me to my conclusion," Graves began. He was busy setting out a number of medical instruments on the side of the pod, including the metal scalpel that Graves favored over modern laser equivalents. "However, the key indicator was the specific types of venereal diseases that this woman has been infected with and treated for," the medical officer added.

"The key indicator of what, Commander?" asked Sterling, feeling like he was pulling teeth to drag the information out of his officer.

"Where this woman originated from, Captain," Graves said, glancing across to Sterling. "These specific diseases and treatments are common to prostitutes that work at the spaceports in Oasis Colony. The drug used to treat them is native to the third planet."

Sterling then realized why he'd found the woman's appearance familiar. Her clothes were similar to those that Dana, the owner of the Hotel Grand, had been wearing.

"So Colicos abducted this woman and brought her to this station, is that what you're suggesting?" Sterling asked.

"That part is for you to deduce, Captain," replied

Graves, somberly. "But if you're asking my opinion, then yes, I believe so."

"But why?" asked Banks. "What the hell has he been doing here?"

"Captain..."

The call was from Lieutenant Razor. She had moved away from the stasis pod while Sterling had been talking to Graves and was now in front of one of the main research computer consoles.

"I've found something," Razor added, activating a holo recording and pausing the playback. The image of a late-middle-aged man wearing a smart suit hovered next to Razor, flickering gently. "It's a personal log or journal by James Colicos."

Sterling felt electricity tingle in his spine. Razor's discovery might give them the information they needed.

"Finally, we might actually get some answers," Sterling said, glancing over to Banks.

"And from the horse's mouth too," replied Banks, looking similarly buoyed by the discovery.

Suddenly, the woman in the stasis pod sprang up and grabbed Commander Graves by the throat. The movement was fluid and frighteningly fast, like a mousetrap springing into action. Sterling reacted on instinct, grabbing the woman's hand and trying to pry it free. However, the turned colonist was freakishly strong.

"Sa'Nerra! Sa'Nerra!" the woman cried before her voice cracked and transformed into a series of hisses and warbles. The sounds were not dissimilar to the alien species' own language of waspish vocalizations.

"Mercedes!" Sterling cried, still struggling to unhook the woman's fingers from around his medical officer's throat.

Banks darted in between Graves and the woman and grabbed the colonist's wrists. There was a sickening, organic crack, like a turkey's neck being snapped. Banks had snapped the woman's wrists and bent her hands flat again her forearms. The woman did not cry out in pain, but continued her waspish cries. With Banks still holding the woman back, Graves grabbed a medical injector from the array of instruments he'd set out and quickly pressed it to the woman's neck. Moments later the hisses stopped and the turned colonist flopped back into the stasis pod, knocked out cold from the jab.

"I'm grateful to you, Commander," croaked Graves, rubbing his throat.

Sterling noted the bruises and scratches surrounding Graves' neck. Another few seconds and the woman might have crushed the officer's windpipe.

"Are you able to continue, Commander?" said Sterling. He was aware that his medical officer needed treatment, but he also knew they were short on time.

"I am, Captain," replied Graves, his voice strained and barely louder than a whisper. "The procedure will not take long. And in this instance, I shall also greatly enjoy cutting into this woman's brain."

Sterling frowned, but didn't respond to his doctor's darkly sinister comment. However, it only added to his already firmly held opinion that Commander Evan Graves was one creepy son-of-a-bitch.

CAPTAIN STERLING LEFT his medical officer to dissect the turned colonist then moved over to shimmering, ethereal image of James Colicos. The scientist gave off a grandiose air, even as a frozen hologram.

"Colicos certainly enjoyed the sound of his own voice; there were hours of logs," said Razor as Sterling arrived with Banks at his side. "To save time, I've used an algorithm to isolate key sections and highlight anything of significance relating to neural technology."

"Okay, Lieutenant, let's find out what he's been doing out here," said Sterling, peering into the eyes of the holographic James Colicos. Razor then tapped the computer on her left arm and the image began to move.

"After a number of frustrating setbacks, I have finally made significant progress on the neural education interface," Colicos began. Sterling noticed that the man looked considerably younger than his supposed sixty-plus years. "Pursuing this goal has been my life's work, made all the more challenging by Fleet's blinkered attitude and short-sightedness, especially from Natasha Griffin." Sterling raised an eyebrow. It hadn't taken long for Colicos to stick the knife into the Admiral. "My initial goal for the interface was to provide a mechanism through which knowledge could be directly implanted into the human brain," the scientist went on, becoming more animated as he spoke. "Military knowledge and skills that take years to acquire and nurture could be condensed into a neural education program lasting mere weeks." Colicos then looked skyward, as if addressing dignitaries in an auditorium. "Think of it... Basic training could be completed in a day, and phase two specialist training within a week. A man or woman on the street could go from zero to full deployment status as an officer within a month. And all this with the benefit of years of military knowledge and inherited experience."

"Pause playback," said Sterling, needing a moment to process what he'd just heard. "Neural education? This all stemmed from a Fleet military program?"

Banks let out a low whistle and Sterling noticed that she appeared just as stunned as he was.

"I had no idea this is what Colicos was working on for Fleet," said Banks, meeting Sterling's eyes. "That sounds like one hell of a project. It would have allowed us to expand the fleet by an order of magnitude. We could have squashed the Sa'Nerran threat years ago."

Sterling nodded. "That didn't happen, though, so clearly something went wrong," he added. He had a feeling they were about to find out what that was. "Resume playback," he said to the image of Colicos.

"Unfortunately, the neural education process proved challenging to perfect, despite my best efforts," Colicos went on, suddenly casting his eyes to the ground. "Neural corruption and irreparable brain damage cost me dozens of test subjects, but just as I was getting close to a solution, Griffin pulled the plug."

The last part of Colicos' statement was spoken with venom. Clearly, Griffin had become the focus of the scientist's frustrations and the person Colicos blamed for his failings.

"If Fleet only had the vision and the will to follow this through, I would not be pursuing my research in the darkness of the Void," Colicos continued, growing more bitter by the second. "What is ten or a hundred or even a thousand more lives sacrificed in the name of science, compared to the billions my technology could have saved?" Sterling and the others continued to watch in silence, spellbound by the scientist's curiously theatrical performance. "However, my perseverance has paid off," Colicos went on. The scientist then reached out of shot and picked something up. Moments later his hand returned and in it was a device that Sterling had no difficulty in recognizing.

"That's a damn neural control weapon," said Sterling, while the holo image of Colicos admired the object, as if it were a long-lost, ancient treasure.

"Neural education was a dead end," Colicos continued, cradling the device in his hands. "I should have seen it sooner, but now I realize my error. The mind is too willful, too individual. It rejected the implanted knowledge, like rejecting a foreign body. To the brain, my neural education device was nothing more than a splinter. And the deeper I dug into the human brain the more damage was done when the splinter was finally pushed free."

"I have a bad feeling about where this is going," said Commander Banks. Her arms were folded, muscles straining the fabric of her tunic.

"Control, however, is another matter," said Colicos, peering into the holo lens.

The longer the man talked, the more insane he was beginning to sound, Sterling realized. The zeal with which he was describing his ideas and discoveries was unsettling.

"The solution was to reprogram the brain, not simply to educate it," Colicos said, sounding triumphant. "The mind cannot reject what it is unable to distinguish from the truth." Colicos then held the neural device to the side of his head. Sterling could see that it wasn't activated, though he still felt his stomach knot to see the scientist perform the action. "With this device, we can create better soldiers and better officers. Soldiers that do not feel fear or doubt. Soldiers that are not afflicted by trauma. We can become as ruthless and as single minded as the enemy."

"Pause playback," said Sterling. He let out a sigh and rubbed the back of his neck.

"So if Colicos invented the neural control device in the first place, how the hell did the Sa'Nerra end up with it?" asked Banks.

"I assume you can skip to that part, Lieutenant?" said

Sterling, glancing across to Razor. The engineer nodded then began scrolling through the entries on her computer.

"I think I've isolated the entries that relate to that question, Commander," the engineer replied. "Do you want me to play them back?"

"Can you just summarize the key points, Lieutenant?" said Sterling, turning away from the holo image of Colicos. "I've already heard enough from this guy."

"Aye, sir. Give me a moment," Razor said, continuing to skim read the information on her computer. "I'm refining the algorithm to pick out the key moments of the timeline and condense it for me."

"That's a neat trick, Lieutenant," said Commander Banks. "Were you always so good with computers?"

"My brother was the real genius, Commander," Razor replied, eyes still focused on her screen.

"Well, I'm glad we have access to your abilities," Sterling cut in. He had assumed that Banks was about to inquire about Razor's brother, and since she had no idea what their new engineer had done in order to merit a place on the Invictus, Sterling judged it better to avoid the subject.

"Here, I think I have it," Razor said. "According to his logs, Colicos developed the neural control technology over a number of years, right here in this laboratory," Razor's augmented eyes then skipped ahead, cutting out any unnecessary information. "It says here that in order to test his device, he would drug and kidnap colonists from a number of Void planets, especially those in Oasis Colony. He'd then bring them here and conduct his experiments."

"Jeez, this guy is even colder than we are," said Banks.

It was another of her characteristically inappropriate comments and Sterling let it slide. He was too eager to hear what else Razor had to say.

"Then it appears that Colicos began a side branch of his research that specifically looked at language," Razor went on. "According to these notes, Colicos was obsessed with proving himself to Fleet. He wanted to clear his name and return in triumph. And most especially of all he wanted to prove Admiral Griffin wrong."

Sterling huffed a laugh. He was certain that Colicos was one of hundreds of people who would dearly love to stick a knife in the dictatorial Fleet Admiral's back. However, the scientist's vendetta was immaterial. It was what Colicos had created that mattered.

"Does it explain anything more about this research into language?" Sterling asked.

"From what I can gather here, the research was geared around neural language translation," Razor said, scrutinizing the screen. Sterling was impressed with her ability to so quickly condense what was years' worth of personal logs into only the key facts. "There's a short entry here which may explain it," Razor added.

Sterling nodded. "Let's hear from the great man again," he said, turning back to the holo of Colicos. The image then blurred as the recording fast-forwarded to the pertinent time-code.

"I've just had some very promising results from my latest neural translation experiments on live subjects," Colicos began. His clothes and hair had changed, and he appeared a little older, though he still looked like a man in his forties rather than his sixties. "I believe I can eventually bridge the gap between human and Sa'Nerran minds," the scientist continued, again causing raised eyebrows from the onlookers in the room. Colicos turned and adjusted the holo camera that was recording his log. The image shifted to show two medical bays, side-by-side. On the first was a human male. On the second was a Sa'Nerran warrior.

"You have got to be kidding me," said Banks. She was now tensing the muscles in her folded arms so tightly that the durable fabric of her uniform was on the verge of splitting.

"I was lucky enough to find a number of Sa'Nerran test subjects in the wreckage of a battle near Thrace Colony," Colicos continued. The scientist was now pacing up and down in front of the medical bays, making wild gestures with his hands. "By implanting a basic neural interface into their brains and applying my neural linguistic technology, I believe I have formed a bridge."

Sterling shook his head. "I'm beginning to think we've discovered the cause of all our problems," he said, feeling a sudden urge to find the real Colicos and strangle him.

"Several test subjects died in the process, but the results are more than worth the loss of life," Colicos went on, still pacing up and down. "The connection is rudimentary, but enough to allow for basic communication between the two species for the first time. Such a discovery could lead the way to peace." Then Colicos stopped pacing and adjusted the camera lens to focus only his face. The scientist again raised his eyes skyward, slowly and reverently. "I'm going to go down in history. I will be forever remembered as the man who ended the first inter-species war." The holo image then flickered and Colicos became suddenly agitated. "No, no! You must not!" the scientist cried, suddenly running out of shot. The holo camera recorded the sound of struggle then the image became blurry and the feed went dead.

"What happened?" asked Sterling. "Who was Colicos talking to?"

Razor's white eyebrows were bent into a sharp vee as she worked furiously on her computer. "I think I can clean up that final image, sir," she said, her fingers moving faster than a pianist playing Flight of the Bumblebee. "Here, I think I have it."

Razor stopped tapping on the screen and the holo image stabilized and sharpened. Instead of a blur there was now the clear image of a naked Sa'Nerran warrior, reaching out to grab the holo lens. A neural interface was clearly visible on the side of the alien's head. Banks cursed and Sterling felt like doing the same, but there was still more they needed to learn.

"Where is Colicos now?" asked Sterling, his eyes still fixed on the Sa'Nerran warrior. "Does the log indicate what might have happened after this recording ended?"

Razor began working on the computer again then shook her head. "That's the end of the recording, but I can tap into the security feed from the station," she said.

Razor continued working for a few seconds then stopped and recoiled away from the screen. She looked disgusted, as if she'd just watched a video of a puppy being run over.

"Out with it, Lieutenant," said Sterling. "It can't be any worse than what we've just learned here."

Razor's eyebrows raised up a fraction then she tapped the screen of her computer. The holo of the Sa'Nerran warrior disappeared and was replaced with a holo security feed. The recording began to play back and Sterling watched in silence as the alien warrior beat Colicos senseless. Then with the scientist out cold on the ground, the Sa'Nerran gathered up the neural equipment that had littered the lab before hauling Colicos over its shoulder and walking out of shot.

"Several minutes after this footage was captured, a shuttle departed the research station," Razor said. She had finally lowered her arm to her side. The computer screen was deactivated and wrapped around her wrist again.

"Could you track its destination?" asked Banks.

"The shuttle's course suggested it was on route to one of the apertures leading toward the Sa'Nerran half of the Void, Commander," Razor replied.

This time Sterling did curse. "Gather whatever you can that may be of use from this lab, and let's get the hell out of here," he said to his engineer.

Razor nodded then set to work as Sterling turned back to his chief medical officer. He wished he hadn't. During the time they had been watching the logs and security holos, Commander Graves had removed the left hemisphere of the colonist's skull. The medical officer's hands were painted red with blood. Then Sterling noticed that Graves was holding what he could only assume was a section of the woman's brain in his hand.

"Do you have what you need, Commander?" Sterling asked, stepping closer to the scene. It looked like something out of a horror movie.

"I believe so, Captain," said Graves, lifting up a bloodied clump of organic material. However, now that he was closer, Sterling could see that there was something metal lodged in the mass too.

"What the hell is that?" asked Sterling, scowling at the lump, which was dripping blood onto Graves' boots.

"This is a section of the colonist's neural implant," Graves replied, pointing to one half of the mass. "It is corrupted, but also contains a significant amount of new technology. Something I've not seen before," the doctor then clarified.

"So what's the other part?" Banks wondered. Her face was also scrunched up, though she had asked the question with genuine curiosity.

"That is a section of the subject's brain, Commander," Graves replied, coolly.

"I wish I hadn't asked," replied Banks.

Suddenly they were interrupted by Lieutenant Shade. She had run over to them from her position guarding the entrance to the lab. Her weapon was in her hand and she looked ready to use it. However, unlike Sterling and Banks, she was oblivious to the blood-stained doctor.

"The scanning equipment that Lieutenant Razor placed inside has detected movement, sir," Shade said. As usual, she was composed, but spoke with urgency. "Two clusters of five. From their heat signatures, formation and the way they're moving, I'd say they were squads of Sa'Nerran warriors."

Sterling and Banks both drew their pistols in perfect synchronization with one another. Sterling tapped his neural implant and reached out to Ensign Keller.

"Ensign, warm up the engines, I want us ready to move out as soon as we get back on board," Sterling said. He'd opened the link so that the other members of the away party could monitor.

"Aye, sir," the helmsman replied, though Sterling could tell his pilot had more to say. "Can I suggest you make it quick, sir?" Keller added.

"Why, Ensign?" Sterling replied, though he had a sinking feeling that he already knew the answer.

"Because that heavy cruiser has just turned toward the research station, Captain," Keller said, "and it's coming in fast."

THE NEWS of the approaching Sa'Nerran cruiser and squads of warriors inspired a frenzy of activity inside the laboratory. Boots thudded across the deck as Lieutenant Shade and the commandoes repositioned themselves, ready to take on the enemy. Lieutenant Razor and Commander Graves hurriedly collected up their equipment and finished transferring as much data from the lab's computers as possible.

"How long until that cruiser gets here, Ensign?" said Sterling over the still open neural link.

"It will be on top of the station in ten minutes, Captain," Keller replied. "The Invictus is docked on its blind side, so unless it chooses to obliterate the station from standoff range, we should be safe right up until it arrives."

"Understood, Ensign," Sterling replied. He then tapped his neural interface to close the link.

"If they're like the other Sa'Nerrans, they'll want to capture us, rather than blow us to atoms," said Banks as they both moved over to where Lieutenant Shade was positioned, at the entrance to an adjoining corridor.

"I hope so," replied Sterling. "Luckily, the mining lasers on that cruiser don't have the range to take us out from its current position, so we have some time." Sterling then glanced back to Razor and Graves, who were still frantically gathering equipment and data. "Pick up the pace, let's move!" he called over to them, trying to instill an even greater sense of urgency.

The computer attached to Sterling's left forearm then vibrated, alerting him to an update. He checked it and saw that the approaching Sa'Nerran squads had split up.

"They're moving around to flank us, Captain," said Lieutenant Shade, swiftly moving to his side. "The first squad is coming in at the rear of the lab," she continued, pointing to the markers on Sterling's computer screen. "The other squad is trying to cut us off before we reach the dock."

Sterling nodded. It was the alien equivalent of a flanking maneuver. "They're trying to funnel us into the loading dock," said Sterling, indicating the area next to the docking hatch on the level below. "What are our options, Lieutenant?"

Shade shook her head. "Limited, sir, it's a bad position," she replied. "If it weren't for the cruiser, I'd say we attack, before they have chance to get into position. But we don't have the time."

Banks moved closer and also peered down at the screen on Sterling's arm. "Then we fight our way out, plain and simple," she said, her eyes becoming steely. "Let them think we're falling into their trap. Then we hit them hard."

Shade nodded her agreement, then she and Commander Banks both looked to Sterling, waiting for his decision.

"We're done playing hide and seek in this system," Sterling said, lowering his arm. The computer screen automatically dimmed and warped around his forearm as he did so. "Let's give these bastards a fight."

"Aye, sir," replied Shade, coming alive as she only did when the prospect of battle was close. The weapons officer then ordered two of the commandoes to the rear and waited for Razor and Graves to finally join the group.

"Razor, Graves, move up in front with Lieutenant Shade and two of the commandoes," Sterling said, turning to his officers. "We have to get this intel back to Admiral Griffin."

The two officers turned to face Sterling, slightly red-faced from the frantic effort of gathering up as much gear as they could.

"Aye, Captain," they said, one after the other, before moving out as ordered.

"Commander Banks and I will take the rear," Sterling then added, nodding at his first officer.

There was a chorus of acknowledgments then Shade, Razor and Graves departed, with the weapons officer out in front, as was her way. Sterling then turned to Banks and raised his pistol, adjusting the power level of the weapon up by a notch.

"Remember what we talked about," Sterling said,

meeting his first officer's eyes. "If I'm taken or I'm hit and fall behind, you shoot me in the head. No heroic rescue attempts, understood?"

"I haven't forgotten," replied Banks, sounding annoyed that Sterling had raised the subject again. "But that's not going to happen," she was quick to add. Sterling could see that her resolve had hardened, like a scab over a wound. "It's my job to keep you alive, Captain, and that's what I'm going to do."

One of the commandoes at the rear signaled that the Sa'Nerran squad were close by. Sterling raised his left arm and glanced down at the screen as it solidified. The warriors were highlighted on the map as moving markers and Sterling could see they were closing rapidly. The sound of plasma weapons fire then filtered into the room from along the corridor that Shade and the others had already advanced though. Sterling slapped his first officer on her shoulder, which felt as hard as a heavy punchbag.

"Ready to kill some aliens?" Sterling said, taking up a position behind one of the stasis pods. The surgically mutilated remains of the woman Graves had operated on stared up at him with the one eye that his medical officer had left untouched.

"Always," said Banks, moving into cover a few meters to Sterling's side.

Plasma blasts erupted into the room and the commandoes returned fire. A warrior then bustled through, taking a hit as it charged into the laboratory. Sterling fired, blasting the alien's head clean off its shoulders.

"Fall back," said Sterling, steadily withdrawing out of

the lab, through one of the other adjoining corridors. Banks and the commandoes also began to move as plasma blasts crisscrossed the room.

Sterling's route would take him longer to reach the Invictus, but it would also ensure that the Sa'Nerran warriors remained separated for as long as possible. One way or another, though, he know that it would all eventually come to a head in the docking section. Then, whoever was left, would slug it out.

Plasma blasts continued to thud into the ceiling and walls as the warriors pushed Sterling and the others back. Sterling and Banks moved into the stairwell, sweeping their weapons up and down the flights of stairs as the commandoes retreated.

"We go straight down here, then right onto the cargo and docking level," said Sterling, cautiously stepping down the first flight of stairs.

Banks called out to the commandoes, urging them to move fast then practically jumped down the stairs to reach Sterling's side. He then felt the computer on his arm vibrate and he raised the screen, frowning down at the display. Four more markers had appeared.

"Is that the same squad that's tracking Shade's group, or another one?" wondered Banks, glancing over Sterling's shoulder while covering the door.

Sterling tapped his neural interface and opened a link to his weapons officer. "Lieutenant, where is your group? Do you have anyone on the docking level, section seven?"

Shade did not respond immediately, though Sterling knew the connection was strong. It wasn't possible to hear the sound of weapons fire through a neural link, but he could feel Shade's emotions, and he knew she was in the middle of a fight.

"Negative, sir, we're approaching from the north corridor, section one," Shade eventually replied. "The warriors are closing in from section two. Two aliens down. We've already lost our commandoes."

Sterling cursed. "Understood, Lieutenant," he replied, his eyes tracking the movement of the new group of aliens on his screen. "Be advised we have another squad of four warriors in section seven."

"Copy that, Captain," Shade replied. "We're almost at the dock. We'll hold the position until you arrive."

Sterling touched his interface to close the link then glanced up at the door into the lab. One of the two commandoes was now through, but the firefight was intensifying.

"Seal that door!" Banks called out as the final commando stepped on to the landing. A plasma blast struck the back of the man's head and Sterling felt flesh and bones splatter across his face and armor. It was like someone had just smashed a pumpkin with a sledgehammer. "Damn it, seal that door!" Banks yelled again, running up the stairs and shoving aside the remains of the dead commando. She slammed the door shut and braced it as alien fists hammered the other side. Banks roared and gritted her teeth, pushing back against the warriors on the other side with the power of a bulldozer. Sterling set his pistol to cutting mode and raced up to assist the remaining commando, who had already begun melting the seams.

"That'll have to do," said Sterling, pulling away and resetting his pistol's firing mode. "We only need to delay them long enough to reach the Invictus."

Sterling moved ahead, closely followed by Banks and the commando. Then at the foot of the stairwell the door flung open and a warrior burst inside. Sterling surged forward and shoulder-tackled the alien against the far wall, stunning it long enough for the commando to blast three holes through its armor. Pressing himself against the wall where the alien had been moments earlier, Sterling saw two more warriors in the corridor outside.

"They've split up," Sterling said, glancing at his computer screen. "I only see two on the scanner, and they're directly ahead."

Banks jumped down beside Sterling and glanced through the door, spotting the other two aliens.

"Straight up power play?" she said, meeting Sterling's eyes. "We come out firing. The other two must have already advanced to the dock."

Sterling was about to reply when he felt a connection form through his neural link. It was Ensign Keller.

"Captain, the cruiser is almost on us, and it's launched Wasps," Keller said. Like Shade, he could feel the tingle of energy surging through his helmsman's body and knew that they'd already engaged the enemy. "They're trying to disable our engines. I diverted all available power to the regenerative armor in that section, but these things are swarming around us like... well..."

"Wasps, Ensign?" said Sterling, finishing Keller's sentence.

"Aye, sir," Keller replied.

"Just hold them off, Ensign, we're on our way," replied Sterling, tapping his interface to close the link. He turned to Banks. "We don't have time for anything subtle or clever. A straight up power play it is."

Sterling, Banks and the commando got into position then Sterling gave the countdown on his fingers. He'd only reached two before the door they'd sealed shut above them was blasted open and the hiss of Sa'Nerra warriors filtered down the stairwell.

"Damn it, go!" Sterling called out, moving through first and immediately firing at the two Sa'Nerrans, lying in wait for them. The combined firepower from all three of the Invictus crew overwhelmed the warriors, but the aliens did not understand the meaning of surrender. Both stood tall and advanced, plasma blasts flying back and forth like burning arrows. Sterling felt a blast hit his chest armor, but the pain of the burn only spurred him on. Intensifying their fire, the two warriors were swiftly obliterated, so that only their fractured, burned carcasses remained. The familiar smell of charred alien flesh filled Sterling's nostrils.

"Keep going!" Sterling called out, pushing the commando on.

Sterling turned to cover the door, expecting the Sa'Nerrans from the level above to burst through at any moment. Then another blast rang out from much closer. Spinning around, Sterling saw the commando lying dead on the floor. A plasma blast had hollowed out the back of his head. Before he could identify the shooter, Sterling was then struck to the back and knocked flat. Flipping over he saw a warrior standing over him. The alien was covered in dust and cobwebs. Sterling realized that it had been hiding in the cooling ducts in the ceiling, waiting for its prey to walk into its trap. The warrior hissed and raised its weapon but a plasma blast exploded its head before it had chance to fire. Sterling felt a hand underneath his arm hauling him up, and he knew it was Banks. Only she had the strength to manhandle him like he weighed little more than a child.

"Can you try not to get captured?" Banks called out, releasing Sterling then firing through the door and killing one of the Sa'Nerrans that had pursued them from the lab. "I'd hate to have to kill you too."

"Noted, Commander," replied Sterling, also firing through the doorway as they both back-pedaled swiftly toward the docking section. Then Sterling felt a lump in his throat, realizing that there had been four warriors on his scans. "Wait, there's another one in here somewhere," he said, conducting a visual search of the ducts and rafters above them.

Banks cursed, also peering up, but keeping half an eye on the door. The bodies of three Sa'Nerran warriors were piled up over the threshold, smoke wisping up from the burned carcasses.

"I don't see it," Banks said, "and we're out of time. We need to go."

Sterling turned to the door leading into the docking area, but before he could pull it open the door was slammed into his face. The impact sent him rocketing into the wall and for a moment he blacked out. Sterling tasted blood and spat a globule of red saliva onto the deck. He then slapped the side of his head, trying to hammer some sense back into himself. When his vision cleared again, Sterling saw Banks locked in a struggle with three Sa'Nerran warriors. Two were holding her arms, twisting them behind her back and pushing her down onto her knees. The third was trying to slide a neural control weapon over her head. He could see that Banks had taken a couple of plasma blasts to her body armor. She was clearly hurting.

Sterling was about to charge at the warriors when he saw his plasma pistol on the deck, just out of reach. He scrambled for it, but his movements alerted the aliens. The warrior fighting to attach the neural control device to Banks' head drew a plasma pistol and turned it on Sterling, but then stopped. Its egg-shaped yellow eyes looked at his collar, where Sterling's four gold captain's bars resided. The alien then hissed to the others, who both also turned their eyes to Sterling. They were clearly aware of his rank and Sterling knew they would try to capture him, rather than kill him. However, this gave Sterling an advantage. The warriors may have hesitated, but he would not.

Standing tall, Sterling raised his plasma pistol and aimed it at the group of aliens surrounding Banks. The warriors pulled Banks to her feet, twisting her arms so fiercely that Sterling thought they might snap at any moment. The third alien moved behind Banks, using her as a shield. It was a tactic that Sterling had seen the aliens employ before. The warrior race liked to use the emotional weaknesses of human beings to their advantage. However, this warrior had clearly never faced an Omega Captain before. Sterling did not want to kill Banks – but he would.

"Do it!" Banks yelled, though her cry was raw with pain. "Do it now!"

Sterling aimed the weapon at his first officer's head and sucked in a breath of air, which was tainted with the stench of death. He began to squeeze the trigger, though the act of doing so felt more arduous than trying to string a bow. He knew he had to shoot, but it was like an unknown force was resisting him and preventing his finger from depressing the trigger fully. *Do it, damn you!* Sterling cursed in his mind. *Shoot!*

Then a plasma blast rang out into the room, followed by another and another. Moments later the three warriors fell to the ground, dead. Standing behind Banks, Sterling saw Lieutenant Shade in the doorway, the barrel of her plasma pistol glowing hot. The shots she had just executed were nothing short of phenomenal, considering the circumstances. They had also saved Banks' life.

Commander Banks nodded to Shade, who returned the solemn gesture of respect. Then she reached down and picked up the neural control weapon before crushing it in her grasp like a soda can.

"Your timing is impeccable, lieutenant," said Sterling, feeling a weight lift from his shoulders. "Another millisecond and I would have had to take Commander Banks out myself."

"I'm surprised I'm not already burned to a crisp," replied Banks, raising an eyebrow at Sterling. "Not that I'm complaining, of course."

Sterling considered a lie, perhaps explaining that the trigger had stuck or the weapon had jammed. However, while he had no issue lying to people, he cared nothing for, lying to Banks was different. The truth was he shouldn't have hesitated and it bothered him that he had.

"Is that Sa'Nerran Heavy Cruiser still out there?" Sterling called out to Shade, deciding to swiftly move the conversation on.

"Aye, Commander," Shade replied, coolly.

Banks picked up her plasma pistol from the deck then walked over to Sterling. She appeared strangely composed considering she had almost died seconds earlier, but Sterling could see in her eyes that she was raging.

"I don't care how big that ship is, I want to blow it back to the shit-hole planet it came from," Banks said. The veins in her neck and temple were throbbing.

Sterling rested a hand on his first officer's shoulder and met her eyes. "I think that can be arranged," he said.

STERLING STORMED onto the bridge of the Invictus with such purpose that Ensign Keller almost fell off the command platform. Sterling tore open the straps of his body armor and tossed it to the deck, revealing the circular burns to his uniform where the Sa'Nerran plasma blasts had penetrated. With the pressure from the body armor gone, the wound stung like hell, but he shut out the pain. His mind was focused on only one thing – the Sa'Nerran Heavy Cruiser. The alien vessel was approaching from across the far side of the planetary fragment. It only had to orbit the fragment to get a clean shot, but Sterling had no intention of allowing the alien ship to fire first.

Commander Banks reached her station next with Lieutenant Shade close behind. Separated from her body armor, Banks' wounds were also clear. And it was also apparent that they were more severe than his own. Banks had taken several hits and the burned flesh on her ribs, stomach and back told the story of her encounter with the warriors on the station. However, he also knew the wounds could be treated, and that they would heal. The aliens on the heavy cruiser would not be so fortunate.

"Ensign, keep the planetary fragment between us and that heavy cruiser," Sterling ordered, grabbing the sides of his console. His fingers slid into the polished grooves in the metal that he'd worn down over the last year as commander of the Invictus. "Then be ready to brake hard and make an attack run directly through the research station. I want you to practically skim the rooftops of those structures"

"Aye, Captain," replied Keller. The ensign had now recovered from the shock of seeing Sterling charge onto the bridge like a Scottish clan warrior.

Sterling could feel the thud of the plasma turrets through the deck plating, beating like war drums. On the viewscreen, a dozen Wasps circled around the ship and the station, stinging the Invictus with their low-yield weapons. The combined effect of the swarm's attacks whittled down the ship's regenerative armor and in places it was already wearing thin. However, if Sterling's plan worked it wouldn't matter. He had no intention of slugging it out with a heavy cruiser. That was a battle he couldn't win. But while the modified cruiser was powerful, it was also slow. More importantly, its hollowed-out structure had been converted for hauling ore and was weak. So long as they timed their maneuver correctly, one full attack should be all they needed to take it down.

Sterling tapped his neural interface and connected to Lieutenant Razor. On Sterling's instructions, she had diverted to engineering, rather than return to the bridge.

"Lieutenant, are you ready to give us the kick we need?" Sterling asked, as a wasp took a direct hit from their plasma turrets and exploded on the viewscreen.

"Aye, Captain, I can give you a boost, but it will blow out a dozen relays in the process," Razor replied. "The blast will also fry the main rail guns, so we might want to avoid any more unwanted attention on the way home."

Sterling huffed a laugh. Trouble always seemed to have a way of finding them, no matter what they did.

"Noted, Lieutenant," Sterling replied. "Transfer the power and stand ready to fight some fires," he added, tapping his interface to close the link.

"We're down to the last six wasps," said Lieutenant Shade from the weapons console. "Armor integrity is failing in multiple sections and there are reports of minor hull breaches. Everything is contained."

"Are there any casualties?" asked Commander Banks.

"If there aren't yet, there soon will be," said Sterling, quick to cut off any answer from Shade. "Let's save counting the butcher's bill until after we've shut up shop."

An alert rang out on the bridge and Sterling glanced down at his console.

"Another hull breach..." Banks said, as always quick to assess the situation. "Emergency seals in place."

"Ensign Keller, are you ready to impress me with your piloting skills?" Sterling called out to his helmsman.

"Aye, sir. Always," Keller replied.

The helmsman had been growing in confidence more strongly over the last few months, Sterling realized. Now, in addition to possessing the ability, he had the belief too.

Sterling then glanced across to Lieutenant Shade. His grip on the side of his console had become so tight that his fingers were going numb.

"Lieutenant, when that cruiser comes into view, fire everything we have at its secondary reactor core," Sterling said. "We only get one shot at this."

"Aye, Captain," Shade replied. She then locked her eyes onto the viewscreen and hovered her hand over the top of her console, ready to fire.

Sterling checked their position. They'd been running rings around the heavy cruiser for the last few minutes, using the planetary fragment as a shield. However, their flight pattern had not been random. The sprawling arrangement of structures built onto the surface of the fragment were all interconnected. It was like a patchwork quilt of different designs that had been added to over many years. A ship the size of a heavy cruiser couldn't navigate through them, but the Invictus could. That was, so long as you had a pilot that was up to the task.

"Time to earn your paycheck, Ensign," said Sterling, waiting for the ship to reach the perfect position. "Start your run... now!"

Keller sprang into action, fingers flashing across his console. Sterling felt the kick of the thrusters and the punch of their main engines. Reduced from full power, the inertial negation systems struggled to counteract the sudden, ferocious acceleration. Keller skimmed the Invictus barely meters above the surface of the planetary fragment, weaving through jagged outcroppings toward the research station. Buildings and towers and long connecting tunnels flashed past with dizzying speed, and Sterling found himself needing to widen his stance in order to stay balanced. Lieutenant Razor had shunted so much power into the engines and weapons that secondary – yet still vital – systems were being starved. Sterling hoped that his engineer hadn't been too liberal when stealing power from the inertial negation system, otherwise they'd all end up as pulpy splats on the rear of the bridge.

Suddenly the wail of alarms gripped Sterling like a knife to the throat, but Keller continued to push the Invictus on. Making an adjustment a fraction of a second too late, Keller clipped a support scaffold with their port wing, slicing through the base like an axe. The jolt almost sent Sterling to the deck, but he just managed to hang on.

"Sorry!" Keller called out, compensating and improvising to get back on course.

"We'll knock it out back at the COP, Ensign," replied Sterling, focusing on his console. The damage control panel was flashing like a pinball table, but the only reading he cared about was the position marker for the heavy cruiser.

"Ten seconds..." Commander Banks called out. "Prepare to fire."

The Invictus surged out from beneath the last of the structures then cut through a fissure in the planetary fragment. The modified alien heavy cruiser was now directly ahead. Sterling had intended to catch the behemoth unawares and with its belly exposed, but as the ship came into clearer view, he realized the Sa'Nerra had not been fooled. Instead of the Invictus pointing at the cruiser's guts, they emerged from the planetary fragment almost nose-to-nose with the massive ship.

"Ensign, take evasive maneuvers!" Sterling called out as the barrel of the cruiser's enormous mining laser began to glow.

Keller pushed the ship in a hard turn and this time Sterling was thrown off his platform. Smashing into the side of Banks' console, he felt his ribs crack. He hugged the metal control station tightly to bear down against the pain. The mining laser then fired, sending an intense column of energy across the Invictus' bow. The beam missed and slammed into the planetary fragment, slicing through the rock like it was cake.

Keller banked hard to reacquire the cruiser and Sterling felt himself sliding off the console. The crushing impact to his ribs, combined with his other injuries, had caused his strength to fail him. Barely inches away from losing his grip, Banks grabbed the back of his tunic to steady him. Peering out through the screen, Sterling saw that Keller's maneuver had positioned them above the cruiser. It wasn't where he'd intended to be, but it would have to do.

"Fire!" Sterling yelled, barely able to get the words out. "Fire, now!"

Shade practically punched her console and the viewscreen momentarily went white as every weapon on the Invictus unleashed concentrated bursts of plasma at the cruiser. The plasma blasts ripped through the Sa'Nerran vessel's hull like it had been perforated by an invisible spear. Sparks arced out from the hull and fires erupted inside and outside the vessel. Then the Invictus was rocked by the shockwave of the cruiser exploding like an atom bomb. More alarms rang out, but quickly silenced again as the fireball from the ship gave way to the blackness of space.

"Woohoo!" yelled Ensign Keller, punching the air. "Great shot!"

Sterling would have also congratulated his crew, though with his ribs broken and his breath gone, he was scarcely able to utter a whisper.

"Enemy cruiser destroyed, Captain," said Lieutenant Shade, though her confirmation of the kill was hardly needed. Sterling staggered back to his own console unaided. Banks knew better than to offer him any more help, and he would have refused it even if she had.

"That's an understatement," said Banks, peering down at her scanner. "I think we could have destroyed a small moon with that blast."

"Plasma rail guns offline, Captain," Shade continued, showing no emotion. "Regenerative armor at twenty-six percent, and climbing. Half of our plasma turrets are also destroyed. Point defenses are still active."

Sterling nodded while cradling his aching ribs. "Casualty report," he asked, directing the order to Banks.

"We lost three commandoes on the station and two crew in the attack, Captain," replied Commander Banks. "I'd estimate Sa'Nerran casualties at one hundred and forty-six."

"Not a bad butcher's bill," said Sterling, forcing himself to stand tall, despite the effort causing him intense pain.

"We've had worse, that's for sure," replied Banks, with a fatalistic air.

"Set a course for the aperture and surge when ready," Sterling called out to his ensign.

"Aye, sir, but shouldn't you get to the med bay?" Keller answered, adjusting course with one hand while glancing at Sterling over his shoulder.

"I'll go to med bay when I'm sure we're in the clear, Ensign," Sterling hit back. His response was crabbier than he'd intended on account of the pain. "The same goes for you two," Sterling added, glancing at Banks then Shade. Both returned disgruntled expressions, like toddlers who had just been told to go to bed. Sterling then met Keller's eyes again. "When we're in the med bay, you'll have the bridge, Ensign," Sterling added, causing the flicker of a smile to appear on Keller's lips. "You've shown that you can handle it."

"Aye, sir," replied Keller. "Thank you, sir."

The helmsman then spun his chair back to his controls and continued piloting the battle-scarred Marauder toward to the aperture. Sterling felt a familiar neural link forming in his mind.

"Are you going soft on me?" said Banks, through the neural link to Sterling. "That almost sounded like encouragement."

Sterling glanced across to Banks, who was grinning at him. "Truth is, if I don't get off this damn platform in the next few minutes, you're going to have to carry me off the bridge," he said over the link.

Banks smile fell away. She would have been able to feel the mental stress of his pain through their neural link.

"Well, don't die on me just yet, Lucas," replied Banks. The statement sounded distinctly like an order.

"I'll do my best, Mercedes," Sterling replied, making a concerted effort to smile, though it ended up as more of a grimace. Then he became serious again. "Hey, I'm glad I didn't have to shoot you today," he said. "It was close though. Too close."

Banks returned a weak smile of her own. "Me too," she said. Then her smile broadened. "After all, who else would wake your sorry ass up in the morning if I were dead?"

Sterling laughed, but then regretted it as pain spasmed throughout his body.

"Go to the med bay, already, before you die at your post, like some ancient mariner," Banks said in a scolding tone.

However, Sterling merely shook his head. "No. My place is here, on the bridge," he said, defiantly. "And this is where I'll be until we've beaten those alien bastards back to their own world and crushed them for good."

Captain Lucas Sterling stood tall and aimed his plasma pistol at Commander Ariel Gunn. A Sa'Nerran warrior stood behind her, its long fingers wrapped around Gunn's slender neck. The alien glared at Sterling with its yellow eyes, while the neural control weapon it had attached to Gunn's implant blinked furiously. The warrior let out a hiss at Sterling, no doubt cursing him in the incomprehensible language of the Sa'Nerra. Then its alien vocalizations warped and twisted and suddenly Sterling realized he could understand them.

"You don't care about anyone..." the alien hissed at Sterling. "Go on, kill her again. Blow her head off her shoulders and prove that you are no better than the Sa'Nerra."

Sterling gritted his teeth and tightened his grip on his pistol. "You force me to do this!" Sterling snarled at the alien. "You invaded our space. You murder my people without reason and without mercy. You're why I have to do this!"

The alien's thin, slug-like lips twisted into a smile. It was an expression that no Sa'Nerran warrior had ever made before. The faces of the alien race were as plastic and as inexpressive as a mannequin. That this warrior dared to mock him with such a twisted sneer only made Sterling loath the creature more.

"Do it then..." the Sa'Nerran hit back, tightening its stranglehold around Ariel Gunn's neck. "Prove that you have the stomach to see this through. Prove you are worthy of the uniform and the silver stripe..."

Sterling felt his pulse pounding in his neck and temples. He averted his gaze from the gloating face of the alien and met Gunn's eyes. They were fearful, pleading.

"Lucas, no!" Gunn cried. "Don't you care about me at all? How can you kill me so easily? You could save me, Lucas! Why won't you try?"

Sterling tightened his grip on the pistol. Gunn's pleading would not change what he had to do. What he had already done. Suddenly Gunn's expression hardened and her voice became bitter and toxic.

"But you won't, will you?" Gunn spat. "The truth is that you're the monster, Lucas, not the Sa'Nerra!"

Sterling had heard enough. He squeezed the trigger and sent a blast of pure energy directly into Ariel's Gunn's face. Her head exploded and her lifeless body fell to the deck. Sterling turned back to the Sa'Nerran warrior. It's plastic face and yellow eyes were still smiling at him.

"You'll never win," the warrior hissed. Then the alien began to morph before Sterling's eyes. Seconds later Captain Lana McQueen was standing before him, wearing her unique Sa'Nerran warrior's armor. "The Sa'Nerra are stronger, smarter and there are more of us," McQueen said. She was calm, logical and cold. "You can't win, Lucas. You will be forced to kill all those you care about, and still you will end up with nothing, begging for your life." Then McQueen's features softened and she held out her hand to Sterling. "Join me, Lucas. Become an emissary with me. I will show you the way."

Sterling adjusted the aim of his pistol and pointed it at McQueen. The former Omega officer just smiled back at him.

"I don't care how many I have to kill to get to you," Sterling hit back, angrier than he'd ever felt in his life. "You can test me. Mock me. Threaten me. But you'll never beat me. And I'll never join you."

Sterling squeezed the trigger and fired, but McQueen melted into nothingness as if she was merely a mirage. Then his eyes went dark and he felt himself floating out of his body. All that remained was the voice of the Sa'Nerran warrior hissing in his mind.

"You will lose..."

Sterling shot up in bed, sheets soaking wet with sweat. His heart was thumping so hard in his chest that it physically hurt. The lights in his quarters on the Invictus were already switched on, though the light level was low, like a sunrise. Sterling cursed then drew in a series of long, slow breaths while gathering his senses and regaining control of his body. At the same time the lights grew steadily brighter.

"Are you okay, Captain?" came the voice of the computer. It spoke in its usual cheery tone, which was at odds with the concerned nature of the question.

"I'm fine, computer," replied Sterling, using the sheet to mop up the sweat on his face and neck before sliding his feet over the side of the bed.

"Your neural activity was especially high during the moments before you awoke," the computer continued. "My analysis suggests that you were suffering another one of your nightmares."

Sterling smiled. The quirky AI was persistent, though oddly well-intentioned. "If you're about to suggest contacting Graves, or giving me a psychoanalysis yourself, then save it," Sterling replied. "I'm fine."

"Perhaps a nice cup of tea then?" the computer added. "My studies of various Earth-based cultures suggest that the British, in particular, find that drinking tea helps to sooth frayed nerves."

This time Sterling laughed. "When the hell do you have time to study Earth-based cultures?" he asked.

"I am a gen-fourteen AI, Captain. I was the first of my kind," the computer replied, sounding a little affronted. "In a ship this size, performing the functions required of me occupies less than ten per cent of my processing capacity," the computer then added, far more cheerfully. "As such, I find myself with a great deal of time to think."

"I thought we talked about you and thinking," Sterling

said, walking over to the compact head in his quarters and running the cold tap. He splashed the icy water over his face and neck, which were still hot and sticky.

"If you would prefer that I cease my activities then of course I will," the computer replied, now choosing to mimic a despondent tone.

Sterling raised an eyebrow and peered at himself in the mirror. He didn't know whether the computer was intentionally trying to manipulate him, or was just playing around with different vocal inflections.

"So long as you do what I need of you, I don't care what you do with the other ninety percent of your time," Sterling replied. He then grabbed a towel and patted his face dry. "Though I suggest you spend some of it thinking about how we can find James Colicos," he added, tossing the towel in the sink, "and how we can defeat the alien assholes that threaten humanity."

"Thank you, Captain, I will give it some thought," replied the computer. "By the way, Commander Mercedes Banks is approaching your door. You forgot to activate your neural link after you woke up, and she is no doubt concerned."

Sterling straightened up and frowned. "Why would she be concerned?" he said. Then he thought better of asking the AI such a question and quickly withdrew it. "On second thoughts, don't answer that and just open the door."

"As you wish, Captain," replied the computer. The door then swooshed open to reveal Commander Banks outside. Her hand was reaching for the door buzzer.

"Well, that was spooky as hell," Banks said, gingerly

removing her hand from the buzzer, which she hadn't managed to press before the door had opened. "I know we have a neural connection, but I didn't know you were psychic too."

"I have the computer keep track of you," said Sterling, stepping out of the rest room. "Just to check on whether you're up to no good."

Banks stepped inside and the door swooshed shut behind her. "I'm sure there are regulations against that, sir," she said, smiling. Then she noticed the state of Sterling's bed, with the sheets twisted into a mangled pile in the center. She frowned then her eyes looked Sterling up and down, noting that he was still in his bed clothes. "Rough night?" she said, raising an eyebrow.

"You're as bad as the damned computer," Sterling replied, shaking his head. "I'm fine." Then he realized that he had yet to undertake his usual morning routine of fifty push-ups. "Though, seeing as you're here, you can make yourself useful if you like?"

This appeared to intrigue Banks. "I'm sure that sort of thing is against regulations too..." she said, with a playful smirk.

Sterling rolled his eyes. "Actually, it's not," he said, just to be pedantic. He then dropped into a plank position, which just caused Banks' eyebrows to raise even further up her forehead. "I'm finding fifty push-ups to be too easy these days," he said, still holding his position. "I don't want to increase the number, as it takes too long. So how about you increase the weight instead and sit on my back?"

Banks folded her arms. "You know, I may not look it, but because of my muscle density, I'm probably a lot heavier than you are."

"Well, this will be a challenge then, won't it?" replied Sterling, undeterred. "Now sit down, Commander."

Banks shrugged and unfurled her arms. "Okay, you asked for it," she said, straddling Sterling. "But I won't let you give up before fifty."

"I never give up," said Sterling. He then raised his eyes to the ceiling. "Computer, ship's status report."

Banks lowered herself onto Sterling and it felt like someone had just parked a shuttlecraft on his back. "Hell, how much do you weigh?" Sterling complained.

"Start working, Captain," said Banks. "Fifty push-ups. No more, no less."

"I'm glad you're not my captain, slave-driver," grumbled Sterling. He then began the first push-up as the computer relaying the usual morning updates.

"Fleet Marauder Invictus is operating at sixty-seven percent efficiency," the computer began in its trademark, cheery voice. "G-COP engineers are proceeding with repairs. The current estimated time for completion is seventy-two hours, fourteen minutes."

"Three more days stuck at G-COP?" Sterling said, squeezing out his fifteenth push-up. It felt like he'd already done a hundred.

"I'm afraid so, Captain," the computer replied. "The damage to the Invictus was extensive, as is to be expected when taking on a Sa'Nerran Heavy Cruiser, solo."

Sterling frowned, or as much of a frown as his pained

facial muscles could manage under the circumstances. It sounded like the computer was admonishing him for taking on the Sa'Nerran mining vessel.

"Thanks for the observation, computer, now get on with the report," Sterling said before dropping down for his twenty sixth push-up.

"Fleet Admiral Griffin is due to dock at G-COP within the hour, aboard the Fleet Light Cruiser Centaur," the computer continued. "She has requested a meeting at oh nine hundred in the G-COP conference room on command level three."

"Noted, thank you, computer," said Sterling. He was more than two-thirds of the way through the set of fifty, but his arms felt like jelly.

"Stop stalling, Captain..." said Banks. She was clearly enjoying tormenting him. "Another twelve and we're done."

Sterling glowered at Banks over his shoulder then resumed his set. "Anything else, computer?" he asked, lowering his nose to the deck.

"There were no Sa'Nerran incursions into Fleet space overnight," the computer resumed. "Relay probes detected seventeen Sa'Nerran warships in the Fleet half of the Void, close to the aperture to G-sector."

"Damn it, we're allowing the enemy right up to our gates," Banks complained. Sterling would have agreed, but the effort of the workout had rendered him unable to speak.

Sterling squeezed-out his fiftieth push-up then collapsed onto the deck with Banks still on his back. His first officer rolled off him then knelt at his side, offering Sterling her hand.

"Good job, Captain," she said, smiling. "I was worried you weren't going to get that last one."

Sterling took Banks' hand then she lifted him onto his knees with infuriating ease. "Remind me never to do that again," he said, rubbing his aching arms and chest. "You're like the human equivalent of a neutron star."

Banks scowled. "I'll try not to take that personally," she said, though it was clear she had. "Anyway, I disagree. I think we should do this more often to work on your upper body. I also think we could also add in some squats with me on your back."

Sterling laughed, though it came out as more of a breathless cough. "Or, I could just go to the gym?"

"Where's the fun in that?" replied Banks, springing to her feet and helping Sterling to stand.

"Would you like me to continue with my status report, Captain?" said the computer. "Assuming you and Commander Banks are finished with your witty exchange?"

"I thought you had already finished," Sterling replied, flexing his chest and shoulders.

"I have only one more item of note," the computer said. "The ambassador-ship, Fleet Light Cruiser Franklin, is en route back to G-COP from Sa'Nerran space. It is expected by twelve hundred hours."

Sterling stopped stretching and met Banks' eyes. The news had grabbed her attention too.

"It's returning from within Sa'Nerran space?" asked

Banks.

"Yes, Commander," the computer chirruped. "Initial reports transmitted through aperture relays indicate the mission was a success."

"What?" Sterling hit back. "A success how?"

"Unknown as of this time," the computer answered. "The report only details that contact with the Sa'Nerran rulers was achieved and that the ambassador's peaceful overtures were received positively."

Sterling couldn't believe what he was hearing. "We don't even know how to say, 'hello' to those alien bastards," he argued. "How can the ambassador have communicated our intent and understood the reply?"

"Unknown, Captain," replied the computer.

Sterling sighed and shook his head. "Well, that's another item to add to the list when we meet Admiral Griffin later," he said.

"Shall I meet you in the wardroom for breakfast in fifteen?" suggested Banks. Then she scrunched up her nose, as if a skunk had just sauntered into the room. "I think you may need to shower and change first," she added, pointing to Sterling's sweat-soaked sleeping clothes.

"Thank you for that keen observation, Commander," replied Sterling, with a touch of snark. He then pulled off his t-shirt and used it to mop up the fresh sweat that had formed on his face from exercising. Banks folded her arms and cast her eyes critically over his body, studying him as if she were examining a painting in a gallery.

"Yes, I definitely think we still need to work on your upper body," she said, unable to hide a smirk.

"Nice," replied Sterling, tossing his sweaty t-shirt into Banks' face. She hysterically clawed it off and threw it onto the bed, as if it had been a tarantula crawling on her skin. "Now, if you don't mind, you can get out."

"Aye, Captain," said Banks, moving to the door. "Though I'd hurry up, I hear they have some twenty-sevens in this morning," she added, still clearly teasing him.

"I'm not falling for that again," said Sterling, moving back into the rest room and opening the shower room door.

Banks shrugged. "Suit yourself, Captain," she said, nonchalantly. "I'll perhaps see if they can save you one, though I'm not making any promises."

The door swooshed open and Banks stepped outside, but she held on to the frame to prevent the door from closing again.

"Or, maybe I'll just eat your one myself," Banks added, coolly. Then before Sterling could answer, Commander Banks had slid her hand off the door and was gone.

Sterling laughed. "I'm not falling for it," he said out loud to himself. Then he shook his head and sighed. "Who the hell am I kidding?" he added, practically tearing off his pants, while trying to turn on the shower at the same time.

CHAPTER 21
PEOPLE ARE LIKE MUSIC

STERLING SLUMPED down into the chair opposite Commander Banks, looking like a man who'd just lost his job. It had taken twice as long as usual for him to shower and get dressed on account of the stiffness that had set in to his chest and shoulder muscles. While he was quietly proud of his ability to do fifty push-ups with the lean, yet unfeasibly solid mass of Mercedes Banks on his back, the activity had also taken its toll. The need to return salutes and pleasantries to the rest of the crew en route to the wardroom meant that by the time he reached the serving hatch, all the number twenty-sevens had gone.

"It's not that bad," said Banks. There was already an empty meal tray in front of her, and another unopened one to its side. "The thirteen is pretty good, I hear."

"I'd rather eat your socks after a full duty shift," replied Sterling, grumpily.

"Let's hope it never comes to that," said Banks, smiling.

Banks then lifted the unopened meal tray off the table,

revealing another one stacked beneath it. Sterling's eyes narrowed as his first officer slid the lower tray across the table then looked at him expectantly. Sterling felt a sense of anticipation rising inside him then lifted the corner of the foil and peeked underneath. A smile beamed across his face as he saw the familiar form of his beloved grilled ham and cheese.

"Someone's bucking for a promotion, I think," said Sterling, unable to contain his glee. "But thanks, Mercedes. You're one in a million."

"A compliment!" Banks said, reveling in her victory. "Wonders never cease."

One of the wardroom staff arrived to replace the coffee jug on the table. The man then offered to process Sterling's meal tray and he readily accepted. Now that he'd sat down, Sterling's weary body didn't feel like standing up again any time soon.

"Where are the others?" he asked, adding some creamer to his coffee and peering around the wardroom.

"Keller and Graves decided to try out the wardroom on G-COP," replied Banks. She had torn the foil off her second meal tray and was working her way through some sort of fried rice dish. "Shade has been and gone, as usual. As for Razor, I honestly don't know."

The wardroom staff member who had taken Sterling's number twenty-seven for processing then returned and slid the tray in front of him. Sterling thanked the man then peeled back the foil, savoring the smell of artificial cheese and lab-engineered ham. The aches and pains in his body immediately bled away.

"Computer, locate Lieutenant Katreena Razor," said Sterling, while picking up the sandwich.

"Lieutenant Katreena Razor is in crawlspace fourteen-alpha, deck four, forward section," the computer replied.

"What the hell is she doing in there?" said Sterling, with his mouth full of grilled ham and cheese. He hadn't actually intended the question for the computer, but his ship's AI answered anyway.

"She is tuning the power distribution network for the new plasma rail cannons," the computer replied. "Prior to this, Lieutenant Razor recalibrated the life-support systems, increasing energy efficiency by four per cent, and increased the output of the main fusion reactors by three percent." There was a pause before the computer added, "With my assistance, of course." Sterling thought he detected a hint of pride in the AI's voice.

Banks then blew out a long, low whistle. "Has she slept or eaten any time in between these feats of engineering genius?" she asked.

"Lieutenant Razor sleeps on average four hours per night and generally visits the wardroom at oh six hundred and at nineteen hundred hours," the computer answered.

"She must be a damned robot," said Banks, throwing down her fork and moving on to eating a stack of fruit biscuits.

"My father only slept a few hours per day," said Sterling, dropping the crusts of his grilled ham and cheese back onto the tray. "Or so I was told, anyway. I don't really remember much." Suddenly, like a snake striking at its prey, Commander Banks grabbed the crusts from Sterling's tray and dropped them onto her own. "Don't you have enough food already?" Sterling wondered. How much Banks ate and the speed with which she could put it all away never ceased to amaze him.

"I'm hungry," Banks said, with a shrug. She was then silent for a few seconds, though Sterling could tell that she was working up to asking a difficult question. "Do you miss them?" Banks then said, regarding Sterling with a quizzical eye. "Your folks, I mean?"

This time it was Sterling who shrugged. "I didn't really know them," he said. "People are like music to me. When you're listing to music, it surrounds you and fills you, and it's all you can think about. But when it's gone the memory of it fades into the background. The tune might come into your head again every once in a while, but you don't miss it. Something else fills that void instead."

Banks scowled at Sterling then picked up her coffee cup and hovered it just in front of her lips. Sterling could again practically see the cogs working in her mind, as she chewed over how to respond.

"So, when I walk out of here and we go our separate ways, you don't think about me at all?" Banks asked. "Or anyone else? It's like we don't exist, or are just a distant memory."

"Something like that," replied Sterling. He realized how cold and detached that sounded, though it was the truth.

"Well, I'll try not to take that personally," said Banks, taking a long, indignant slurp from the coffee cup.

Sterling was suddenly reminded of his dream about

Ariel Gunn and his Omega Directive test on the Hammer. As usual, he'd forgotten about the dream almost as soon as he'd woken up, but his conversation with Banks had caused the memory of his dead friend to resurface, like a familiar tune. Sterling toyed with the some of the remaining food on his tray trying to understand the reason why that incident kept returning to him as he slept.

Do I really not give a damn about anyone? He asked himself. It was, strangely enough, a question he had never asked himself before. *And what does it matter if I don't...* he continued, still toying with some of the snacks on his tray.

"Everyone on this ship could be dead in a few days, including me," Sterling then said out loud to Banks, who was still studying him with interest. "It's better not to form attachments. It's better to wake up each morning and expect that each face you see that day might not be there tomorrow."

Banks continued to watch and listen with interest, though her expression gave nothing away. If she was shocked by Sterling's statement or agreed with it, or downright didn't care either way, he couldn't tell.

"We're just machines when you boil it down, and like any machine we have a specific job to do," Sterling went on. "We need all the parts of that machine to work, but if one breaks it can simply be replaced. That's how we'll win, Mercedes," Sterling continued, his enthusiasm building as the speech progressed. "That's how we'll beat the Sa'Nerra. They prey on our human weaknesses. Our emotions. Our fear of loss. We have to show them no fear. And we have to show them no mercy."

Banks placed her coffee cup down on the table and shot Sterling a soft smile. "My god, you really are the consummate Omega Captain, aren't you?" she said. "You're making me feel cold just by looking at me."

Sterling tossed a biscuit into his mouth then dusted off his hands. "The calorie count of what you've just eaten probably matches the output of the sun," he said, noting that Banks had completely cleared two full meal trays, and his sandwich crusts. "I think you probably have enough stored energy to withstand my chilling presence."

Banks reached over the table and stole the remaining biscuits from Sterling's tray. "I don't know, I think I need a bit more fuel, especially considering how chilly you are this morning," she said before tossing one of the snacks into her mouth.

"Captain Sterling, Fleet Admiral Griffin has requested your presence immediately in G-COP conference room, command level three," the computer announced.

Sterling checked the time on the clock on the wall then frowned. "It's only ten minutes past eight," he said, raising his eyes to the ceiling and responding to the computer. "Our scheduled meeting was at nine."

"The Admiral has altered the time of the meeting, Captain," the computer replied. "She is already waiting for you. And she requests that you also bring Commander Banks."

Sterling sighed then tore the top off a pack of wet wipes and used the contents to freshen his hands and face. "I guess that's the end of breakfast then," he said, pushing his chair back and tossing the used wet wipe onto his empty tray. Banks also stood up then grabbed Sterling's wet wipe and used it to clean her own hands and face. "You do have one of your own, you know?" said Sterling, scrunching up his nose. "Two, in fact, considering you doubled up on breakfast."

"I had to claw your sweaty t-shirt off my face not that long ago, so I think sharing a wet wipe is okay," replied Banks, tossing the cloth down onto one of her two trays. "It doesn't mean we're married or anything." Sterling laughed then invited Banks to move ahead. "It's a good thing too," Banks continued, heading toward the door. She then paused and glanced back at Sterling. "Because based on what you just told me, you'd struggle to remember who the hell I was most days."

DESPITE BEING the Fleet space station closest to the Void, the command outpost in G-sector was a poor cousin to its city-sized counterpart in F-sector. At roughly two-thirds the size of F-COP, the station certainly wasn't small, but it had much more of a forward operating base feel to it. It was relatively stripped back, lacking the many luxuries that F-COP offered, and had a far smaller population of civilian contractors. There were also no families or children allowed on the station. Its use was purely as a military asset. Along with Fleet Gatekeeper Halberd - a powerful weapons platform with a suitably menacing designation – G-COP was the first line of defense against a Sa'Nerran invasion.

"I can't say that I'm thrilled to be back here again," said Commander Banks as she and Sterling moved through the station toward the conference room where Admiral Griffin was waiting.

"I'm not surprised," replied Sterling. He knew that G-

COP had been the location of Mercedes Banks Omega Directive test. "I guess this place dredges up some pretty bad memories."

"I don't think about it much," replied Banks, "but when I do, I find myself getting angry more than anything else."

"How come?" asked Sterling, while returning the hurried salute of a Fleet Lieutenant who was walking in the opposite direction. The officer had clearly noticed the silver stripe on his uniform and increased her pace in order to escape the two "Void Recon Unit" officers as quickly as possible.

"Because those other officers and crew didn't have to die," Banks replied.

Admiral Griffin had recruited Mercedes Banks after Sterling himself had undergone an Omega Directive test. Banks' ordeal was quite a different one to the situation Sterling had found himself in, but the choice had been no less challenging. Griffin had essentially engineered an isolated "prison break" in the detention area of G-COP. A dozen Sa'Nerran warriors had got loose. The Fleet guards had been outnumbered by two to one, and had surrendered to the aliens, rather than stand and fight. As a then Lieutenant Commander in charge of the detention sector, Banks was left with two choices. The first was surrender. The second was to airlock the entire section into space, including the warriors, Fleet crew and even herself. She chose the latter. Griffin, in her cold-hearted wisdom, had known these would be her only choices. The crew who chose to surrender therefore wound-up dead, frozen in space. Banks, however, had been blown out into space through a different airlock and found herself sailing into the waiting hold of a prison ship. She had still suffered extensive injuries from her exposure to the vacuum of space, but she had survived, and she had proven herself to be made of the sort of mettle that Griffin was looking for.

"Griffin likes the tests to be 'real'," Sterling replied, playing through the scenario in his head. "If the stakes aren't real, the choices a person makes aren't genuine either."

"I don't mean that," replied Banks, glowering at a Fleet crew member who passed them by. The man had made the mistake of staring at Banks and the silver stripe on her uniform like she was a member of the Gestapo. "I mean if they'd made different choices, they'd have come through it, like I did. That's what makes me angry."

Sterling huffed a laugh. "If they'd made the choice you made then they'd be Omega officers too," he said. Then he shook his head and sighed. "The fact is, Mercedes, most people believe that when faced with an impossible situation, they'd make the hard choice. They believe that they'd take the bullet, accept the sacrifice, make the kill or whatever it is. But the truth is they don't. Emotions overwhelm them. It's just human nature."

Banks nodded in agreement. "The trouble is that our problem isn't a human one," she said, as they turned the last corner before reaching the conference room. "The Sa'Nerra aren't human. To fight them, we have to be something different. We have to be just like them."

Sterling stepped up to the conference room door and pressed the buzzer. The strident, powerful tones of Fleet

Admiral Griffin replied, commanding them to enter. The mere sound of the Admiral's voice was enough to send chills rushing down Sterling's spine. The door then swooshed open and he stepped inside, closely followed by Commander Banks. Fleet Admiral Griffin was standing by the window. She had her hands pressed to the small of her back and appeared to be absorbed by the view of the north docking ring. The conference room was one of the more impressive facilities in G-COP and the long, floor to ceiling glass wall provided a dizzying view out into space. As he approached the window, Sterling realized he could see the formidable form of Fleet Gatekeeper Halberd in the distance. In the foreground, between the gatekeeper and G-COP was a Fleet ship on approach. The comm chatter from the control tower was being played through the speakers in the conference room, at a low volume. The vessel was already under G-COP's control and was being brought in on automatic with its weapon systems powered down, as per standard procedure. The only thing unusual about the docking maneuver was where the ship was headed. It appeared to be on-course to the north docking port on command level one, which meant that a member of its crew was clearly someone of extreme importance.

"Which ship is that?" asked Sterling, dispensing with the usual formalities when greeting the most senior military officer in the Fleet. Like himself, Griffin was not interested in trading pleasantries and preferred to get down to brass tacks as quickly as possible.

"That is the Franklin. The ambassador ship that's returning from its diplomatic mission into Sa'Nerran space," Griffin replied. Her surly tone and stiff body language suggested she was not pleased to see the vessel.

"Its mission was apparently a success, or so I've heard," replied Sterling, peering out at the sleek light cruiser.

"I will be the judge of that," said Griffin, her words as stiff as her posture. The Admiral then turned to Sterling and he found himself straightening to attention, as if Griffin had just paralyzed him with her piercing eyes. "I am due to meet Captain Serrano to debrief her about her diplomatic mission as soon as the Franklin docks, so I don't have much time."

Sterling grabbed the back of one of the conference room's plush chairs, with the intention of sitting down, but Griffin jammed her foot against the castors.

"We can do this standing, Captain," Griffin said, pushing the chair back under the table. "I've already reviewed your data from Far Deep Nine and have a team forensically working through the details for clues as to Colicos' possible whereabouts." Griffin had again turned to the window and was staring out at the ambassador ship. "To be honest, I'm not surprised this neural weapon is his doing." Griffin was the least approachable person Sterling had ever known, but the Admiral seemed to be seething with rage under the surface, even more so than usual. "If Colicos is still alive then he's being used as a pawn by the Sa'Nerra. We must find him. His knowledge of the neural weapon is crucial to finding a way to counteract its effects."

"Understood, Admiral," replied Sterling, agreeing with her conclusion. "I'll have our new engineer study the data too. Hopefully, we can be underway again soon, once repairs are complete."

The ambassador ship had docked to command level one during the time they had been speaking and Griffin now looked anxious to leave.

"I will relay any new information directly to your ship, via the secure communication chip I gave you," Griffin said, turning back to Sterling. "Once I am finished with Captain Serrano, I have a meeting back on Earth with the War Council. The information you have uncovered will strengthen my argument for a continued presence inside the Void."

"Assuming we haven't struck up an accord with the aliens before then," Sterling said, glancing up at the belly of the ambassador ship.

"We both know that the Sa'Nerra are not interested in peace, Captain," Griffin hit back with such bite that Sterling could practically feel her teeth clamped around his throat. "Get underway again as soon as possible."

"Yes, Admiral," replied Sterling, realizing that Griffin's patience was already at its limits.

Suddenly the conference room was rocked and Sterling was thrown off-balance. A rumble resonated through the deck and the walls and a bowl of fruit on the conference table rattled off and smashed on the floor.

"What the hell was that?" said Sterling, pressing his face to the window and peering around the station. Then he saw a fireball on the main docking ring and felt his mouth go dry. "A ship just exploded on the dock," Sterling said.

Griffin and Banks both rushed to the window and peered at the docking ring.

"It's the Centaur," said Banks, her breath misting the window. "That's the ship Admiral Griffin arrived in."

Griffin pushed away from the window and tapped her neural interface. Sterling and Banks were both permitted to monitor.

"Captain Roth, what the hell is going on?" Griffin demanded. Roth was the commander of G-COP, though Sterling had never met him. "Captain, answer me!" Griffin called out again after no response was forthcoming.

"For Sa'Nerra!"

For someone whose expression was usually so hard that even a diamond couldn't scratch it, Griffin's reaction was telling.

"Who is this?" demanded Griffin.

"I am an aide to the emissaries," the voice of Captain Roth replied. "The Sa'Nerra now control this station."

Griffin immediately tapped her neural interface to close the link then rushed over to the conference room controls built into the table. The screen wall at the top of the room activated and Griffin used her command access to bring up a security feed. Captain Roth was in the middle of the command center, weapon in hand. The bodies of Fleet officers and crew were scattered at his feet.

"How the hell did the Sa'Nerra turn the commander of a COP?" wondered Sterling, peering at the viewing wall with his arms folded across his chest.

Then they all watched as the inner docking hatch opened and Captain Amy Serrano stepped off the ambassador ship followed soon after by a squad of Sa'Nerran warriors. Captain Serrano walked up to the turned commander of G-COP and the two clasped hands in a gesture of solidarity and camaraderie.

Sterling cursed bitterly. "This whole thing was a set-up," Sterling said. "The diplomatic mission wasn't a success. It was just a way to get the Sa'Nerra and those turned traitors on-board the station."

Then another figure emerged from the docking hatch. It was a man, wearing the distinctive armor of a Sa'Nerran warrior. A section of the man's head was partially covered in metal plating. The figure turned, giving Sterling and the others their first clear view of the traitor's face. However, Sterling already knew who it was; his former chief engineer, Clinton Crow.

THE SECURITY FEED of the command operation center went dead, but the image of the Invictus' former engineer was still imprinted on Sterling's retinas. Another series of powerful thuds resonated through the deck and walls of the station, as if G-COP itself was being struck by an asteroid-sized hammer.

"Command levels one through three have been locked down," said Admiral Griffin, who was scowling down at the console built into the conference table. "It's a failsafe mechanism that can only be triggered from the command center by the station commander or a flag officer."

Sterling understood the significance at once. "That means that Crow and the other Sa'Nerra have control of G-COP."

Sterling felt Lieutenant Shade reach out to him through a neural connection and he accepted the link.

"Captain, we just monitored a detonation aboard the

Centaur. The ship was completely destroyed and the docking ring heavily damaged."

"We saw it, Lieutenant," replied Sterling, moving over to the window and peering down at the diminutive form of the Invictus. "Be advised that G-COP has been seized by Sa'Nerran operatives, led by the emissary, Clinton Crow. They were aboard the ambassador ship."

"Is Admiral Griffin okay?" Shade asked. She then quickly adjusted her question. "I mean, is the Admiral safe?"

Sterling scowled then glanced across to Griffin. She and Banks were working on the console built into the conference table, oblivious to Sterling's neural call. He remembered how Griffin had personally enlisted Shade and vouched for her. Clearly there was more to their relationship than he knew, but now was not the time to get into it.

"The Admiral is safe and with us, Lieutenant," replied Sterling. "What's the status of the Invictus?"

"The mag locks engaged moments after the Centaur was destroyed, sir," Shade answered. "Lieutenant Razor informs me that mag locks and weapons fail-safes have also engaged for all ships docked to G-COP. We're trapped here."

"Is Razor on the bridge with you?" Sterling asked.

"Aye, Captain," replied Shade. "She's at the aft consoles."

Sterling tapped his neural interface and opened the link to include his chief engineer. "Lieutenant Razor, I need you to hear this too," he said.

"I'm here, Captain, go ahead," Razor replied.

"The Sa'Nerra have control of G-COP," Sterling began. Even as he spoke the words in his mind his statement sounded unbelievable. "We don't know their intentions yet, but I think we can assume more Sa'Nerra are on the way."

"What are your orders, Captain?" replied Razor. She was impressively calm, matching even Lieutenant Shade's glacial level of composure.

"Work fast to circumvent the mag locks and prepare to repel boarders," Sterling replied. "If that ambassador ship was carrying an assault force, there could be hundreds of warriors already on-board G-COP. You must not allow yourselves or the Invictus to be taken and turned."

Shade and Razor both chorused, "Aye, sir," their voices harmonizing in his mind.

"Stay alert, I'll be in contact when I know more," Sterling added. He then tapped his neural interface to close the link and turned back to Banks and Admiral Griffin.

"Some of the other vessels have put out distress beacons," said Banks, noticing that Sterling's attention was now focused on her. "The Sa'Nerran invaders are already overwhelming the security forces on decks one through three." Banks highlighted the enemy movements on the computer console. "We're also picking up dozens of squads of warriors moving through to the lower decks."

Sterling hurried over to the conference table and peered down at the information on the console.

"How come they've haven't come for us?" said Sterling,

noting that none of the squads of Sa'Nerran warriors were approaching their location.

"I prefer not to let anyone know exactly where I am likely to be or when, unless I can help it," replied Admiral Griffin. "This meeting was not logged. So as far as the Sa'Nerra, and the station commander knows, I was on the Centaur when it detonated."

Sterling sighed and nodded, suddenly realizing why the Admiral's vessel had been the only ship Crow had targeted.

"Thanks to the distress signals, we can at least expect reinforcements to arrive within thirty minutes," said Banks. "We're going to need them."

"Unfortunately, no ship that comes to our aid will get within a kilometer of this station," replied Sterling. "With G-COP under Crow's command, any vessels surging into the area will get pulverized if they stray too close."

Banks cursed and began pacing up and down. "What about the Halberd?" she said, motioning toward the gatekeeper weapons platform that was visible in the distance at the mouth of the aperture. "Can we contact the crew on board and request their assistance?"

Sterling looked to Griffin, who was contemplating Banks' idea, though she still appeared pensive. Sterling then watched as the Admiral attempted to access the station's communications array, but her request was denied.

"Damn it, they've locked down all access to deck one only," Griffin spat, hammering her fists down on the conference table. "Contact your ship and have them relay a message to the Halberd," Griffin added, looking across at

Sterling. "We must act quickly, before they jam all outgoing communications."

Sterling nodded and reached for his neural interface. However, before he could activate a link, the conference room was shaken by a series of thumping tremors. At the same time light flooded through the conference room windows, as if someone had shone a flashlight directly into Sterling's face. He squinted his eyes shut to block out the dazzling light. Through his narrowed gaze he saw what had caused the flash and the vibrations. G-COP's powerful battery of plasma railguns had opened fire, unleashing a concentrated burst of energy aimed directly at Fleet Gatekeeper Halberd. Sterling, Banks and Griffin watched in silence, helpless to intervene, as the blasts of plasma hammered into the weapons platform and obliterated it.

For several seconds no-one spoke as they observed the mighty weapons platform disintegrate in a fiery blaze. They all knew the implications of the Halberd's destruction. With the gatekeeper destroyed and G-COP's significant arsenal of firepower at the Sa'Nerra's command, nothing could prevent an invasion fleet from flooding into the sector. To state the fact out loud would have been pointless, Sterling realized, so it was no surprise that neither he, Banks nor Griffin did so.

As the glare from the explosion died down, Admiral Griffin turned away from the window and moved to the rear of the conference room. The Admiral then removed a simple silver chain from around her neck. Sterling saw that there was an ID chip attached to it, similar to the one

Griffin had given Sterling in the past to allow for secret encrypted communications to flow between them.

"We cannot allow G-COP to fall into enemy hands," said Griffin, as she inserted the chip into a large, secure storage compartment built into the wall. "I think we all know what needs to be done."

Sterling knew Griffin well enough to predict her intentions. It helped that they were the same as his own.

"If we're to take back the station then we'll need weapons," said Sterling. "This conference room is on command level three, which means we're only two decks below the command operations center."

The Admiral lifted her left wrist and pulled back the sleeve of her tunic. Embedded into her arm was a simple screen, on which was displayed a seemingly random string of numbers and letters. Sterling frowned as the code changed, flashing up a new sequence of letters and numbers. Glancing down at her wrist, Griffin entered the new code into the secure compartment's control panel and the door unlocked.

"There are some benefits to being a flag officer, Captain," said Griffin, pulling open the door to reveal six plasma pistols and six sets of body armor.

Griffin removed three pistols and three sets of armor, tossing each one onto the conference table like a sports coach tossing items from a kit bag onto the field. The Admiral then removed the ID chip from the door, but kept it in her hand, rather than placing the chain back over her head.

"This is a command override key," said Griffin, walking

calmly over to Sterling. "You can think of it as a skeleton key." She offered the chip to him. "If you insert this into the command console on deck one, you will be able to override the station commander and take control of G-COP."

Sterling took the key and placed the chain over his neck. "What's with the code on your wrist?" he added, tucking the chip beneath his tunic.

"This is the authenticator," said Griffin again pulling back the sleeve of her tunic. "The code changes every ninety seconds. Without the authentication code the key is useless."

Sterling frowned. "Without cutting your arm off and brining it with me, I don't see how that helps us, Admiral."

"Cutting my arm off wouldn't help you either, Captain," replied Griffin through narrowed eyes. "Believe me, if it would then I would have had you remove it already." Sterling's eyes widened. He had no doubt in his mind that Griffin was being serious. "If I die, or the authenticator is removed, it automatically ceases to function." Griffin pulled her sleeve back down over the screen and held Sterling's eyes even more firmly. "Unfortunately, I cannot risk joining you on the assault," she added, her dissatisfaction with this state of affairs written plainly across her face. "If the Sa'Nerra were to capture and turn me, the knowledge and access they would gain would be devastating to the entire fleet."

"I understand, Admiral," replied Sterling. He couldn't deny that the tenacious flag officer would have been a welcome extra gun, but her reasoning was sound.

"The Sa'Nerra will likely still search this room," said

Banks. "I can help to barricade the door and give you some added protection."

Griffin looked around the room then frowned at Banks. "Barricade the door with what?"

Banks stepped up to the conference table and moved the plasma pistols and body armor onto one of the plush conference chairs. She then gripped the side of the table and began to tip it onto its side, scattering the chairs on the opposite side like pool balls. Considering the table was more than twenty feet long and likely weighed the same as a horse, the ease with which she accomplished the feat clearly surprised Griffin.

"I'll drag it against the door after we leave," said Banks, dusting off her hands.

Griffin raised an eyebrow. "Should this succeed, I trust you will not forget to release me from this prison, Commander," she said.

Sterling tapped the ID chip hanging from the chain beneath his tunic. "Once Commander Banks and I reach the command console, I'll contact you over a neural link to receive the code."

Griffin nodded then picked up one of the pistols from the conference chair and tossed it to Commander Banks. She caught it without hesitation. The admiral then handed a pistol to Sterling and the two officers locked eyes.

"The Omega Directive is in effect, Captain Sterling," Admiral Griffin announced. The words sent a shiver down Sterling's spine. Griffin holstered the final weapon then again locked her icy stare onto Sterling. "Your orders are to retake this station, no matter the cost. Is that clear?"

"Perfectly clear, Admiral," Sterling answered, holstering the plasma pistol then grabbing a set of body armor. He held out the armor to Banks and his first officer took it, meeting Sterling's eyes with a look of raw determination that he'd learned to recognize and trust implicitly. "No matter the cost," Sterling added.

Sterling then held the eyes of Commander Mercedes Banks, drawing strength from her strength, and steeling himself for what would be the toughest test either of them had ever faced.

STERLING AND BANKS prowled along the corridor outside the conference room, weapons held ready. The sound of raised voices and plasma weapons fire was filtering into their ears from gun battles that had already begun on command level three. Sterling glanced down at the computer wrapped around his left arm, which displayed an architectural schematic of G-COP. Despite being considerably smaller than its cousin in F-sector, the space station was still larger than a mega-sized shopping mall. Their location two levels below the main command operations center was an advantage, but Sterling guessed there were still dozens of warriors between them and where they needed to be.

"Any genius ideas for how we get to level one, without getting killed?" asked Sterling. He then remembered his first officer's last plan that involved reaching a higher level and glanced over at her, eyebrow raised. "Preferably ones that don't involve climbing through service crawlspaces into rest rooms."

Banks smiled. "That had crossed my mind, but it wouldn't work on G-COP," she replied. "Level one is sealed off from the rest of the station. The only conduits that link the two are for utilities like power and water. Maybe a cat could make it through, but not us."

"In some ways, that's a relief," Sterling said, returning to studying the schematic. "This level is mainly dedicated to administrative operations," he continued, thinking out loud. "Crow was smart enough to block off the lower levels, trapping the bulk of G-COP's security forces below this deck."

"What about making our way through the central garden?" said Banks, stabbing her finger toward the screen. "There's a stairwell leading up to the command level two offices at the far end."

Sterling focused in on the area, chewing the inside of his cheek. "There's not much cover in there, save a few fake trees," he said. "And since the route up to level two is directly beyond the east exit, that's where we should expect the heaviest resistance."

Banks considered Sterling's comments, scrunching up her nose as she did so, but then she conceded the point.

"Okay, so we might not be able to reach command operations through the crawlspaces, but we can still use the service areas to reach level two," Banks said. She pointed to the maintenance doors at the end of the adjacent corridor. Sterling frowned, but Banks was quick to clarify her plan. "Don't worry, it doesn't involve crawling across a rest room floor this time," she added. Banks then zoomed in on the map on Sterling's computer and tapped her finger onto the screen. "There are voids behind all of the interior walls, where the utilities conduits are routed through. We can get inside using Griffin's keycard, then climb up to level two. After that, we'll need a new plan."

Sterling nodded then lowered his arm, automatically deactivating the computer. He didn't like the idea of climbing around inside the station's voids, but he also didn't have a better idea.

"Okay, let's move," said Sterling, checking along the corridor then hustling across to the next intersection with Banks covering their rear. The sound of weapons fire was growing louder by the second. It quickly became clear to Sterling that they were heading toward the battle, rather than away from it.

"The nearest maintenance door is right across this landing," said Banks, nodding in the direction they needed to go.

Sterling peeked around the corner and saw that they had reached the eastern edge of the central garden. It was a manufactured sanctuary of largely fake flora, bathed in artificial sunlight that was designed to emulate early evening summer sun. For the Fleet crew on G-COP, stranded light years from Earth or any other planet, it was a necessary sanctuary that helped to keep people sane. However, Sterling could see that this particular haven had already been violated by the alien invaders that now rampaged through the station.

"I count maybe sixteen Sa'Nerra and a dozen Fleet,

fighting it out just ahead," said Sterling, pulling back out of sight. "That maintenance door is completely exposed. We'll be sitting ducks if we go out there."

Banks shuffled around the side of Sterling and scouted the surroundings. "I have an idea," she said, though from the look in her eyes, Sterling could tell he wasn't going to like it. "Those co-working tables are made of solid metal," she went on, pointing out the object in question with the barrel of her pistol. "We move out then I grab a table and use it as a shield while you unlock the door with Griffin's skeleton key."

"They're just office tables, Mercedes," replied Sterling with a skeptical frown. "It's not going to take a plasma blast like the regenerative armor of the Invictus."

"It only has to take a few hits, not survive a prolonged attack," said Banks, undeterred. "They're tough enough for what we need."

A plasma blast then flashed past the end of the corridor and burned a hole into the wall a few meters from where they were hiding. Sterling took another cautious glance into the garden space and saw more warriors were advancing. Cursing under his breath, he turned back to Banks, holding his pistol ready.

"I don't think we have a choice," he said, honestly. "Go on three and I'll cover you."

Banks ran out from cover and sprinted toward the nearest co-working table that was nestled just inside the garden space. Plasma blasts were racing back and forth through the artificial leaves and branches and Sterling saw three of the Fleet security forces go down. Fleeting shapes moved through the undergrowth and Sterling fired, hitting one warrior and setting a fake tree alight. However, from his new vantage at the edge of the garden, it was now clear that the Sa'Nerran forces vastly outnumbered the Fleet defenders.

"Mercedes, hurry, this place is about to get overrun," Sterling called out to his first officer, who had just reached her target. He fired three more blasts from his pistol, killing another two warriors. Then a shot flew past his ear in return, so close he could smell the singed hair around his ears.

Banks reached the table and grasped her hands around the thick, stem-like base. She then lifted it off the deck and held it out in front of her, like an umbrella caught in a strong gust of wind. A second later, plasma blasts thudded into the surface of the improvised shield.

"Get behind me!" Banks yelled, crouching low and side-stepping out of the garden area toward the maintenance door on the side wall.

Sterling moved in close behind his first officer as more blasts smashed against the table. Already he could see the effects of the impacts on the reverse side of the table's surface. Firing blind over the top and sides of the table in an attempt to drive his attackers back, Sterling then tapped his neural interface and reached out to Admiral Griffin.

"Are you there already, Captain?" replied Griffin, clearly surprised to have been contacted so soon.

"Not yet, Admiral, but I'm going to need an ID code from you to unlock a maintenance door," replied Sterling.

He reached inside his tunic and grabbed the chain around his neck.

"Very well, Captain, let me know when you need me to read it out," Griffin replied. "And remember, the code cycles every ninety seconds."

Banks reached the door then dropped to one knee, maneuvering the table to shield them both.

"Make it quick," Banks called out, as sparks flew over the top of the table, scorching her face.

Sterling removed the ID keycard then went to insert it into the locking mechanism. However, his hand had barely stretched out in front of him before a plasma blast thudded into the door. Sterling spun around and spotted the shooter, the keycard falling from his hand as he raised his pistol to fire back. Another blast raced past his shoulder, striking the reverse side of the table and missing Banks by barely an inch. Sterling fired, hitting the warrior first in the leg then in the face, blasting the alien's head clean off. Suddenly, the image of Ariel Gunn popped into his mind, stupefying him like a sharp slap to the face.

"Lucas, the key!" Banks yelled.

Sterling snapped out of his sudden daze, grabbed the key from the deck and turned back to the door. The table that Banks was using as an improvised shield was now buckling. Sections were burned through, exposing them to a lucky shot or well-aimed blast.

"Admiral, give me the code!" Sterling called out in his mind, while slotting the keycard into the reader. There was silence on the other end of the link. "Admiral, the code!" Sterling said again, feeling his pulse thump in his neck.

"Lucas, I can't hold them off for much longer!" Banks called out, as a blast flew through the table and burned into the wall beside the door.

Dark scenarios invaded Sterling's thoughts. What if Admiral Griffin had already been killed? What was his plan B? Was there even a plan B?

"Seven, Two, Five, Zulu, Echo..." began Admiral Griffin in Sterling's mind.

Sterling cursed and hurried to catch up, tapping the code into the numeric pad on the door.

"Three, Nine, Romeo, One," Griffin continued.

"I thought we'd lost you for a moment, Admiral," said Sterling, while he continued to enter the sequence.

"I was waiting for the code to refresh, Captain," Griffin replied, sounding considerably calmer than Sterling felt. "Did it work?" she added, as more blasts penetrated Banks' makeshift shield.

"I'll let you know in a second..." replied Sterling, entering the last digit of the sequence. There was a painful wait before the lock turned green. Sterling yanked the keycard out of the door, almost snapping it in the process, threw it over his neck then grabbed the door handle. To his relief it opened.

"Mercedes, let's go!" Sterling yelled, pushing the door and holding it open for his first officer.

Banks drew the broken and burned table closer to her chest then pushed it away from her body, letting out a shot-putter's roar as she did so. The table soared through the air and smashed into two advancing Sa'Nerran warriors. The aliens had barely hit the deck before Banks had drawn her pistol and fired. Two more warriors were hit and killed by the time Banks had backed through the opening. Sterling slammed the door shut then took two steps back and launched a kick at the handle with the heel of his boot. The adrenalin surging through his bloodstream helped to give him the power needed to smash the handle clean off.

"Admiral, we're through," said Sterling in his mind. "I'll contact you again when we've reached level one."

"Pick up the pace, Captain," replied Griffin, sounding like an angry customer waiting on her lunch order. "Griffin out."

Sterling managed to huff a laugh then flopped back against the inside wall of the maintenance area and closed his eyes. Banks thudded into the wall at his side, so close he could hear her labored breathing. Sterling glanced over at his first officer, observing scorch marks and burns to the skin on her cheeks, neck and hair from the splinters of hot metal that had showered her face.

"Well, that went well," said Banks, staying true to form and responding to their near-death experience with a glib remark. Then she became serious. "What happened with you out there?" she then said. "It was like you zoned out."

"Nothing happened," Sterling hit back. He was angry and embarrassed enough at himself for his moment of paralysis, and didn't want Banks reminding him of what had occurred. The memory of Ariel Gunn had previously only invaded his sleeping mind. This was the first-time it had troubled his conscious thoughts, and he was determined that it would also be the last. "I was blinded by the muzzle flash from a warrior that was firing at us, that's all."

Banks' eyes narrowed a fraction and Sterling could see she was itching to press him further, but she chose not to.

"Aye, sir," replied Banks, pushing herself away from the wall. She then peered around the narrow confines of the new location, scouting for the best route up to level two. "But that won't be the last flash of plasma we see today."

"No, it won't," replied Sterling. "But it will be the last time I hesitate, no matter what happens from this point on."

STERLING'S BOOTS clanked and clattered on the steep metal staircase that led up to the maintenance area on command level two. Compared to the main area of G-COP, the maintenance space was cold and felt damp. However, it also had the virtue of being devoid of Sa'Nerran warriors.

"Keep climbing, this should take us all the way to level two," said Banks as Sterling reached the first landing.

The staircase was designed like a fire escape, using steep flights of steps that zig-zagged up the side of the station. It was harder work than Sterling expected.

"Remind me to take the stairs more often on the Invictus," Sterling said, calling down to Banks. "My legs are already burning."

Suddenly, the sound of banging filtered to Sterling from above and he halted his ascent. The noise quickly disappeared, but Sterling stayed where he was and signaled Banks to also stop.

"What is it?" asked Banks. Evidently, she had not picked up the sound.

Sterling glanced down at Banks and pressed his finger to his lips. Then the banging came again, louder and more persistent than before. Sterling moved back across the narrow landing and peered up. He could just make out the maintenance door at the top of the stairs.

"I think they might be on to us," said Sterling, keeping his gaze focused on the door. Then the fizz of a plasma-cutting beam echoed through the cold and dank maintenance area and Sterling saw the glow of melting metal.

"I think they're definitely on to us," replied Banks, sarcastically.

Sterling scanned the surrounding area, but he was caught in a limbo between the two levels. He couldn't go up, but he also couldn't retreat back to level three, which was already crawling with alien warriors.

"Any ideas?" Sterling said, jogging down the stairs to join Banks on the landing below.

"Only one, but I'm not sure you'll like it," replied Banks.

"I'm sure I'll like it a lot more than getting filled with holes from Sa'Nerran plasma rifles," Sterling hit back.

"I'll hold you to that," said Banks. Then she turned around and threw her leg over the top of the railings that surrounded the narrow metal landing. Sterling watched with morbid interest as his first officer then swung her other leg over and balanced precariously on the outer ledge.

"I don't think jumping to our deaths will help,

Mercedes," Sterling said, giving in to his curiosity. "What the hell are you doing?"

"Finding us an alternative route up," replied Banks. She then leapt across the chasm between the landing and the outer wall of the maintenance space, grabbing onto the thick structural beams with her pincer-like grip.

Sterling peered up the stairwell again as sparks and molten metal began falling through the open grating of the deck plates. The Sa'Nerra were almost through.

"Well, whatever you have in mind, do it fast," Sterling said, following Banks' lead and stepping over the railings.

With one hand still clamped to the metal beam, Banks then dug her fingers into the seams of one of the thousands of panels that formed the outer wall. Yanking back with her formidable strength, she then tore the panel clean off. Her foot slipped in the process and for a second Banks dangled precariously over the precipice. Sterling's heart-rate spiked, as it seemed for a moment that she would fall to the level below. However, as on many occasions before, her strength saved her.

"Jump across and climb through," Banks called over to Sterling. "We'll have to climb up using the structural supports in the Void between the maintenance area and the station's inner hull."

Sterling could already feel an icy breeze flowing out of the hole that Banks had created. However, it was the thought of having to free-climb all the way to level two that sent a chill down his spine.

"You're right, I don't like this idea," said Sterling, preparing himself to jump. Then another hard thump resonated through the maintenance space and Sterling glanced up to see that the door had been smashed through. The impact of the metal slab crashing into the landing rattled the staircase and almost caused him to lose balance.

"Lucas, jump now!" Banks called out. She was also peering up, one hand clasped to the structural support and the other clinging onto the metal wall panel.

Sterling sucked in a breath of the freezing air then launched himself across the chasm. He caught the lip of the opening and felt the sharp metal bite into his hands. However, this time Banks could not use her strength to help him.

"They're coming," urged Banks as Sterling dragged himself up and threw his body through the opening. His feet found the edge of a horizontal support beam and he managed to inch himself away from the opening.

"I'm through," cried Sterling, shaking the pain and numbness from his fingers.

Banks swung her body into the opening then held out the metal panel. "Take this while I climb through," she cried.

Sterling adjusted his footing then took hold of the metal panel with one hand, holding onto a structural beam with the other for support. Banks then released her hold on the panel, suddenly exposing Sterling to the full weight of the metal slab. He was pulled forward and almost fell headfirst through the gap, but his grip just held.

"Mercedes, hurry..." Sterling gasped through gritted teeth as Banks hauled herself through the opening. She then grabbed the edge of the panel and Sterling felt her take the strain.

"Help me to fit it back in place," said Banks, rapidly adjusting her hold on the panel so that she was gripping the moldings on the reverse side.

Using all the strength he had remaining Sterling lifted the panel so that the edges aligned with the gap. Banks pulled the metal slab hard toward her then there was a satisfying thunk as the panel locked into place. Moments later, Sterling heard the sound of heavy boots clattering down the staircase on the other side of the wall. He and Banks froze and waited. The bootsteps grew louder and were followed by a concerto of waspish hisses from the alien warriors. Sterling could only imagine what the Sa'Nerran soldiers were thinking and how they were trying to reconcile the fact their quarry had seemingly vanished into thin air.

"They must have retreated to level three!"

The voice sent another chill down Sterling's already freezing cold body. It was the voice of Clinton Crow.

"Follow them!" Crow yelled, somehow managing to be understood by the warriors, despite speaking English. "I want Sterling and Banks brought to me alive. I wish to present them to Emissary McQueen as a prize."

Boots again clattered across the stairwell outside, quickly growing quieter and more distant. Then the sounds vanished and all that remained was the hum of energy flowing through the station's conduits. Sterling tapped his neural interface and reached out to Banks, still afraid to speak out loud for fear that a warrior was hiding just beyond the wall.

"We'll need to climb across as well as up," Sterling said through the link. "Hopefully, we'll get lucky and manage to punch through into the Void behind an empty office or corridor space."

Banks nodded then answered through their link. "You take the lead," she said, moving closer to Sterling with the ease of a champion rock climber. "That way, if you fall, I'll have a chance to catch you."

Sterling managed a weak smile. "If I die today, it won't be from something as anticlimactic as falling to my death," he answered. Then he adjusted his hand holds and took the first step on the sheer vertical climb up. "If today is my day, I'll die with my hands around that bastard Crow's neck."

Sterling then pulled himself up and grabbed the next support beam. The icy-cold metal burned his hand and instinctively he let go. Banks reached over and pressed her hand to Sterling's back, acting like a safety harness.

"You were saying?" said Banks, with a wry smile.

Sterling pulled the sleeves of his shirt through the cuffs of his tunic and over his hands, then tried again to grab the ledge. This time his grip held firm.

"Fine, I officially designate you as my safety net," said Sterling, pulling himself up. His breath was misting in the freezing cold air, but the effort of the climb was helping to keep him warm.

"That's just part of my job, Captain," replied Banks, climbing up behind Sterling with enviable ease.

Sterling and Banks continued in this way for what felt

like hours until finally they had scaled the wall and reached level two of G-COP. Finding a nook to rest in, Sterling released his grip on the freezing metal panels and squeezed the pain from his throbbing hands.

"If this map is right, we should be outside one of the level two meeting rooms," said Banks, peering down at the computer wrapped around her muscular left forearm. "I could be way off though," she added. "G-COP is throwing out a ton of EM jammer interference so I can't get a clear reading."

"Anywhere is better than here, Commander," said Sterling, folding himself up into a tight ball in an attempt to ward off the cold. Banks shrugged, seemingly concurring with her captain's assessment.

"Okay, here goes nothing," said Banks. She then adjusted her position, grabbing onto a vertical support beam with both hands and leant back. She then leapt into the air, causing Sterling's heart to momentarily stop beating before she swung down and hammered the heels of her boots in the metal wall panel.

"Damn, Mercedes, a little warning next time!" Sterling said, taking a firm hold of a support beam. "I thought you were calling it quits for a moment then."

Banks smiled. "Like you said, I'll be damned if I'm going to die out here," she said, leaping up and hammering another kick into the wall. This time the metal slab gave way and clattered into the inner void. Banks shuffled into the opening then gestured toward the new hole that she'd just made.

"Age before beauty," she said, inviting Sterling to move through first.

"What the hell does that mean?" replied Sterling.

"It means you go first," said Banks, still smiling.

Sterling frowned then shuffled into the opening. "How about, 'captain before first officer'?" he added, dryly, hauling his weary frame through the gap and into the inner void.

Banks then pulled herself through and joined Sterling in the Void. It was like a building site, with the remains of part-used materials and old tools littered across the deck.

"Out of sight out of mind," commented Banks, kicking some of the detritus with the toe of her boot.

"What you see on the outside always hides a darker truth, once you scratch through the veneer," said Sterling, stepping up to the wall that would lead them back inside the station. "Take this uniform, for example," Sterling added, turning back to Banks and brushing his still throbbing hands across his scuffed body armor. "We might look like we're just part of Fleet, but inside we're not. We're different. Dark, cold and a little bit grubby, just like this void."

Banks eyes widened. "Wow, that's very poetic, Captain," she said, more than a little sarcastically. Then she kicked another broken piece of pipe and gave an acquiescent shrug. "But I guess you're not wrong."

Sterling gently rapped his knuckles against the wall of the inner void. "Come on, let's get out of here, before I freeze my ass off," he said.

Banks and Sterling began to inspect the wall panel,

looking for a way to force it open. However, it quickly became apparent to Sterling that it was considerably more robust than the relatively rudimentary panel in the engineering space.

"I'll see if I can find some tools to help prize it open," said Sterling, doubling back and scouring the floor.

However, the work crews that had built the station had obviously been diligent enough to remove any tools of value. All he could find were some rusted old crowbars and off-cuts of metal beams and conduits.

"Here, these will have to do," said Sterling, returning to the wall and handing Banks a hefty metal bar that had been shorn off at the end, like a pike.

Together, Sterling and Banks dug the crude tools into the seams of the wall panel. Then, with the aid of Banks' strength, they began to break the panel open.

"It's moving," said Sterling, again gasping the words through gritted teeth.

Suddenly, Sterling detected the familiar hiss of the Sa'Nerra's indecipherable alien language and he froze. Glancing across to Banks, it was clear from her wide-eyed expression that she'd heard it too. Neither moved, hoping that the sound had just been in their imagination. Then a plasma blast thudded into the other side of the panel, punching through the wall inches from Sterling's head. He cursed and pushed himself clear.

"Kick it down!" Sterling yelled, still gripping the metal bar in his hand.

Banks nodded then took several paces back as another blast punctured the wall and slipped past them into the freezing darkness of the void. A second later, Banks charged at the wall and slammed the heel of her boot into the dead center of the panel. The power of the kick dislodged the wall and sent the slab of metal smashing into the body of the alien warrior on the other side. Sterling moved through first as Banks recovered from the shock of the impact. A second alien warrior was inside. Its egg-shaped, yellow eyes turned to Sterling and it raised its weapon. Reacting on pure instinct, Sterling slapped the weapon out of the creature's leathery hand then kicked the warrior in the gut. The alien reeled back then pulled a serrated, half-moon blade from its belt and came at Sterling again. He caught the warrior's wrist and wrestled the weapon away. The pain and weariness in Sterling's body was suddenly gone, erased by a rush of adrenaline. However, in addition to the cascade of hormones, enzymes and proteins that were flooding through his body, Sterling was also gripped by rage.

I've not come this far to be stopped now... he told himself, gritting his teeth and tearing the blade from the Sa'Nerran's grasp. The alien stepped back, stunned by Sterling's visceral display of aggression. However, before the warrior could react further, Sterling had swung his arm and opened the alien's throat with its own weapon. The warrior clasped its long fingers around its neck, but the cut was deep and the crimson alien blood flowed like water from a faucet.

Banks appeared at Sterling's side and together they stood in silence, watching the alien bleed out and die at their feet. Sterling could still feel Banks through their neural link, which neither of them had severed after first moving into the void beyond the station's walls. Like her, Sterling felt no pity for the alien, nor a need to grant it mercy and a swifter death. The alien warrior deserved neither, and like the warriors they would still have to face, it would get shown no quarter. The Omega Directive was in effect, and Sterling would stop at nothing to ensure the Sa'Nerran invaders failed in their attempt to seize the station. Even if that meant reducing G-COP to atoms along with all souls on board.

A SERIES of bright flashes lit up the office, each one popping off in rapid succession like camera bulbs at a red-carpet movie premiere. Sterling turned to the window, attaching the blood-stained half-moon blade to his belt as he did so before drawing his plasma pistol. Far out in the distance he could see shapes moving against the starry backdrop of space. Two more flashes then forced him to squint and shield his eyes.

"That's the fourteenth Sa'Nerran warship that's surged in," said Banks, as another three flashes of light appeared at the mouth of the aperture. "Make that seventeen. It's hardly an invasion fleet, though."

"It's not an invasion fleet," Sterling replied, glancing back at Banks. "If it was, we'd be staring down the nose of the super-weapon we discovered at Omega Four."

"What is it then?" said Banks, moving to Sterling's side and folding her powerful arms.

Sterling shrugged. "I think they're just testing us, and

testing their new army of turned drone fighters to see how they perform," he suggested. "But if they can hold or destroy G-COP in the process, it makes it a whole lot easier to push into Fleet space."

The sound of plasma weapons filtered into the office, but it was distant and muted. Sterling moved away from the external window and cautiously glanced into the corridor outside. It was still clear. Remarkably, their sudden and violent arrival onto level two had so far gone unnoticed by the other Sa'Nerra on the station, which gave him and Banks a brief moment of respite. Then another series of flashes lit up the room, though this time they were much more intense. Sterling felt a vibration thrum through the deck plates and realized that these new surges were much closer and from a different aperture.

"It's the Praetor," said Banks, who had remained by the window, looking out into space. Sterling re-joined his first officer and saw the third-generation Fleet Heavy Cruiser moving slowly toward the station. "And it looks like the Prince Regent and the Hawthorn too. The others I can't make out."

Sterling then heard the familiar whir of powerful gears and motors resonating through the structure of the station. It was the sound of G-COP's plasma rail guns moving into position.

"Damn it, get clear you fools..." Sterling said, urging the new Fleet arrivals to increase their distance from G-COP and its devastating arsenal of weapons. However, he already knew it was too late for the Praetor. Its captain had surged into the system too close to G-COP, sealing its fate in a matter of milliseconds.

Moments later the station shook again and a dozen plasma blasts rippled through space, striking the Praetor across its belly. Sterling cursed as the blasts pulverized the two-kilometer-long battleship. Electrical energy crackled and fizzed along its hull and the ship listed out of control, thrusters firing chaotically. It remained intact, but Sterling had been in enough battles to know that the Praetor was already out of the fight. Banks spat out a curse and thumped her fist onto the window ledge, cracking the smooth, artificial material. Sterling, however, didn't react. He was saving his anger for later, bottling it up ready to explode at Clinton Crow when they finally caught up with him.

"The other Fleet ships are moving clear and advancing toward the approaching Sa'Nerran battlegroup," said Banks, having regained her composure. She was again gazing out at the advancing fleet of alien vessels. "Without reinforcements, they won't be able to hold them off for long."

"They'll last long enough for the Hammer and others to arrive," said Sterling, turning away from the window. "But if we can't retake G-COP, we'll be forced to destroy it. And that will leave this sector ripe for the picking."

"Then we have to hurry," said Banks, failing to contain her anger as Sterling had done. "If the Hammer surges in too close to G-COP, it will also get pulverized. We could not only lose the sector, but some of our most powerful warships too."

Sterling nodded while glancing out toward the Praetor, which was still on fire and listing further away from the battle. However, they could stand the loss of several heavy cruisers. G-COP was a far more important military asset, and the Hammer was arguably even more vital. The dreadnaught was essential to the defense of the outer sectors. If the Hammer was lost then Fleet wouldn't stand a chance against a full-scale alien invasion. It would put even more pressure on the United Governments to capitulate and surrender.

"Come on, let's move out," said Sterling, slapping Banks on the shoulder. She was right. There was no time to lose.

Sterling crept back over to the other side of the office and peered through into the corridor outside. The sound of fighting again filtered into his ears, but the coast was still clear. Glancing down at the map on his computer, Sterling quickly assessed the best route for them to reach level one.

"There are only three ways to get into the command operations center," said Sterling, as Banks slid alongside. "The main elevator in the north section," Sterling continued, highlighting the area on the map. "Or the two emergency stairwells on the east and west hallways."

Banks considered the options for a few moments then tapped the elevator on the map. "I know it might sound crazy, but I think this is our best way in," she said. "The doors at the top and bottom of those stairwells will be sealed up tighter than a starship's hull. It would take a plasma railgun to breach them." Banks then tapped Sterling on the sternum, where Admiral Griffin's skeleton key was still tucked away beneath his armor. "With this, we could override the elevator lockdown and ride up to the command center."

It was certainly a bold idea, Sterling thought, but in principle Banks' suggestion might work. The tricky part would be getting inside the elevator.

"Hopefully, Crow has returned to the command center with only a handful of guards," replied Sterling. "With the element of surprise, it might work. Though if we can score some better weapons first, it would help."

Banks hurried back inside the office and grabbed the Sa'Nerran plasma rifle off the warrior that Sterling had killed earlier. She tossed it to Sterling and he caught it. Holstering his pistol, he inspected the weapon. Its design was naturally better suited to the long-fingered aliens, but it wasn't the first time he'd used the alien rifle. Banks then checked the dead warrior's armor, pulling out two devices and a spare energy cell. She returned to Sterling, handing him the cell and one of the devices. It was then that he recognized the alien object as a Sa'Nerran fragmentation grenade. It was a particularly nasty weapon that the aliens had specifically designed to cause a maximum number of casualties. It rarely killed immediately, unless it landed right by a person's feet, but it was effective at maiming Fleet crew that were unfortunate enough to be caught in its wide radius. In contrast, the Sa'Nerra, with their tough, leathery skin and hard armor were often able to withstand the blasts and continue fighting.

"What about you?" said Sterling, stowing the new gear. "A frag grenade and a pistol won't get you far."

"A frag grenade, a pistol and super-human strength," Banks corrected, cocking an eyebrow at Sterling.

"Mercedes, I'm serious," said Sterling. He wasn't in the mood for Banks' ill-placed humor.

Banks held up her hands in a conciliatory gesture then moved over to the slab of wall that was in the middle of the room. She gripped underneath it then dragged the rectangular block of metal off to the side. Sterling winced as he got his first look at the Sa'Nerran warrior that had been pancaked beneath it.

"Now, we're both ready," said Banks, grabbing the squashed warrior's rifle and its spare cell. She then recovered the alien's two grenades and slid them into the utility pouches on her armor.

"Let's move," said Sterling as several more flashes from G-sector's apertures lit up the room. Sterling could see that more Fleet ships had arrived to join the fight. This time, they were all giving G-COP a wide birth, but the constant thump through the deck told him that the station was still engaging the ships at long range.

Banks moved out ahead and they both crept through the corridors as quickly and as quietly as possible. Level two was mostly reserved for offices and meeting spaces for G-COP's senior crew, as well as for official and ceremonial occasions. It was also a more compact level, occupying less than half the floor area of the main levels below.

The sound of weapons fire continued to reach them from multiple directions as they advanced, but they had managed to make progress unopposed. Then as Sterling cut across a junction toward the wide corridor that led to the bank of elevators, he caught his first sight of the enemy. Cursing, he turned back to Banks and tapped his neural interface.

"There are six warriors guarding the elevators," said Sterling through a neural link.

Banks peeked down the corridor then ducked back into cover. "We can take them," she replied, confidently.

"Not without alerting every other damn alien on the station," Sterling hit back.

"Then we'll take them out too," said Banks. This time, however, there was no suggestion she was joking.

Sterling raised an eyebrow. "What meal packs did you eat this morning to make you so feisty?" he asked, for once being the one to make an ill-timed quip.

"Sooner or later, we're going make an almighty racket," said Banks, switching the rifle to her left hand and drawing her pistol. "It's do-or-die time, Lucas."

Sterling nodded then copied Banks, switching the rifle to his off hand and grabbing his pistol with the other.

"Then let's do it," he said, matching his first officer's gritty determination. "On three..."

Sterling began the countdown in his mind then both he and Banks sprang out from cover in perfect synchronization. Sterling had already nearly squeezed the triggers of his weapons before he realized that the warriors had gone.

"What the hell?" he wondered, frowning at the now unguarded elevator shafts at the foot of the corridor. "Where did they go?"

Banks cautiously moved ahead to get a better view of

the landing area surrounding the bank of elevators. Then she suddenly ducked out of sight and pointed toward the east side of the station.

"They're by the east viewing gallery," Banks said, still speaking to Sterling in her mind. "It looks like some sort of meeting."

Sterling moved closer then also chanced a look around the corner. The six warriors had moved up to the floor-to-ceiling glass wall that enclosed the east viewing gallery. It was one of the ceremonial rooms that overlooked the east docking ring, giving a grand view of the vessels moored there. Through the glass wall, Sterling could see more warriors inside the room, counting up to a dozen. However, then he realized that the aliens were not the only occupants.

"It looks like there are Fleet crew inside that room too," said Sterling, glancing back at Banks.

His first officer frowned then took a second look. From her position, she had a clearer vantage on the room. Sterling could practically feel the rage bubbling inside her through their neural connection.

"They're turning them," said Banks, again meeting his eyes. "I couldn't see the whole room, but there have to be forty or more Fleet personnel in there."

Sterling again cursed under his breath. Twenty alien warriors was already too many for them to handle, but if the Sa'Nerra turned the Fleet crew too, they'd be overwhelmed in a matter of minutes. Then he spotted that the door to one of the offices beside the bank of elevators was open.

"Get ready to move," said Sterling, tapping his neural interface and reaching out to Admiral Griffin.

"What are you thinking?" Banks replied, pulling back and raising both weapons to her side.

"I'll be damned if I'll let those aliens turn our own people against us," Sterling said, feeling the link to Griffin form. He widened the connection to allow Banks to monitor.

"Are you in position, Captain?" said Griffin through the neural link. Her voice sounded weak as well as strained. The distance between them was one cause of the poor connection, Sterling realized, but there was more to it than that.

"We're just outside the elevators to level one, Admiral, but we have a situation," Sterling replied. "I need a verification code."

"This had better be important, Captain," Griffin replied, her frustration still coming through cleanly despite the weak link.

"It is," replied Sterling.

"Very well, stand by," replied Griffin. "I have immediate problems of my own."

Sterling frowned. "Are you in danger Admiral?"

"Concern yourself with your own mission, Captain," Griffin hit back. "I can handle myself."

Banks smiled. The Admiral's customarily prickly response was no less than either of them had expected from her.

"Understood Admiral, standing by," replied Sterling.

"What do you have in mind?" said Banks, speaking out

loud in hushed tones. Trying to maintain two separate neural conversations was taxing enough in itself, never mind in their current stressful condition.

"We get to the computer terminal in that office without being seen then I initiate the emergency shutters and seal the viewing gallery, along with everyone inside," Sterling replied.

Banks looked toward the office across the hall then again turned her gaze to the gathering inside the viewing gallery.

"They still have enough firepower inside that room to blast their way out," she replied, sounding skeptical of Sterling's plan.

"That's why you're going to roll all these alien grenades inside before I lock it up tight," replied Sterling, handing Banks the one grenade she'd given him earlier. "Four alien frags should be enough to put them all down, at least for long enough so that we can finish this thing with Crow."

Banks appeared surprised by Sterling's answer. "The Fleet crew in there will get hit too," she replied. "Most of them won't make it."

"They're not Fleet, anymore," Sterling hit back. In truth, he didn't know how many of them had already been turned. However, he did know that if they did nothing, all of them would soon join the ranks of Emissary Crow's servant army. "The Omega Directive is in effect, Commander," Sterling added, gripping Banks with a determined stare. "We do whatever it takes, okay?"

Banks sighed then nodded. "Aye, sir."

Checking across the hall again, Sterling saw that the six

aliens that had been guarding the elevators were still standing at the windows of the viewing gallery. They appeared to be watching the other warriors turn the Fleet crew. They were perhaps enjoying the occasion in the same way that the Romans once enjoyed the bloody spectacle of gladiatorial combat. Signaling Banks to move out, they crept across the hall and managed to slip into the office unseen. Sterling then pulled the ID chip out from beneath his armor and slotted it into the computer terminal.

"I'm ready, Admiral, give me the code," he said through the neural link. There was a moment of hesitation before Griffin answered.

"One, Tango, Three, Charlie, Seven..." Admiral Griffin began. Sterling tapped the code into the terminal's display and waited for the rest of the code. However, Griffin had gone quiet again.

"Admiral, is that it?" asked Sterling, but still there was no response.

"Lima, Sierra, Five, Bravo," Griffin finally continued.

Sterling could feel the tension and discomfort in the Admiral's voice, even through their weakened neural link. He knew that she was hurt, but this time he resisted the urge to ask the Admiral her status, knowing that it would only prompt another rebuke.

"Got it, Admiral," Sterling replied, entering the remainder of the code. He then unlocked the computer terminal and accessed the security overrides for level two.

"Contact me again when you reach level one," Griffin said through the neural link between them. Sterling could feel the connection growing weaker by the second.

"Aye, sir," replied Sterling, activating the emergency shutter system and setting a countdown timer for sixty seconds. "I'll contact you again soon. Hang in there and give them hell." He knew the last part wasn't strictly necessary, but Sterling felt that he needed to show some solidarity.

"I'll give *you* hell if you don't hurry up, Captain," the Admiral replied. "Griffin out." Sterling felt the link sever, and this time he also couldn't help but smile.

"Ready?" said Banks. She had stowed her weapons and was holding a grenade in each hand. The other two were waiting in the pouches on her armor.

"Ready..." replied Sterling, picking up his weapons and moving over to the door. He glanced back at the terminal and saw that the timer had hit thirty seconds. Sucking in a deep breath, he nodded to Banks then charged out into the hallway.

The first two warriors standing outside the viewing gallery were hit and killed even before the sound of the plasma rifle had reached their alien ears. The remaining four spun around, their egg-shaped yellow eyes widening as Sterling and Banks surged toward them. He fired again killing two more warriors as blasts raced back in their direction. However, while his aim was true the Sa'Nerran's shots were wild and loose. *So, you can be rattled, you alien bastards!* Sterling thought as he fired again. The notion that he might have scared the warriors gave him a perverse sense of pleasure.

Banks activated the first two grenades then hurled them through the open door, using her strength to bounce them off the rear window, deep into the room. Pulling the last two grenades from her armor, Banks was then hit in the chest by a blast from one of the two remaining warriors. Sterling fought to contain the swell of panic in his gut then fired again, putting the aliens down. He dropped the rifle and grabbed Banks under the arm, hauling her up.

"I'm okay," Banks said, grabbing the grenades and hurling them through the door.

Two warriors managed to slip outside before the shutters slammed down, entombing the rest of them in the viewing gallery. Sterling launched himself at the closest of the two aliens as the deck beneath his feet was rocked from the explosions only a few meters away. However, the thick sheets of metal covering the walls and windows shielded him from the effects of the grenades.

The warrior grabbed Sterling and tried to wrestle him down. Using the alien's mass against it, Sterling spun the warrior onto its back and pressed his hands around its leathery throat. Banks had recovered enough to intercept the second warrior before it had managed to draw its weapon. Sterling couldn't see the fight, but he heard the crunch of sinew and tendon and crack of bone and knew that Banks had overpowered the creature. Meanwhile, the alien beneath Sterling hissed and spat as he tightened his grip around the warrior's throat. Then it reached for the semi-circular blade attached to Sterling's body armor and tore it clear. Sterling again felt the swell of panic as the alien prepared to thrust the serrated weapon into his flesh. Just in time, a regulation-issue Fleet officer's boot landed on the alien's wrist, trapping it to deck. Sterling glanced up to see Banks peering down at the imprisoned alien, her eyes wild. She could have helped him and killed the alien in an instant, but this was Sterling's kill and she knew it. Putting all of his weight into the effort, Sterling pressed harder and harder until the warrior's hiss faded to a pathetic rasp then vanished altogether.

Sterling flopped back off the strangled alien, himself gasping for breath. Banks helped him to stand and for a moment they both stood in silence, allowing their heart rates to recover. Yet as they waited, no more alien warriors rushed in to attack. Whatever remained of the forces on level two were now trapped in the east viewing gallery, along with the dead or dying bodies of the Fleet crew. Sterling realized that all that now stood between them and Clinton Crow was the metal above their heads. And, from the look in his first officer's eyes, he knew that if it came down to it, Banks would tear a hole through the ceiling with her bare hands in order to reach their target.

STERLING RECOVERED his Sa'Nerran plasma rifle from the deck and moved back inside the office beside the bank of elevators. Banks followed, but kept watch at the door in case any more warriors showed up. Sliding into the chair in front of the computer console, Sterling then brought up the elevator control systems. Thanks to Griffin's skeleton key, he was still able to access many of the station's core functions. However, as he attempted to override the elevator controls the command was refused.

"Damn it, I can't unlock the elevator to level one," said Sterling, attempting to input the command for a second time. He thumped his fists onto the desk as it was denied again. "Crow has the command level sealed up tight."

"It doesn't help that he knows exactly how our systems work," said Banks, remaining by the door. "I do have one more crazy idea that you probably won't like," she added, glancing back at Sterling.

"So long as it works, Mercedes, I promise you that I'll like it," Sterling replied.

Banks moved away from the door and stood behind Sterling. Leaning across him, she brought up the schematic of G-COP levels one and two on the computer terminal.

"Crow docked the ambassador ship directly to the command operation center," said Banks, pointing to the docking port on the map. "But that's not the only dock on level one," she added, sounding like a detective revealing a subtle, but important clue. "If we can get Keller to launch in the Invictus' combat shuttle then we can fly close enough to the station to avoid its guns and dock directly to the command operations center."

Sterling frowned and rubbed the back of his neck as he studied the maps. "That's a great idea in principle, but there is a problem," he said, highlighting level two on the screen. "There are no docks on this level, so how do we get on-board the shuttle?"

Banks zoomed the map into the west side of level two and highlighted the west viewing gallery. "We make our own dock," she said, tapping the screen. "Keller latches on to the glass with the shuttle's docking port and cuts through."

Sterling nodded. "Griffin's key should allow us to access to the docking port controls on level one directly," he said, feeling a lifting of his spirits. "With any luck, it should take Crow by surprise too." Sterling then reached for his neural interface. "Let's just hope that the Invictus hasn't been overrun already," he added, tapping the interface and attempting to reach Lieutenant Razor, who was in temporary command of the Invictus.

"Lieutenant, what's your status?" said Sterling, feeling the connection take hold. He opened the link so that Banks could monitor. As with Admiral Griffin, the distance between him and the Invictus meant that the connection was weak.

"Mag locks are still holding, sir, but I'll have them down in twenty," replied Razor through the neural link. She sounded vexed, as if Sterling had interrupted her in the middle of something important. "But the Sa'Nerra are running rampant throughout the station, turning more crew than they're killing."

"Is the ship secure?" asked Sterling. In all the excitement of their own endeavors, the fate of his own ship and crew had fallen to the back of his mind.

"The aliens have breached the dock, but Shade and the commandoes are holding them back," Razor replied. "Honestly, Captain, she's kicking their asses so hard I think they're having second thoughts." Sterling smiled and glanced up at Banks, who also appeared to have appreciated the comment.

"Keep working, Lieutenant," replied Sterling, feeling confident that the Invictus was still in good hands. "Is Ensign Keller with you?"

"Aye sir," replied Razor. Sterling felt the link widen and another voice appeared in his mind.

"Keller here, Captain," replied the voice of his gifted young helmsman.

"Ensign, I need you to take the combat shuttle and hard

dock to the glass wall outside the west viewing gallery on level two," Sterling said. He realized there was no point in mincing his words. There was a pause, which Sterling allowed, accepting that Keller might need a moment to process the magnitude of the instruction.

"Aye, sir, understood," Keller eventually replied. The helmsman's confusion was evident in the tone of his voice, but Sterling appreciated that Keller had not asked him to repeat the order, or explain it.

"Make it quick, Ensign," Sterling added. "We're running out of time."

Sterling felt the ensign leave his mind and he focused back in on Lieutenant Razor.

"What's the condition of the Fleet?" Sterling asked, removing the ID chip from the terminal and hanging the chain over his neck again. He and Banks then exited the office and began moving toward the west viewing gallery.

"The Praetor is crippled and we've lost six Fleet ships already," Razor replied. "The enemy have lost seven, including two battlecruisers. More Fleet ships are arriving every minute, but the Sa'Nerra continue to surge into the system too."

"Any sign of the Hammer?" Sterling asked, sweeping the barrel of the alien plasma rifle along corridors as he moved toward the west side of the station.

"Negative, Captain, though it's en route," replied Razor. "And there's something else, sir," Razor then added, suddenly sounding tense. "One of the alien ships that just surged through the portal is Heavy Destroyer M4-U1."

Sterling sighed. "MAUL..." he replied through the link.

"Aye, sir," replied Razor. The mere mention of the ship's name was enough to inspire dread, even into the hearts of the toughest officers. And while Sterling was used to his engineer's unflappable nature, everyone had their limits.

"It's just another ship, Lieutenant," replied Sterling, as the west viewing gallery came into view ahead of him. "Work on freeing those mag locks. Then once we take care of Crow and get back on-board, we'll put MAUL to the test."

"Understood, sir," replied Razor. There was then a brief pause before the Lieutenant spoke again. "Keller is in the launch bay," the engineer added. "G-COP still has all ships on remote security lockdown, so I'll need to blow the doors to let him out."

"Do what you have to do, Lieutenant," said Sterling, stepping through the door of the west viewing gallery. "And keep the Sa'Nerra off my ship."

"Aye, Captain," replied Razor.

"And Lieutenant, remember that the Omega Directive is in effect," Sterling then added, with a more sober tone. "Anyone who is turned is the enemy. Anyone, you understand?"

There was another momentary pause. "I understand, sir," his engineer replied. Despite the weak neural link, Sterling could feel that has engineer genuinely comprehended the gravity of his order.

"Break those mag locks, Lieutenant," Sterling continued. "Sterling out."

Sterling tapped his neural interface then moved over to

the floor-to-ceiling glass window that looked down onto the west docking ring. A dozen Fleet ships were still magnetically tethered to the station, but Sterling could also now see Sa'Nerran Wasps buzzing around outside. The trapped vessels were doing their best to shoot the agile, one-man fighters, but the wasps were succeeding in scoring hits onto the engines of the docked vessels. True to their names, the Sa'Nerran fighter craft were like flying insects paralyzing their prey with their painful stings.

"There!" Banks cried suddenly, pointing to the lower sections of the station.

Sterling adjusted his gaze and saw the familiar shape of the Invictus' combat shuttle. It was weaving through the station and between the docking rings like a stunt plane. Several of the wasps had broken off their attacks to pursue it, but it was clear to Sterling that none of the alien pilots possessed Keller's skill.

Plasma blasts continued to flash out from the docked ships and several of the pursuing wasps were destroyed. Keller than suddenly disappeared from view. Sterling pressed his nose to the glass, trying to get a better angle, but the combat shuttle was nowhere to be seen.

"Where the hell did he go?" wondered Sterling, his breath misting the armored glass of the viewing gallery.

Suddenly the deck rumbled and the shuttle surged up from below level two, mere inches from the glass. Sterling darted back into the room, heart pounding in his chest. It was like someone had just sprang out at him, shouting 'boo!'. Moments later there was a hard thud against the glass as the combat shuttle attached its docking ring. Then plasma cutting beams set to work.

Sterling had barely recovered from the shock of the combat shuttle appearing out of nowhere when a plasma blast raced into the room and struck the wall. Turning to the door he saw a squad of warriors running toward them. Sterling cursed then returned fire.

"Start cutting through from the other side!" Sterling called over to Banks, tipping a table in the center of the viewing gallery to use as cover. Banks adjusted the power level on her pistol and set to work as Sterling continued firing. One of the warriors was struck to the knee and went down. The squad then stopped and took up positions outside, using offices and corridors for cover.

What the hell are they doing? Sterling thought, wondering why the aliens had halted, considering they had the advantage of numbers. Then he saw one of the warriors pull a grenade away from the stow on its armor.

"Mercedes, get behind the table!" Sterling shouted, realizing what the warrior intended to do.

Banks spun around, spotted the warrior with the explosive device in hand, and rushed to the table. The warrior threw the grenade, which sailed into the room, but Banks had already ducked behind cover alongside Sterling. An explosion shook the room, but Banks' strength was equal to the force of the blast. The table held, though dozens of sharp splinters of metal perforated its surface. Sterling pushed himself away, feeling blood wet his skin. Some of the fragments had sliced into his arms and legs, but the wounds were superficial.

However, had it not been for the protection of the table, they both would have been shredded like pulled pork. There was another hard thump behind them and Sterling turned to see that the shuttle had succeeded in cutting through.

"Captain, come on!" cried the voice of Ensign Keller from inside the shuttle.

"Go!" Sterling called to his first officer.

Banks moved toward the opening as Sterling stood up and fired over the top of the battered table. Clearly surprised to still see them alive, the warriors had broken cover, allowing him to take down two more with easy shots. Plasma blasts then rained into the room again, striking the already perforated table. Further out into level two, Sterling could see more warriors closing in. Ducking behind what little cover remained, Sterling turned and crouch-ran for the docking hatch, throwing himself into it with a superman dive. Banks dragged him the rest of the way through then the hatch sealed and moments later, Keller detached. The punch from the acceleration of the shuttle winded Sterling far more than the dive through the opening had done.

"Hey, Captain!" said Keller from the cockpit, though the ensign's eyes were firmly fixed ahead. "Hell of a day, huh?"

COMMANDER BANKS HELPED STERLING to his feet and he staggered into the cockpit, falling into the seat alongside Keller. The combat shuttle then jerked right and swooped beneath a docking pylon, nearly sending Sterling flying through the cockpit glass.

"Do you know where you're going, Ensign?" asked Sterling, hurriedly pulling on the harness. Banks appeared behind him, her hands gripping the headrest of his and Keller's seats tightly so as to keep her balance.

"I do, Captain," Keller replied, turning hard for a second time then diving through a narrow gap between levels seven and eight. Plasma blasts flashed past, slamming into the station as he did so. "I just have a couple of insects on my tail."

Sterling glanced behind to the see two wasps in pursuit. Considering the dizzying speed and insane maneuvers of the combat shuttle, he was even a little impressed that the alien pilots had managed to keep pace.

"Make short work of them, Ensign, we're on the clock," said Sterling.

"Aye, sir," replied Keller, skirting across the surface of the station in yet another direction.

The moves and changes of direction were so rapid that Sterling literally didn't know which part of the station was up or down. The combat shuttle was then punched hard on the side and alarms wailed inside the cockpit.

"Hang on!" yelled Keller, turning past yet another pylon then racing over the top of the Light Cruiser Jemison. Sterling glanced behind, but incredibly the alien wasps were still on their tail.

"That last hit took out the targeting systems," said Commander Banks, who had hung on to the chairs despite the rollercoaster ride of maneuvers. "Give me manual control. I'll take care of these pests."

Banks hauled herself toward the rear of the shuttle and dropped down into one of the tactical combat seats. Working fast, she activated the virtual gunnery systems and was soon staring out into space.

"Start climbing toward level one," said Sterling. He then pulled the ID chip out from beneath his now cut and scorched armor and shoved it into the ship's computer. "This had better work, or we just jumped out of the frying pan and into fire..." Sterling added, his fingers fumbling across the keys while attempting to access G-COP's docking computer. He then tapped his neural interface and reached out to Admiral Griffin. This time, even the effort of connecting to Griffin's mind across the maelstrom of activity on the station was a struggle. He gripped the sides of the chair and closed his eyes, trying to shut out everything other than the sound of Griffin's voice.

"Captain, tell me you're on level one..." he heard Griffin ask, though the voice was barely a whisper in his mind.

"I'm on my way, Admiral," replied Sterling as another thud punched the ship. He then heard the combat shuttle's plasma turret unload. "I need one more code from you first."

"Standby, Captain," replied Griffin, her voice faint and exhausted. It sounded like she was dying.

The thud of the plasma turret erupted again, followed by a whoop from Banks. "Got one!" she cried out to the front of the cockpit.

Sterling opened his eyes and glanced to the rear as another flash of plasma from the remaining wasp raced overhead. It was so close, Sterling thought he could feel the heat from it on his face.

"We're running out of time, Mercedes," Sterling called back. "Do or die, remember?"

Banks continued to wrestle with the virtual gun controls. Despite Keller's brilliant piloting, the alien was still on their tail. Another plasma blast glanced off the cockpit glass, leaving a distorted smear in its wake.

"Any time now!" Sterling called out.

Banks squeezed the triggers, blasting the wasp cleanly on the cockpit, destroying its canopy and exposing the alien pilot to the vacuum of space. Moments later, the craft collided with the station and was atomized.

"Great shot, Mercedes!" Sterling called out. He turned

to Keller and gripped the pilot's shoulder. "Take us in, Ensign, as fast as you dare."

"Aye, sir," Keller replied, smartly. The young helmsman threw the shuttle into a hard series of maneuverers, forcing Sterling to release his hold and grab the arms of the chair for stability. Not for the first time in the last hour, Sterling found himself gritting his teeth as the station came racing toward them, so fast it was a blur. Then Keller spun the shuttle around and thrust hard to arrest their velocity before using their remaining momentum to butt up hard against the docking port of command level one. It was an astonishing maneuver and one that Sterling would have raved over had it been any other occasion. But their window to act was short and closing fast.

"Now, Admiral!" Sterling called out in his mind.

Griffin read the code out, though Sterling had to force his eyes shut in order to concentrate on her voice. More than once, he thought he misheard the Admiral and was compelled to take a guess. There wasn't time to ask Griffin to repeat herself. He remembered that the Admiral's authentication codes changed every ninety seconds. However, to Sterling, it sounded like she may not even have that long left to live.

Sterling finished entering the code then waited for the docking computer to authenticate his request. Banks was already standing by the docking hatch, weapons ready, anxiously watching Sterling. Then the lock around the level one docking hatch thudded open and there was a hiss of air though the seals.

"Get ready to haul our assess out of here when we're

done," Sterling said to Keller, unfastening his harness and jumping out of the seat.

Keller then unfastened his harness and drew a plasma pistol. "Let me come with you, Captain," he asked. All traces of the green and hesitant young ensign were gone. "You'll need the extra gun."

Sterling nodded then together he and Keller moved up to side of the hatch.

"Ready?" said Banks.

"Do-or-die time," replied Sterling. "Let's go."

COMMANDER MERCEDES BANKS hit the button to release the hatch and the metal slab hissed open, thudding into its housing. Banks immediately opened fire through the opening, but plasma blasts raced toward them with equal speed. Banks jumped through the hatch and Sterling followed, spotting four Sa'Nerran warriors. Straight away he took a blast to the chest and fell, but managed to scramble into cover behind one of the workstations in the command operations center.

"Captain, are you okay?" Banks called out, as Keller moved through, firing at the warrior and making it safely into cover.

"I'm a little singed, but okay," Sterling called back. He tore open the straps of his body armor then pulled it off. The material was still smoldering and threatening to set his tunic on fire.

"You're already too late, Captain," a voice called out from further into the room. Sterling immediately recognized it as belonging to Clinton Crow. "Though I must admit I'm impressed you got this far."

"I don't give a damn what you think, Crow," Sterling hit back, reloading the energy cell in the alien plasma rifle. "Or should I call you 'emissary'? Or how about 'traitor'? That would seem to fit better."

Through gaps in the workstations, Sterling could see Crow moving between the four warriors in the middle of the room. His former engineer then stopped directly in front of the command computer.

"History will remember me as the savior of the human race, Captain," Crow hit back. "If Fleet or your precious Admiral Griffin had their way, humanity would be simply eradicated. The Sa'Nerra will never document this war. They will not belittle their history with mention of the human race. All that will be recorded is that we discovered a nest of vermin and eradicated it. Humanity will be forgotten. It will be as if you never existed at all. Unless, that is, you surrender."

Sterling laughed. "Surrender and become mindless servants, like you and McQueen?"

Crow's expression suddenly hardened. "My mind is perfectly intact, Captain," he hit back. "I remember well the scorn I received on a regular basis from you and Commander Banks." He reached up and tapped the metal cranial plate that covered half of his head. "And I remember this too, Captain," he spat. "I begged you for help, and not only did you abandon me like a coward, you tried to kill me first."

"It would have been better for you if you'd died on that

shipyard, Crow," Sterling replied, feeling no remorse over his actions. "I was trying to spare you from becoming the thing you are now."

Crow advanced, though he was still cautious of where Keller and Banks remained concealed behind cover. The Sa'Nerran warriors, likewise, had their weapons aimed in the directions of his two other officers, ready to blast them should they poke their heads into view.

"I should thank you, really, Captain," Crow continued, sounding more like his former engineer. "You helped me to evolve and move beyond the bumbling man you so clearly looked down upon. Now, I am superior to you and to the rest of the human race."

"Well why don't you call off your pets and we can test that theory?" Sterling replied. "How about it, Crow? You and me, man to man. Or man to whatever the hell you are now."

Crow smiled, though it was a cruel look that did not suit the man's still curiously studious appearance, even despite the armor and metal plate in his head.

"I would dearly love to entertain that notion, Captain, but I'm afraid our time together is short," the emissary replied. "In a few minutes, this station's reactor will overload. Then our armada will crush what's left of your Fleet, bringing us one step – or should I say one sector – closer to your eventual, inevitable defeat."

Sterling laughed again. "You always did talk too much, Crow," he replied, sick of hearing the man's voice.

"Stand up and fight then," Crow snapped back. "You

are outnumbered and outgunned. My honor guard will crush you as easily as they crushed this station's crew."

Crow reached down and lifted the body of a Fleet lieutenant commander into the air. The woman was limp and lifeless, and Sterling could see deep gashes across her body caused by the serrated Sa'Nerran blades. Crow tossed the body aside, reminding Sterling of the enhanced strength that the turned humans possessed.

"Let me take him," said Banks, through a neural link to Sterling. "You and Keller lay down fire and I'll charge at him. Once I have my hands around his neck, maybe his honor guard will back down."

Sterling considered this, but he couldn't believe that a Sa'Nerran warrior would back down over anything, even to save their emissary. He also couldn't ignore the fact that there were four rifles pointed in their direction.

"We have to take them together, Mercedes," Sterling replied, making his decision. "But we likely all won't make it. Whoever survives has to take the key and regain control of the station, even if that means taking it off my dead body."

Sterling could see Banks' jaw clench up as he said this, but whatever his first officer wanted to say, she kept it inside.

"Understood, Captain," Banks replied. However, even though his first officer was speaking through her mind, it still sounded like the words had been forced through gritted teeth.

Sterling opened the link to Keller and adjusted his grip on both the Sa'Nerran rifle and his plasma pistol.

"On three, we take out the honor guard," said Sterling, glancing across to Banks and to Keller. Both looked ready and for a moment he felt a swell of pride. Omega officers were made of sterner stuff than regular Fleet, and his crew had proved that again and again. Now, they would do so one more time.

"Three..." Sterling said, beginning the countdown in his mind. However, that was as far as his count got.

Suddenly, an intense flash of light flooded though through the windows, blinding Sterling. He halted his count and spun around. Hanging above G-COP, so close that he felt like he could reach out and touch it, was the Fleet Dreadnaught Hammer. Sterling smiled – he'd never been happier to see his former ship – but his smiled faded as he saw flashes pop off across the hull of the giant vessel. The Hammer was firing at them.

Plasma blasts lashed the hull of G-COP and the command center was rocked. The Hammer was taking matters into its own hands. More brilliant flashes flooded the level, each one accompanied by a powerful pneumatic thud. G-COP was firing back. It was a contest of epic proportions. The unstoppable force versus the immovable object. Sterling had a feeling that the universe would finally get an answer to this paradox.

Shutters thudded down across the windows of the command level as it was rocked again by blasts from the Fleet's flagship. Consoles exploded and the ceiling partially collapsed, raining debris down onto Sterling. Glancing across to Crow and the Sa'Nerran honor guard, Sterling saw that the warriors had been knocked from their feet. Crow was clinging onto the main computer with his enhanced strength, but he too was distracted.

"Now's our chance, go!" Sterling cried out to the others though their neural link.

Banks was up and moving first, firing from the hip with both weapons. Crow took a hit and went down, but Sterling couldn't see if the emissary was alive or dead, and there was no time to check. Advancing toward the other warriors with Keller keeping pace at his side, Sterling opened fire. Blasts flew past him in the opposite direction, but he managed to hit and kill another of Crow's guard with a lucky shot to the alien's face. If the fizz of weapons fire and the hammering of his heart didn't tell him he was in a fight for his life, the smell of burning flesh left Sterling in no doubt.

Banks was then hit by a blast from another of the honor guard, but her momentum propelled her into the alien. They both went down and Sterling lost sight of his first officer. Keller then hit the warrior, but the blast deflected off the alien's armor. A hiss escaped the Sa'Nerran's lips and he shot back. Keller went down, but still Sterling did not check his advance. Pulling the serrated Sa'Nerran blade from its stow on his armor, he launched himself at the warrior, blade stretched out again. The alien's yellow eyes turned to him a moment too late and Sterling plunged the weapon into the warrior's flesh. Landing on top of the creature, Sterling raked the blade across the warrior's thick neck, opening its throat and putting it down permanently.

Heart still pounding and lungs heaving for air, Sterling spun around looking for Crow, but was met with a kick to the face. He spiraled backward, tumbling over the bodies of the dead warriors before hammering into the base of a workstation. Shaking the pain from his head, he looked up to see Clinton Crow advancing toward him. The emissary's armor was melted through next to his heart, but the man showed no sign of pain or fear.

"Such a waste," said Crow, bending down and stripping a half-moon blade from the body of the warrior Sterling had killed. "If you would only allow yourself to be re-educated, you could be a valuable asset. Another great emissary of the Sa'Nerra." Crow tutted and shook his head. "Now, you will merely become another drone in our army of turned human servants. Such a pity."

Still holding the blade in one hand, Crow reached to the rear of his hip and removed a Sa'Nerran neural weapon. Sterling's eyes widened as he saw the device in Crow's hand, knowing that he didn't have the strength to resist his former engineer. Scrambling to his feet, he looked for another weapon, but there was nothing within reach. Instead, he forced his battered and bruised body to stand tall and raised his guard.

"Man on man, is that how it is?" Crow smiled as he continued his measured advance. The emissary then flicked a switch on the neural control device and it began to hum with energy. "Let's see how you handle yourself in a fair fight, Captain." Crow raised both the blade and the neural weapon in readiness to attack.

"Who said anything about a fair fight?" said Sterling.

A blast of plasma then struck Crow in the chest, burning another hole in the emissary's Sa'Nerran armor. Crow glanced right and saw Banks, draped over the top of a computer console, plasma pistol in hand. She was bleeding from a gash to the head.

Sterling then charged forward and hammered a kick into Crow's body, sending the emissary tumbling over the main command computer and on to the deck. Sterling pursued, tossing the blade aside as he did so and collecting a Sa'Nerran rifle from one of the dead aliens. He orbited the circular computer console then aimed the rifle down at Clinton Crow.

"I think it's time I gave you another education," said Sterling, dialing up the power of the rifle to its maximum setting. "This time, I'm going to make sure there's nothing left of your head for those alien bastards to patch up."

Sterling went to squeeze the trigger, but the station was rocked by another series of powerful explosions. Thrown off his feet, he landed hard on the deck, cracking the back of his head as he did so. His eyes darkened and the sounds of crackling consoles and rumbling explosions faded in and out in his ears. The next thing he knew, he was being hauled to his feet. He could hear voices, but he wasn't sure if they were real, in his mind or merely part of his imagination.

"Lucas!"

This time the sharp yell roused him from his dazed stupor. Mercedes Banks was staring at him, blood smeared across her face and neck.

"Lucas, the key! Banks continued. "We have to stop the reactor overload."

Sterling shook his battered head and yanked the key out from around his neck, snapping the chain in the process. He tried and failed to stab the chip into the computer, but Banks grabbed his hand to steady his aim.

"Where's Crow?" Sterling asked, finally slotting the authenticator chip into the computer.

"He got away," replied Banks, spitting the words out in disgust. "He took our shuttle while we were all knocked down."

Sterling glanced over to the docking hatch and saw that their combat shuttle had gone. Cursing, he turned back to the computer and brought up the main menu. The console was active and some options were available to him, but as expected he was still locked out of the command functions. He tapped his neural interface, though the act of doing so felt like needles being jabbed into his temple.

"Admiral, I'm at the command computer, give me the code," Sterling said, reaching out to Griffin in his mind. However, this time, he could not form a link. "Admiral Griffin, are you there?" Sterling said again, but still there was no response.

"I can't reach Griffin through the link," Sterling said to Banks. "See if you can make contact. We need the authentication code."

Banks tapped her interface and a look of intense concentration gripped her face. Sterling waited impatiently for a response, but then noticed Ensign Keller. His helmsman was lying face down on the deck, not moving. He felt his gut tighten into a knot and his instincts told him to run to the officer's aid, but he knew he couldn't.

"I can't reach her either," said Banks, slamming her palms down on the console. Then her eyes fixed onto another section of the computer and she cursed.

Sterling frowned and followed the line of his first officer's gaze. Then a curse escaped his own lips as he realized what she had seen. The authenticator chip had been hit by debris that had fallen from the ceiling during the attacks on the station. It was now smashed and useless.

"What the hell do we do now?" said Banks, looking and sounding more despondent that Sterling had ever seen her.

More explosions rocked the station, forcing Sterling to grip the console tightly to steady himself. However, compared to the earlier barrages, Sterling judged these latest attacks to be less severe. The thud of G-COP's plasma turrets had also diminished. Sterling accessed the status screen on the computer, which was one of the few functions available to him. He could see that the Hammer had abandoned its attack on G-COP and was now heading toward the aperture to assist the rest of the fleet. He could also see that five of the fourteen Fleet vessels docked to the station had been compromised. The seals around their docking tunnels were flashing red, showing that they had been breached by Sa'Nerran boarding parties.

"Lucas, what the hell do we do?" Banks asked again, after Sterling's answer had been conspicuous by its absence.

"We abandon the station," Sterling said, meeting his first officer's eyes. "It's over, Mercedes. Crow wins this round." Banks growled and thumped the command computer, smashing one of the screens into a thousand pieces. "We take the ambassador ship, and get clear. Maybe we can still help in the battle out there," he added, staring out toward the aperture.

Sterling then felt a link form in his mind. His pulse quickened in the hope that Griffin was reaching out to him, but when the voice spoke it was Lieutenant Razor.

"Captain, the mag locks are free and I have control of the Invictus," Razor said. "Lieutenant Shade has repelled the Sa'Nerran forces. We're sealed up and ready to go. What are you orders?"

Sterling glanced down at the command computer and again scanned the list of ships docked to the station.

"Lieutenant, this station is going to blow at any moment," Sterling began. "Detach immediately then I want you to blow the docking clamps of every other ship still locked to the station, with the exception of the following." Sterling highlighted the five ships that had been compromised. He had no way to know for sure that those crews had all been turned, but he couldn't take that chance. "Do not free the ships at docks six alpha, six delta, five echo, five bravo and five charlie. Is that clear?"

"Aye Captain," replied Razor, though Sterling could sense her unease. "There are over two thousand crew split between those ships, sir. If we leave them, they'll be killed when the station blows."

"I know that, Lieutenant," replied Sterling, flatly. "The Omega Directive is in effect."

"I understand, Captain," replied Razor. Sterling could sense that she had accepted his order, but he could also sense that she did not like it. He didn't like it himself. "What about you, Captain? How will you get off the station?"

Sterling turned to the second docking hatch at the other side of the command deck. "Don't worry about us, Lieutenant," he replied. "I have my own ride out of here."

Sterling tapped his neural interface to close the link. His eyes then fell onto the body of Ensign Keller.

"We should at least take him back with us," said Banks.

"Griffin would call that sentimental nonsense," Sterling replied. "Dead is dead. Now, he's just a hunk of meat, like the rest of these corpses."

"I don't care," replied Banks. "He was one of us."

Sterling sighed and nodded, and together he and Banks moved over to Keller.

"He did his duty," said Sterling, kneeling at his helmsman's side. "He was a good officer."

"And one hell of a pilot," Banks chipped in.

Sterling flipped Keller onto his back and grabbed his wrist, ready to haul the man up and onto his shoulders. He knew that Banks could carry the ensign with far greater ease, but this was something he had to do himself. However, as his fingers tightened around the man's flesh, he felt something push back against his skin.

"Wait..." said Sterling, adjusting the position of his

fingers on Keller's wrist. He then let go and pressed them to the ensign's neck instead. "He's not dead."

Banks scowled. "He took a blast directly to the chest, without armor. How the hell can he still be alive?"

Sterling shook his head and stood up. "I don't know and I don't care," he replied. "Thousands will die today, but I'll be damned if Keller is one of them."

Banks nodded then picked up the ensign as easily as if he were a newborn baby. Sterling set off at a sprint in the direction of the docking port.

"Do you still know how to fly a light cruiser?" said Banks, following at his side.

"Not as well as the guy you're carrying," replied Sterling, reaching the dock and activating the hatch mechanism. Then he turned and met Banks' eyes. "We'll figure something out," he added, with more assurance than he had any right to display at that moment. "We always do."

Banks nodded then moved inside the ambassador ship, with Ensign Keller still draped across her powerful arms.

Sterling sucked in a deep breath of the air on the command level, tasting burned flesh and electronics, then turned to enter the docking hatch.

"Captain Sterling..."

Sterling froze and closed his eyes, concentrating on the voice. He felt the link strengthen.

"Captain, are you in position?" said Admiral Griffin. Her voice was weaker than ever, and it took every last ounce of concentration Sterling had to maintain the link.

"Captain, I'm..." Griffin continued, but then her voice trailed off, and the link was severed.

Sterling cursed again. He had another choice to make, though in actuality he realized he'd already made it. Griffin would not approve, but he didn't care. If the Admiral was still alive then he was going to get her back, because in the dark days that lay ahead, Fleet and the United Governments were going to need her.

STERLING AND BANKS made their way through the deserted corridors of the ambassador ship, Fleet Light Cruiser Franklin. For a ship that usually had a crew of two hundred, the empty spaces were eerily quiet. *A ship without a crew is like a body without a mind,* Sterling thought, as he and his first officer made their way to the bridge. Banks was still carrying Ensign Keller in her arms. The helmsman's pulse was weakening, but the young officer was still alive, if only barely. *If Keller can cling to life, then an old battle-axe like Griffin can,* Sterling told himself, glancing at his helmsman, limp in Banks' arms.

Stepping onto the command platform of the Franklin, Sterling entered his emergency command override codes to take control of the vessel. The captain's console, along with the other consoles on the bridge flickered back into life. Then the viewscreen turned on, displaying a view of the battle raging out close to the aperture. Sterling didn't need a sensor analysis to know that it was going badly for the fleet warships. The Hammer was still caught in a no-man's land between the bulk of the engagements and G-COP. The dreadnaught may have been the only ship in the Fleet that could stand toe-to-toe with a heavily armed and armored command outpost, but in doing so it had not escaped unscathed. Its engines had been damaged and it was now limping toward the battle.

"See if you can stabilize Keller then take the weapons console," Sterling called over to Banks while he ran through a hasty pre-launch checklist. He bypassed every check possible then powered up the engines.

Banks rested Keller on the deck then grabbed an emergency medical kit and cracked it open. She tore open Keller's tunic, revealing the plasma burn to his chest. Sterling could see that it was bad and had gone through the bone, with charred flesh giving way to blackened ribs.

"How the hell that kid is still alive, I don't know," said Sterling, hopping over to the weapons console to arm the Franklin's plasma rail guns. He then moved to the helm controls and prepared to detach from G-COP.

"He won't be for much longer, unless we can get him to Graves soon," replied Banks.

She applied a field dressing designed specifically for plasma burns to the wounds. Then she hit Keller with a cocktail of drugs designed to numb any pain the ensign was feeling and keep him alive for as long as possible.

A distant thud resonated through the deck and Sterling checked the helm control console. "We're clear," he said, while maneuvering the light cruiser away from the docking pylon. Then another thud, louder and harder than the first rumbled through the bridge, followed by the sound of grinding metal.

"Are we taking fire?" asked Banks, jumping onto the weapons control console and opening the damage report.

"No, that was me," said Sterling, holding up a hand. "I hit the pylon on the way out. This hunk of crap is a lot bigger than I'm used to flying these days."

Banks raised an eyebrow. "Are you sure you don't want me to drive?" she asked.

"How about you just get ready to shoot?" replied Sterling. Banks' condescending tone had irked him, though he was also a little embarrassed.

Sterling switched the viewscreen to show an image of the command outpost and for the first time the damage from the slug-fest with the Hammer became clear. Parts of the station were smashed open and others were on fire. Sterling could see hundreds of bodies floating in space around the most heavily damaged parts of the station.

"Do we really think Griffin is still alive in there?" wondered Banks as the Franklin slowly descended to level three.

"We'll find out soon enough," replied Sterling. He was frowning down at the helm controls, trying to maneuver the hulking vessel close enough to the conference room to get the docking umbilical attached. More hard thuds and reverberating creaks echoed around the bridge and alarms sounded across every console.

"Ease up a little, Captain, we're being hit by collapsing structural supports," said Banks, though this time without the condescending tone. "At this rate, we'll bring the whole of levels one and two down on us."

Sterling sucked in a deep breath then continued to ease the ship into position. It was like trying to fit a square peg into a round hole. The only way to make it work was with brute force.

"There, that should be close enough," said Sterling, initiating the station-keeping thrusters to hold them in position before wiping the sweat from his brow. "Stay on the weapons while I cut through into the conference room. And keep a neural link open to me at all times."

"Aye, sir," replied Banks, tapping her neural interface.

Sterling ran off the bridge, feeling the link to Banks form in his mind. Stopping en route to the docking hatch, Sterling opened a weapons locker, grabbed a pistol and hastily pulled on a fresh set of body armor.

"Lucas, hurry!" said Banks, suddenly bursting into his mind with crystal clarity. "I'm reading the station's reactor at critical. It could blow at any moment!"

"Understood," replied Sterling, fighting the aches and pains in his body and pushing on harder and faster.

Reaching the docking hatch, Sterling could see that the umbilical had attached and formed a seal. He tried to open the hatch, but it was still shut tight. Cursing, Sterling overrode the safety protocols then yanked the hatch open. The sudden equalization of pressure blew him into the umbilical, as if he'd been kicked in the back by a bull. Pushing himself off the freezing cold surface of the corridor, Sterling raised his pistol and dialed the power level to maximum. The cutting beams were still working to slice through the thick armored glass of the conference room, but he didn't have time to wait. Aiming the pistol, he fired a concentrated burst of plasma into the center of the glass. The glass shattered and Sterling was again blown forward through the rough opening. He landed hard on the deck inside the conference room and felt blood drip down his face from fresh lacerations. However, the pain kept his mind keen and alive.

Shaking his battered head, Sterling glanced up to Griffin, who was lying against the far wall. The conference room doors had been smashed through and the bodies of four Sa'Nerran warriors lay on the deck. Rushing to Griffin's side, Sterling pressed his fingers to her neck and felt a pulse thumping back against his skin.

"Admiral!" Sterling shouted, grabbing Griffin's shoulders and shaking her vigorously. "Admiral, get up, we have to go!"

Griffin opened her eyes then scowled at Sterling like he trying to mug her. "Captain, what the hell are you doing here? Get off the station, that's an order."

"I intend to, Admiral, but not without you," Sterling replied, ignoring the Admiral's directive. "Now can you stand? G-COP is going to blow at any moment."

"That's precisely why you shouldn't be here," Griffin hit back. "The Omega Directive is in effect, Captain. The Directive does not exclude me."

"Sorry, Admiral, I must have missed that section of the tech manual," said Sterling, grabbing the Admiral under her arms and hauling her to her feet. Griffin yelped with pain, and Sterling saw wounds from plasma blasts and Sa'Nerran blades across her back, arms and legs. "I have the Franklin docked just outside," he continued, helping Griffin over to the improvised docking port.

"The Franklin?" said Griffin, shaking off Sterling's hands and standing on her own. "Where is your ship? Where is Crow?"

"I'll explain later, Admiral," Sterling hit back. There were limits even to his tolerance of the grouchy admiral's cantankerousness.

"You'll explain now, mister," Griffin snarled. Then the thump of boots alerted them to a squad of Sa'Nerran warriors outside. The aliens saw Sterling and Griffin then raised their weapons. The admiral sighed and shook her head. "Very well, explain later," she said, admitting defeat on this occasion. "But it had better be good..."

Sterling scoured the floor, spotting a Sa'Nerran rifle close to the feet of a dead warrior. "Here, take this," said Sterling, handing his pistol to Griffin. He then grabbed the Sa'Nerran rifle and raised it. "I'll hold them off while you get inside the tunnel."

Sterling fired at the approaching warriors, hitting one and driving the others into cover.

"We go together or not at all, Captain," Griffin hit back.

The admiral then shot over Sterling's shoulder, almost deafening him. The blast sailed out into the corridor and struck a warrior on the face, hollowing it out like a bowl. Sterling and Griffin continued to back away, maintaining a steady stream of fire until their backs were against the external glass wall.

"Admiral, go!" yelled Sterling, firing and hitting another warrior in the gut.

Griffin handed the pistol back to Sterling and he continued to hold off the warriors while Griffin climbed into the docking umbilical.

"Now you, Captain," Griffin said, extending a hand to Sterling.

Sterling continued to fire until both weapons ran empty. Tossing them down, he spun around and grabbed Griffin's arm. A sharp, hot pain then filled his body and he fell to his knees. Griffin's arm slipped through his fingers.

"Just leave!" Sterling shouted as the smell of his own burning flesh flooded his nostrils.

Griffin scrambled toward him along the tunnel and reached down.

"Grab my arm, Captain," she called out. Her tone was calm, but forceful.

Sterling tried to reach up, but pain shot through his body. More blasts hammered into the wall at his side.

"I can't. Just go, while you still can!" Sterling cried.

"Take my damned arm, Captain, that's an order!" Griffin roared. "I've already lost one Omega Captain. I'm not losing two!"

Sterling bit down hard then thrust out his arm, feeling a hand close around his wrist. His body was then hauled up and into the opening as more blasts flashed overhead.

"Mercedes, get ready to detach," Sterling called out to Banks in his mind.

"I'm ready, but the station is going critical, Lucas," Banks called back. "This is going to be close."

Sterling and Griffin crawled to the end of the docking umbilical and slid onto the deck inside the Franklin. Clawing himself up, Sterling then slapped the button to close the hatch before collapsing to his back.

"Mercedes, we're through, punch it!" Sterling called out in his mind.

The hatch hammered shut and Sterling felt a thud through the deck as the Franklin detached from the station. He and Griffin were then thrown to the opposite wall as the light cruiser accelerated away from G-COP. Pushing himself into a sitting position, Sterling peered out through the viewing window in the docking section as the station began to slip into the distance. He could see the Invictus, snaking between the docking pylons, firing its plasma rail guns to free the last of the ships that had been locked to the station. The nimble Marauder-class vessel then blasted clear, along with the frigate that it had just set free.

Suddenly, there was a blinding flash of light, so bright and intense that it felt like needles being stabbed into his eyeballs. The physical shock of the detonation hit them moments later, along with flying chunks of metal that were all that now remained of G-COP. Fleet's key military asset on the front line of the war was gone, but Sterling knew that the battle for G-sector was not over yet.

THANKS to several injections of drugs and the hasty application of a wound dressing from one of the Franklin's emergency med kits, Sterling was feeling a little more alive. Similarly, the stream of chemicals flooding throughout Admiral Griffin's body had also given her a much-needed boost. Sterling knew that the effects were temporary, but they would last long-enough to finish the battle in G-COP. Then, if he was still alive, the side-effects would kick him harder than a Muay Thai champion.

Sterling staggered onto the bridge of the Franklin and Banks turned to him from her position at the helm controls. Her expression was initially one of relief at seeing him alive, but then her eyes hardened and her smile fell away.

"Lucas, are you okay?" Banks asked. Sterling could feel her concern through their still-open neural link. "You look like you jumped through a window."

"Strangely enough, that's pretty accurate," replied

Sterling, stepping onto the command platform and resting his weary form onto the captain's console.

"Are you okay, *Captain...*" said Admiral Griffin, stressing Sterling's rank. Banks immediately straightened up as the flag officer approached. "This is a ship of war, not a pleasure cruiser, Commander. Reserve first names for social occasions only."

"Aye, sir," replied Banks. She then glanced across to Sterling, eyebrows raised, but neither of them dared speak to one another through their neural link, for fear that the secretive admiral was somehow monitoring.

"I believe you're in my place," Griffin said, standing behind Sterling with her arms pressed to the small of her back.

Sterling initially returned a confused frown to the Admiral, but then it dawned on him what she was referring to.

"Of course, Admiral, the ship is yours," he said, stepping down from the command platform in deference to his senior officer.

"Take the weapons station, Captain," Griffin added, moving up to the command console and resting her palms on the sides. "Let's get this ship into the fight."

"Yes, sir," replied Sterling, hobbling over to the weapons control station and familiarizing himself with the layout.

Despite the apparent folly of taking a light cruiser into battle with a crew of only three, Sterling felt oddly upbeat about their chances. Griffin's seemingly unconquerable confidence was infectious. The Fleet Admiral then noticed Ensign Keller, still lying on the deck at the rear of the bridge, heavily patched up and sedated.

"Is he dead?" she asked, flatly.

"Not yet, though he should be," replied Sterling, also casting a glance back at his helmsman.

"See to it that he stays alive," Griffin ordered. Sterling was curious as to whether this was genuine concern from the Admiral – a spark of light and warmth in her cold, dark heart – but then her next statement answered his question. "I will not be able to find you a better helmsman at such short notice, so make sure this one does not die."

"Understood, Admiral," Sterling replied. Banks again managed to shoot him a sideways glance without Griffin noticing.

The bridge consoles then chimed an alert, signifying an incoming communication. Sterling accessed the comms panel on his console and saw that it was an open broadcast from one of the Sa'Nerran vessels. The ship's identifier was one he immediately recognized – Sa'Nerran Heavy Destroyer M4-U1.

"Put the message onto the viewscreen, Captain," said Griffin. "Let's hear what they have to say."

Sterling accepted the incoming communication then the image of Clinton Crow appeared on the viewscreen. He was still dressed in his battle-scarred Sa'Nerran armor, flanked by new members of his honor guard.

"People of the United Governments Fleet, I am an Emissary of the Sa'Nerra," Crow began, sounding like a preacher giving a sermon. "Due to the refusal by your leaders to negotiate a peace, we have destroyed your command outpost as a demonstration of our might."

Sterling could feel his grip tighten around the sides of the weapons station as Crow spoke. Griffin and Banks were also absorbed by the image of Crow on the screen. Their eyes were shining with hostility and contempt.

"The Sa'Nerra are now left with no option other than war," Crow continued. He then opened his arms out wide, as if embracing his flock. "But you still have a chance at peace. Choose Sa'Nerran rule and your lives will be improved, as my life has been improved." Then Crow's expression hardened and he took a step forward. The lights on the bridge of the alien warship shone off the metal plate in Crow's head, as if it were suddenly red hot. "Refuse and we will continue to drive further into your space, until eventually – and inevitably - we will reach and destroy Earth." Crow's expression switched again, this time offering the viewers a warm, but painfully insincere smile. "The choice is yours, good people of the Fleet," Crow went on, again opening his arms. "The emissary awaits your answer."

The viewscreen went dead and an unnatural silence fell over the bridge. Admiral Griffin then entered a sequence of commands into the captain's console. Sterling saw on his panel that the Franklin had opened a fleet-wide communications channel.

"This is Fleet Admiral Griffin," the flag officer began, again standing with her hands pressed to the small of her back. "I am taking command of the fleet. Target your weapons on Sa'Nerran Heavy Cruiser, designation M4-U1 and fire at will." Griffin then tapped a single button on her console and the channel cut off.

"Take us in, Commander Banks," Griffin called out to the helm station before she turned to Sterling. "Give them everything we've got."

Sterling felt the pulse of the Franklin's engines build as the ship accelerated toward the enemy. Several vessels had already engaged, allowing themselves to take hits from closer and more imminent threats in order to press the attack on the emissary's ship. Three Fleet warships were destroyed within seconds, but the vessels that the Invictus had freed from G-COP were closing fast. Sterling sorted through the mass of signals on his console and locked onto MAUL. The battle-scarred heavy cruiser appeared on the viewscreen, moving through the battlefield with skill and intelligence. The infamous warship fired, adding the Fleet Destroyer Javert to its long tally of kills. Then the vessel was struck by several plasma blasts and fire engulfed a section of its hull.

"Come on, die you bastard!" Sterling urged, muttering the words under his breath. He checked his own console, but the Franklin still did not have a clear shot, such was the mass of Fleet ships that were already part of the engagement.

MAUL turned hard and began to burn for the aperture, but the Fleet vessels were closing in fast. Two more ships exploded in fire – the Rose and the Wolfhound – but now the Hammer was also bearing down on the

Sa'Nerra's top gun. The dreadnaught may have been damaged, but it was still the most powerful piece on the board.

A bank of the Hammer's plasma cannons flashed, sending blasts of energy toward MAUL. There was an explosion and Sterling felt his heart race, but when the debris cleared, MAUL was still intact. Another alien vessel had flown into the line of fire, sacrificing itself for its emissary.

"Captain, are we in range yet?" Griffin called out. She was now gripping the side of the captain's console, much as Sterling often did.

"Ten seconds, Admiral," Sterling called out as more Fleet ships took damage and were forced to fall back. *Come on, come on...* Sterling urged, tapping his finger against the side of the console. Then the target lock on MAUL solidified and held strong. "Firing!" sterling called out, unleashing volleys from all of the Franklin's weapons simultaneously. Blasts of plasma raced out ahead of them, briefly blinding the viewscreen due to the sudden intensity of the glare. A powerful explosion lit up the darkness of space and an orange fireball expanded then quickly dissipated to nothing. However, there was no celebration on the bridge of the Franklin. Their attack had struck true, but not on their intended target. As their blasts had raced toward MAUL, the remaining Sa'Nerran warships had moved in and formed a shield around the heavy destroyer that carried their emissary. Sterling's shots had taken out three enemy warships, but not his intended target.

Sterling cursed and thumped his console, knowing that

their chance had been lost. Crow was going to escape, as was MAUL. However, Sterling had no doubt at all that he would see both of them again.

STERLING STOOD with his arms folded, peering out through the window of the forward observation lounge on deck two of the Hammer. Surrounding the Hammer in the space around the aperture was a fifth of the entire United Governments Fleet. G-sector's Void Defense Taskforce had been all but obliterated in the battle. With the Hammer heavily damaged, Griffin had ordered F-sector's Fourth Fleet, commanded by Admiral Rossi, to shore up the region. Sterling could see the purple markings of three Fourth Fleet light cruisers sitting off the Hammer's bow. Just beyond them was the unique shape of his own ship, the Fleet Marauder Invictus.

"Penny for your thoughts?" said Mercedes Banks.

Sterling jolted around to see his first officer standing behind him. Like him, Banks' wounds had been tended to in the forty-eight hours since the battle for G-sector had ended.

"I'm thinking that I haven't seen this number of gold

stars in a single room since my Fleet graduation ceremony," Sterling said, hooking a thumb toward the adjoining conference room.

The admirals in command of all five United Government War Fleets, plus the commander of the Perimeter Defense Taskforce, were in the room. If this wasn't already a large enough collection of bigwigs, the United Governments Secretary of War, Ernest Clairborne, was also in attendance.

"I somehow don't think it's a good sign," said Banks, glancing across to the closed double-doors. "Personally, I'd rather be anywhere than here right now."

"I know what you mean," replied Sterling, anxiously chewing the corner of his mouth.

Ordinarily, he and Banks wouldn't be called to a meeting of the War Council, but on this occasion Admiral Griffin had requested their presence, though she hadn't explained why.

"They've been in there for hours already," said Sterling, watching a squadron of fourth-fleet destroyers cruise past the window.

The double doors swung open and Secretary Clayborne stood in the center of them. Through the doors, Sterling could see Fleet Admiral Griffin and some of the other admirals, each of whom wore the distinctive symbols of their respective fleets on their shoulders.

"Captain Sterling, Commander Banks, please come through," said Clayborne, with an approachable smile.

Sterling had only met Clayborne once, but he'd heard him speak many times. He was an accomplished politician and all-round smooth talker, which had always made Sterling suspicious of him. Unlike with neural communication, where it was impossible to hide your feelings from another person, an accomplished orator like Clayborne was able to hide his true opinions behind a shield of words. Sterling glanced across to his first officer and flashed his eyes at her before stepping toward the conference room. It felt like he was walking into his own court martial.

"Just there is fine, Captain," said Clayborne, still smiling amiably.

Sterling stood on the spot the Secretary of War had indicated and tried to look comfortable, despite the sea of admirals all peering back at him. Banks stepped alongside Sterling, her hands squeezed tightly into fists at her sides. A neural jammer in the room meant that he and his first officer were not connected through a neural link at that moment. Even so, Sterling could sense her discomfort.

As Sterling examined the faces of the men and women in front of him, he met the piercing gaze of Admiral Ernest Wessel. He winced, realizing that if the commander of the Earth Defense Fleet was in attendance, his son probably wasn't too far behind. However, the recently-appointed head of the Special Investigations Branch was currently nowhere to be seen.

"Captain Sterling and Commander Banks, we have asked you here today to pay tribute to your courage, service and selflessness in the line of duty," Clayborne began, his powerful voice filling the room.

Admiral Griffin then stepped up to the side of the

Secretary of War, holding a wooden box in both hands. Sterling thought that she looked as uncomfortable as he and Banks felt.

"After your courageous endeavors on the F-sector command outpost, where you saved countless lives, I had intended to confer upon you both the Fleet Service Cross," Clayborne continued. He turned to Griffin, who held out the box while Clayborne lifted the lid. Sterling's eyes grew wide as he saw the contents. "However, in light of your recent actions rescuing Fleet Admiral Natasha Griffin and saving close to five thousand Fleet personnel aboard the nine warships the Invictus freed from G-COP, it is only fitting that we award the Fleet Medal of Honor instead."

Sterling felt a lump form in his throat. He had walked into the room anticipating a grilling from the War Council over the circumstances of G-COP's destruction. A medal ceremony was the last thing he expected, or wanted.

"I'm afraid that due to the circumstances, a grander medal ceremony will have to wait," Clayborne continued. "However, the War Council and the admirals felt it important to recognize your exceptional contribution and bravery while we are all gathered here today."

The Secretary of War removed one of the medals from the box, adjusted the ribbon and held it up. Sterling bowed allowing the secretary to place the medal over his head. As Sterling lifted his head again, he could see the eyes of Admiral Wessel narrow.

"Commander Banks, if you will allow me," Clayborne continued, offering the second medal to Sterling's first officer. She also bowed, though when she rose again her cheeks were flushed crimson.

Clayborne began to clap and the admirals all followed suit. However, Sterling couldn't help but notice that Admiral Wessel's gesture was more akin to a sarcastic slow-clap than one with genuine enthusiasm and meaning. After the applause died down, each of the admirals briefly congratulated Sterling and Banks. Then came the turn of Admiral Wessel. As the commander of the Earth Defense Fleet, Wessel's tunic bore a two-tone logo of earth, instead of the usual-colored stripe.

"Congratulations, Captain Sterling," said Wessel, though the words were uttered with such rank insincerity that Sterling almost laughed. "It's interesting how you continue to find yourself at the heart of so many pivotal moments in this war, is it not?"

Though phrased as a question, it was clear to Sterling that the Admiral was suggesting some other reason or motive behind his actions.

"Well, when you're on the front line, Admiral, you tend to come across the enemy quite a bit more often than I expect you do sitting in orbit around Earth," Sterling replied. He had intended just to nod, smile and give a simple response in order to make Wessel go away. However, like his son, Admiral Wessel had goaded him and Sterling had taken the bait.

"It's a shame that you were unable to stop Crow, because now the front-line is now much closer to Earth," Wessel replied, maintaining his cool. "Crow was one of your officers, was he not?"

Sterling smiled, though this time he had to fight a lot harder to maintain his composure. Wessel's insinuation was clear.

"Yes, he was, Admiral," Sterling answered. "Before he was turned, that is."

"And Captain McQueen, the other emissary of the Sa'Nerra, she was part of your taskforce, correct?" Wessel added, with an inquisitive frown.

"Part of the Void Recon Unit, you mean?" Sterling corrected. Sterling then wondered whether Wessel had made the error deliberately, perhaps in an attempt to trip him up.

"Of course, my mistake," replied Wessel, in a smarmy tone of voice before smiling again. "Well, hopefully now that travel into the Void has been prohibited by the War Council, you'll be pleased to know that you and your crew will find yourselves in far less dangerous circumstances going forward."

Sterling frowned. The news that travel into the Void was banned had not yet reached him, and Wessel immediately picked up on this.

"Oh, you didn't know?" said Wessel, clearly enjoying himself. "Perhaps you should speak to Admiral Griffin. I'd hate to ruin any more surprises for you." Wessel then lifted Sterling's medal off his chest with the tip of his finger. "Congratulations again, Captain," Wessel added, his words dripping with contempt. The Admiral then allowed the medal to flop back onto Sterling's tunic before trudging away without even bothering to acknowledge Commander Banks' presence.

"Like father, like son..." said Banks, letting out a long sigh. "What is it with the Wessels, anyway?"

Sterling shook his head. "I don't know, though I think I dislike Admiral Wessel even more than his pissant son."

Admiral Griffin began to walk over. Her movements were stiff and awkward, on account of the numerous surgeries that she was recovering from.

"I take it that Wessel broke the news about travel into the Void?" said Griffin, speaking quietly so that the others in the room couldn't hear. However, most of the other officers, including Wessel and the Secretary of War, had already dispersed.

"He took great pleasure in doing so, yes," replied Sterling, quickly glancing over to the door to make sure Wessel wasn't lurking nearby.

"The United Governments are scared," Griffin said, her voice as stiff as her injured body was. "This incident, and Crow's little speech, has only intensified their desire for a diplomatic solution."

Sterling recoiled slightly. "How the hell has it intensified a desire for a diplomatic solution?" he hit back. "They literally captured our ambassador ship and used it as a weapon against us."

The eyes of some of the remaining admirals briefly flicked in Sterling's direction, and Admiral Griffin ushered them further away from the throng.

"Partly, the UG is bowing to public pressure," Griffin replied, still with half an eye on Admiral Wessel. "There are already violent protests on Earth and many inner colony worlds. Crow's words are being believed."

Sterling cursed. Up until the emissaries arrived on the scene, the Sa'Nerra were easy to predict. They waged war with weapons, not words. Now, thanks to Lana McQueen and Clinton Crow, the aliens had added propaganda to their already formidable arsenal.

"More importantly, the latest intelligence analysis suggests that a Fleet military victory is no longer possible," Griffin continued, speaking in even more hushed tones. "The UG wish to delay the Sa'Nerran invasion while they search for a method to reverse the effects of the neural control weapon."

"But if they've banned travel into the Void, how are we supposed to track down James Colicos?" Sterling asked.

"The War Council wants nothing to do with Colicos," replied Griffin. Her anger and disappointment at this fact was plain to see. "They believe Colicos has been turned. And even if he hasn't been, they wouldn't trust him. The UG is focused on finding a solution without Colicos' help."

Sterling sighed and rubbed the back of his neck. "What do you believe Admiral?" he asked.

"I don't trust Colicos either," Griffin replied. "But in the time we have left, he is the only one who can undo the damage he has caused."

The remaining admirals all began to file out of the room, and Griffin appeared anxious to leave also.

"I have another meeting of the War Council to attend," Griffin said, following the other admirals with her eyes. "Return to the Invictus then head for F-COP. Soon it will be announced that Fleet is pulling out of G-sector entirely."

"We're retreating?" queried Banks, her muscles suddenly becoming taut.

"The Hammer is badly damaged and can only be repaired at F-COP," Griffin said, turning her piercing blue eyes to Banks. "However, deep space aperture relays have picked up a Sa'Nerran armada heading this way. The Hammer cannot be repaired and returned here before it arrives."

"Are we talking a fleet like that one we just repelled, or something new?" asked Sterling.

"This one is new," replied Griffin. Each word hit Sterling like a dart. "It is led by a new kind of warship. The same one that you already discovered. Fleet has given it the designation, Titan, and it is accompanied by hundreds of ships. It is an invasion force, pure and simple."

Sterling shook his head. "Then surely we have to make a stand? We can't just allow them to take G-sector unopposed."

Griffin held up her hands. "I have already been through this with the War Council, Captain," she said, sounding suddenly angry. "Most of the admirals agree that we need to fight, but not all."

Sterling snorted and shook his head. "I'm willing to bet that one of the admirals that dissented was Wessel," he spat, again glancing toward the door.

"The President of the United Governments has made her decision and Clairborne supports it," Griffin snapped. Our hands are tied." It was rare for the Admiral's anger to bubble to the surface, so Sterling knew to back down and keep quiet. "You are to withdraw to F-sector and defend the aperture. That is an order."

"Understood, Admiral," said Sterling, straightening to attention.

"Officially, all our hopes now rest on Fleet scientists discovering a 'cure' to the Sa'Nerran neural weapon," Griffin went on. As was often the case, she was more open with Sterling than she would be with other captains, due to his unique status. "With the neural weapon gone, their advantage is gone. Then we can attack, without fear of our ships and crews being turned against us."

Sterling raised an eyebrow. "And unofficially?"

Griffin again met Sterling's eyes. "Unofficially, I do not intend to sit on my hands and hope for the best."

"What are our real orders, Admiral?" asked Sterling, suddenly eager to get back into the field. "Unofficially, I mean."

"All in good time, Captain," Griffin replied. The Admiral had regained her composure, though her anger was still perilously close to the surface. "I will contact you once I'm through here."

Sterling nodded then turned to leave.

"One more thing, Captain," Griffin said. "Alone, if you please."

"I'll see you outside," said Banks, not waiting to be asked to leave. Like Sterling, she had begun to recognize when it was best to simply get out of the Admiral's hair as quickly as possible.

"What is it, Admiral?" asked Sterling, once Banks had stepped outside.

"I made you an Omega Captain because I trusted that you were willing to make the hard calls," Griffin began. Sterling straightened up. The Admiral's tone was formal and severe, and he already knew where she was heading. "Coming after me was reckless," Griffin went on, confirming Sterling's suspicions. "You risked the lives of three Omega officers, not to mention a powerful warship, in order to save one person. I am no more important than anyone else. The Omega Directive must be followed to the letter." Griffin paused, allowing her opening salvo to land, before following up with the killing blow. "Sentimentality does not win wars, Captain. Cold, hard, merciless choices do. Is that clear?"

"If I may speak freely, Admiral?" replied Sterling. He had been expecting such a dressing down and was ready for it.

"Go on," said Griffin. Sterling thought she even sounded a little intrigued.

"Sentimentality had nothing to do with my decision, Admiral," Sterling began. This caused the Admiral's eyebrows to raise up slightly. "And that's because you're wrong about one key thing. You *are* more important. The Fleet needs you if we're to win this war, whether they know it or not, or like it or not." Sterling then paused, allowing his opening words to sink in, just as Griffin had done. Then he delivered his punchline. "Saving your life was a tactical choice, Admiral. Nothing more, nothing less."

Griffin's eyes narrowed, but she said nothing in reply, and simply scrutinized Sterling's face with quiet intensity.

"Very well, Captain, you're dismissed," said Griffin.

However, Sterling did not adjust his stance. "Admiral, may I ask you a question?"

Again, Griffin appeared intrigued. "Go on," she said again, though a little more cautiously than before.

"When I was shot in the back on G-COP and couldn't make it inside the docking umbilical, why didn't you leave me to die?"

This question had been on Sterling's mind for the last couple of days. The impromptu medal ceremony, plus news that the Sa'Nerran Titan was on the way, had caused it to slip his mind. However, Griffin's dressing down had brought it back to the front of his thoughts.

"How many stars do you see on my collar, Captain?" asked Griffin.

Sterling almost smiled, but managed to maintain a level expression. He knew what was coming next.

"Four stars, Admiral," Sterling replied, stiffly.

"Correct," replied Griffin, snappily. "And remind me, Captain Sterling, what do these four stars mean?"

Sterling straightened his back even more stiffly and cleared his throat. "They mean that you don't have to explain a damned thing to me, Admiral," he answered.

"Very good, Captain," said Griffin. "You are dismissed."

STERLING'S BOOTS clacked against the deck plating as he walked down the long corridor to the docking port where the Invictus was waiting for him. The sound of his boots and the way the noise echoed through the halls of the Hammer was unique among all the ships Sterling had ever set foot on. The Hammer was one of a kind. It was also a vessel that contained many memories for Sterling, some good, some bad and some that continued to haunt him. He was glad to once again be leaving the venerable old war machine in his wake.

Rounding the corner, Sterling saw the docking section directly ahead. However, there was someone standing by the door waiting for him. Sterling smiled, initially believing it to be Mercedes Banks, even though the officer's back was turned to him. However, as he got closer, Sterling's smile fell away as he realized who it actually was.

"I am growing tired of chasing you down," said Captain Vernon Wessel. His uniform was darker than the regular

Fleet blue and there was a glossy black stripe on his shoulder, along with the insignia, SIB.

"I've been busy, Vernon, what do you want?" grunted Sterling, trying to push past. Wessel blocked his path.

"You know damned well what I want, Captain," Wessel snapped. "You were ordered to cooperate, and now I want my interview. I have waited long enough."

Sterling took a step back and glared at the head of the Special Investigations Branch. "Perhaps you haven't been paying attention to the daily briefings, but I've been preoccupied with more important concerns." Sterling wasn't even trying to be nice. He just wanted to get back onto his ship and get on with his mission.

"I know all about your little adventures," Wessel replied, bitterly. "Though your escapades, and your medal, change nothing. You owe me an interview. Now."

Sterling sighed then took a pace toward Wessel. The man's eyes narrowed, but he held his ground. "I will give you an interview when my duties allow it, Captain Wessel," he seethed. "Now get out of my way."

For a few seconds, Wessel held his ground. "Very well, Captain," the SIB officer eventually replied, his tone taking on a more bitter bite. "If you want to make this a battle between us then so be it."

"You don't know a damned thing about battle, Vernon," replied Sterling. At this point, he just wanted Wessel to get out of his way, before he did something he'd regret. "If you'd seen what I've seen, you'd crap your fancy black pants."

Wessel looked shocked and appalled and was suddenly

lost for words. However, this gave Sterling an opportunity to slip past.

"I find it curious how 'Emissary Crow' managed to escape from G-COP," Vessel then called out, having finally found his tongue again. Sterling stopped and closed his eyes, but kept his back to the officer. "And in your own shuttle too," Wessel went on. "Strangely convenient, wouldn't you say?"

Sterling opened his eyes and turned to face the SIB officer. "Do you have something to say, Vernon?" he replied, feeling the rage start to bubble through his veins.

"Oh, I think you know what I'm saying, Lucas," Wessel hit back, speaking Sterling's name like it was an insult.

"Why don't you go ahead and say it to my face then?" Sterling replied, taking a pace closer to Wessel. Wessel's face fell and he backed away, fear showing in the man's eyes. "That's what I thought," Sterling spat, turning his back on the SIB officer and marching away.

"I'll see you in the interview room, traitor..."

Sterling closed his eyes and gritted his teeth, but this time Wessel had gone too far. Spinning around, he surged toward the man and hammered a right hand into Wessel's face, knocking the officer clean off his feet.

"I'll have you on a charge for this!" Wessel blurted out, staring up at Sterling from the flat of his back. The SIB officer pushed himself to a sitting position and dabbed his hand to his nose, which was streaming with blood. "I'll end you, Sterling, just you wait and see!" Wessel roared. "I'll end you!"

"Do your worst, Wessel," Sterling hit back. At that

moment, he could have spat on the man's boots, but this time he managed to reign in his anger. "Interview concluded," he added before taking one last look at Wessel then striding onto his ship with a renewed spring in his step.

STERLING RETURNED another polite nod and a smile to a member of the Invictus crew before finally managing to slip inside his quarters. He waited for the doors to swoosh shut behind him and rested his head back on the cool, dark-gray metal. The quiet and solitude of his room felt like a hot flannel being draped over his face. Unbuttoning his tunic, Sterling slid onto his bed and lifted his boots up onto the rock-hard Fleet-issue mattress. To most people, it would have felt like lying on a bed of soft clay, but Sterling had grown so used to the feeling that he could no longer manage to sleep on anything else.

Closing his eyes, he let the events of the past few days slip into his unconscious mind. He had a few hours before the Invictus was scheduled to undock from the Hammer and head through the aperture to F-COP. He intended to spend that time in solitude. However, although he was alone, Sterling struggled to find any solace in the comfort of his own quarters. His mind was whirling with reflections on the events that had transpired and meditations on what was still to come.

Then he noticed the Fleet Medal of Honor lying on his chest, glinting under the harsh overhead lights in the room. He had tucked it under his tunic for the walk back to the Invictus, but with his uniform now unbuttoned the medal was again exposed. He removed the ribbon from around his neck and took a moment to inspect the medal for the first time. He had never seen one before, at least in the flesh. A handful more than a hundred had been awarded in the entire fifty years of the war, and now he had one. Captain Lucas Sterling, Omega Taskforce. He snorted a laugh then reached over to the table beside his bed. Opening the drawer, he slipped the medal inside.

I wonder if Clairborne would have been so willing to hand me this, if he'd known how many Fleet lives I've taken, as well as how many I've saved... Sterling thought, pushing the drawer shut.

Suddenly, there was a scuffling sound from somewhere in the room. Sterling froze and listed intently, in two minds as to whether he'd simply imagined the sound. Then it came again. It was a rapid pattering, as if something was scampering around under his bed. Panic gripped him, wondering what new alien device the Sa'Nerra might have developed.

The docking gates were breached during the attack on G-COP, Sterling remembered. *Shade held them back, but the warriors could have still got something inside.*

Slowly drawing himself up on the bed, Sterling looked for something he could use as a weapon. However, there was nothing within reach. Cursing under his breath, he reached down and removed his boot. Then the scampering sound came again and this time he could place where it was coming from. Slowly sliding toward the bottom of the bed, Sterling raised the boot above his head, preparing to strike whatever was about to emerge from underneath it. The scampering came again, and Sterling tensed his muscles, ready to attack. Then the source of the noise revealed itself and Sterling froze. What had emerged from under his bed was not a new kind of Sa'Nerran assassination device, but a dog.

The door chime sounded, but Sterling still found himself too stunned to move. "Computer, who is that?" he asked.

The door slid open to reveal Mercedes Banks standing in the hallway. Sterling rolled his eyes.

"Computer, what have I told you about opening the door?" Sterling said, glancing up at the ceiling. "I said 'who is at the door', not 'open the door'."

"Apologies, Captain, though due to your sudden, canine-induced catatonic state, I reasoned that you may require some assistance," the computer replied, cheerfully. "And since you appear not to like visiting the ship's doctor, I thought that the ship's first officer might do instead."

"What have I also told you about thinking?" Sterling said to the ceiling.

"Am I interrupting something?" Banks said, looking a little nervous. "Because I can come back."

"No, come in Mercedes," said Sterling, beckoning her

in. "The computer and I can have our little conversation later."

Banks raised an eyebrow then stepped inside in order to allow the door to slide shut behind her. Then she noticed the dog, which was now sitting at the foot of Sterling's bed, looking completely at home.

"Is that a dog?" asked Banks, pointing at the animal.

"Yes, it's a dog, Mercedes," replied Sterling, a little huffily. He then slipped his boot back onto his foot and slid his feet onto the deck. "The more important question is, why is there a dog in my quarters?"

The dog scampered over to Banks and tapped its paw onto her boot, at the same time emitting a soft, low whine. A broad smile spread across the first officer's face then Banks crouched low and began to pet the animal.

"Who's a good boy then?" said Banks in the sort of silly voice that humans adopt when talking to animals. "Yes, he is a good boy!" Banks added while continuing to stroke the dog, which was clearly loving every second of the attention.

"If you want to maintain your fierce reputation with the crew, I suggest you don't let them see you do that," said Sterling, with a wry smile.

"Come on, Lucas, even an ice-cold heart like yours can't possibly say no to this?" Banks hit back.

The dog looked at Sterling and emitted another strange low whine.

"Unless that dog can fill a slot in the duty roster, it's of no use to me," Sterling replied, drawing a scowl in response from Banks. "How did it get on-board anyway?"

"The canine slipped on-board the Invictus during the

immediate aftermath of the engagement with Sa'Nerran forces attempting to board the ship," the computer replied.

"I wasn't asking you," said Sterling. However, since the computer obviously knew more about the mystery of the dog than he did, Sterling decided to indulge the chipper AI. "Out of interest, though, what else do you know?"

"The canine's breed is a Beagle. Its designation is "Jinx" and it is, in fact, a bitch not a 'good boy'." replied the computer.

"Call her that again and I'll rip out your processors," Banks snapped, while stroking the Beagle's ears.

Sterling shot Banks a disproving look. "It's not an insult, Mercedes, that's just what a female dog is called."

"Not on this ship it's not," replied Banks, forcefully.

"The former owner of Jinx was Lieutenant Commander Fiona Walsh, a senior medical officer stationed on G-COP," the computer continued, oblivious to the ire it had inspired in Banks.

"Former owner?" said Sterling. "Where is Commander Walsh now?"

"Lieutenant Commander Walsh was killed in the destruction of G-COP," the computer replied. The quirky AI maintained its buoyant tone, despite the grim news it had just delivered.

"See what I mean? It's fate," replied Banks. She was now down on the floor with her legs stretched out in front of her. Jinx had its head rested on her powerful thigh.

"Seriously, you want to adopt a ship's dog with the name 'Jinx'?" Sterling hit back. "Why don't you just shoot an albatross and hang it around my neck?"

Banks appeared ready to press the case for her proposed new member of the crew when the computer interrupted again.

"Captain, there is an urgent incoming communication from Fleet Admiral Griffin." The AI announced.

"Put her through in here," said Sterling, moving from the bed to his desk and turning on the console.

"It is a text-only message, Captain," the computer then clarified. "It was transmitted using Omega Taskforce encryption protocols."

"An Omega Directive?" wondered Banks, pushing herself up so that she could also see the screen.

"Let's find out," replied Sterling, removing the encrypted ID chip Griffin had given him from his drawer and slotting it into the console. The message flashed up on the screen. It read, "Omega Directive Griffin Delta Two Alpha." Sterling placed his hand on the authenticator pad. The cloak and dagger tactics from Griffin already had him concerned. "Omega Directive Griffin, Delta, Two, Alpha. Unlock," he said out loud to the computer.

The computer processed Sterling's identity using hand print and retinal scans.

"Identity confirmed: Sterling, Lucas. Omega Captain. Omega Directive Griffin, Delta, Two, Alpha, unlocked."

Sterling scanned the order, his eyes narrowing into a frown the further he read. Banks read the directive over his shoulder, though she had finished before Sterling had.

"She wants us to surge into the Void now, with a Sa'Nerran invasion armada en route?" said Banks, apparently sense-checking what she'd read to make sure Sterling's understanding was the same.

"That's what it looks like," said Sterling, rocking back in his chair. "We're to find and retrieve Colicos at any cost."

Banks sighed then sat on the side of Sterling's bed. Jinx the Beagle wandered over and sat by her foot.

"How are we supposed to get back again?" Banks added, reaching down to again stroke the Beagle's ear.

"I'm sure she'll have a genius plan for that buried somewhere in the fine detail," replied Sterling. However, he was simply hoping this was the case, rather than knowing it for certain.

Banks smiled. "Well, it looks like we won't have time to re-home Jinx after all," she said.

Sterling sighed, pushed up himself up and walked over to his wardrobe. "Then I put Acting Ensign Jinx completely under your charge, Commander," he said, while pulling a clean tunic off its hangar.

"Aye, Captain," Banks replied, continuing to beam at him.

Sterling then tapped his neural interface and reached out to Lieutenant Razor, who was on watch on the bridge. "Lieutenant, make ready to leave," Sterling said, buttoning up his tunic. "But do it surreptitiously. We don't want people to know where we're going."

"Aye, Captain," replied Razor. "Though Ensign Keller is currently running some diagnostics on his helm control console, so I'll notify him to hurry it up."

Sterling glanced over at Banks, wide-eyed. "Keller is already back at his post?"

Banks nodded. "You might consider Graves to be a 'creepy SOB'," Banks replied, using the definition that Sterling had applied to their ship's medical officer. "But he's one Dr. Frankenstein-level genius too. Keller's chest is more metal now than flesh, and his heart and one lung are artificial, but he's back as strong as ever."

"In two days?" Sterling replied incredulously, moving over to the door. Jinx the Beagle followed them.

"I didn't ask how, and I suggest you don't either," Banks replied. "I get the feeling what Graves did was probably not legal."

Sterling huffed a laugh then shrugged. "Hell, so long as it worked, I don't give a damn what he did," he replied. "We need that kid at the helm, now more than ever."

The door to Sterling's quarters slid open and he stepped outside. Two members of the crew walked past and saluted. They then noticed the dog by Sterling's foot and almost tripped over one another. Sterling shook his head at the dog then glanced over at Banks. However, she appeared lost in her own mind.

"Penny for your thoughts?" asked Sterling.

"I was just hoping that we stocked up on number nineteen meal packs before we left G-COP," Banks said. Sterling waited for her to shoot him a wry smile, but when it didn't come, he realized she was serious.

"Come on, Commander," Sterling said, slapping his first officer on the shoulder and setting off toward the elevators. "I'm sure we'll find ourselves in a fight in another bar or hotel somewhere in the Void soon enough. If we survive long enough, I'll buy you dinner when we get there."

The door to the elevator slid open and they both stepped inside.

"It's a date, Captain," said Banks.

Jinx the Beagle wandered inside the elevator and sat down between the two senior officers of the Fleet Marauder Invictus. The doors closed and the elevator began to ascend to the bridge.

Ahead of them was not just another Omega Directive assignment, Sterling realized, but a mission that could potentially decide the fate of the human race. The Sa'Nerran invasion armada, led by the emissaries, Crow and McQueen, was heading for earth. And thanks to the alien neural control weapon, their forces outmatched those of Fleet. G-COP was already lost and the Hammer had almost fallen too. Their only hope now was to nullify the advantage of the alien neural weapon, before it was too late. And even then, in the face of the Sa'Nerran Titan – the new superweapon, the full capabilities of which were still not known – victory was far from certain.

One thing, however, was certain. Captain Lucas Sterling and the Omega crew of the Invictus would stop at nothing in order to succeed. That was his mission. And he intended to carry it out, no matter the cost.

The end (to be continued).

CONTINUE THE JOURNEY

Continue the journey with book three: The Exile.
Available from Amazon.

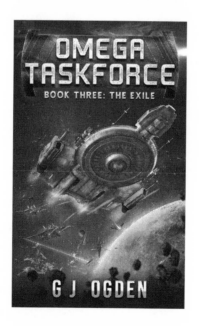

ABOUT THE AUTHOR

At school, I was asked to write down the jobs I wanted to do as a "grown up". Number one was astronaut and number two was a PC games journalist. I only managed to achieve one of those goals (I'll let you guess which), but these two very different career options still neatly sum up my lifelong interests in science, space, and the unknown.

School also steered me in the direction of a science-focused education over literature and writing, which influenced my decision to study physics at Manchester University. What this degree taught me is that I didn't like studying physics and instead enjoyed writing, which is why you're reading this book! The lesson? School can't tell you who you are.

When not writing, I enjoy spending time with my family, walking in the British countryside, and indulging in as much Sci-Fi as possible.

Subscribe to my newsletter:

http://subscribe.ogdenmedia.net

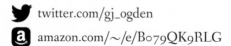

twitter.com/gj_ogden

amazon.com/~/e/B079QK9RLG

If you like Omega Taskforce then why not check out some of G J Ogden's other books? Click the series titles below to learn more about each of them.

Darkspace Renegade Series (6-books)

If you like your action fueled by power armor, big guns and the occasional sword, you'll love this fast-moving military sci-fi adventure.

Star Scavenger Series (5-book series)

Firefly blended with the mystery and adventure of Indiana Jones. Book 1 is 99c / 99p.

The Contingency War Series (4-book series)

A space-fleet, military sci-fi adventure with a unique twist that you won't see coming...

The Planetsider Trilogy (3-book series)

An edge-of-your-seat blend of military sci-fi action & classic apocalyptic fiction. Perfect for fans of Maze Runner and I am Legend.

Audible Audiobook Series

Star Scavenger Series (29-hrs)

The Contingency War Series (24-hrs)

The Planetsider Trilogy (32-hrs)

Made in the USA
Middletown, DE
07 August 2021

45585322R00205